A THOUSAND DEAD HORSES

A Thousand Dead Horses

Rod Miller

FIVE STAR
A part of Gale, a Cengage Company

LIBRARY OF CONGRESS CATALOGING-IN-PUBLICATION DATA

Names: Miller, Rod, 1952– author.
Title: A thousand dead horses / Rod Miller.
Description: First edition. | Waterville, Maine : Five Star, [2020]

Identifiers: LCCN 2019041807 | ISBN 9781432869687 (hardcover)
Subjects: GSAFD: Western stories.
Classification: LCC PS3613.I55264 T48 2020 | DDC 813/.6—dc23
LC record available at https://lccn.loc.gov/2019041807

First Edition. First Printing: August 2020
Find us on Facebook—https://www.facebook.com/FiveStarCengage
Visit our website—http://www.gale.cengage.com/fivestar
Contact Five Star Publishing at FiveStar@cengage.com

Dedicated to fellow Westerner Steve Gallenson,
who introduced me to Pegleg Smith
and horse thieves on the Old Spanish Trail;
and to Western songwriter and singer Dave Stamey,
who gave me Juan Medina and *los machos*.

PROLOGUE

Drifting dust angled down out of the desert sky, the cloud thickening as it neared the ground, pointing the way, as sure as the flight of an arrow, to the retreating herd of thousands of horses. A smaller, shapeless dust trail billowed up from the opposite direction, its source becoming more distinct as it approached the men huddled in the tangles of mesquite and desert willow marking the place called Rabbit Springs.

Soon enough, the drumming of horses' hooves drifted out of the coming dust cloud, and the concealed men clenched the muzzles of their mounts to avoid betraying their presence with a welcoming whinny.

"Here they come." Boone pulled off his wide-brimmed hat, mopped the sweat from his forehead and scalp with a shirtsleeve, and replaced the hat, tugging it down around his ears tighter than it had been before. He stroked the face of his horse before placing his palm over its nostrils and squeezing. The horse tossed its head, rattling the headstall, but the boy held firm.

Nooch watched it all, hissing between his teeth, reminding Boone to be still. Boone grunted in reply, elbowing the young Ute squatting beside him. Three Mexicans, three other Indians, and a white man—Philip Thompson, the leader of this undertaking—were concealed nearby.

Dust settled as the posse reached the spring, and the horsemen—Boone guessed their number to be about thirty—rode to the verge of the shallow ponds and allowed the horses to drink.

A few let their mounts walk into the water, but they soon backed out when one of the men—he must be the leader, Boone thought—shouted something at them. He did not understand the words, for he had no Spanish, but the boy assumed the sheepish-looking men had been chastised for stirring up mud in the water they would soon be drinking.

Boone looked on and listened as the posse's leader spat out orders. The riders, a few at a time, reined their horses away from the water. *Can't let a heated-up horse drink too much,* the boy told himself, surprised that a bunch of ignorant, ragtag Mexicans would know that.

After a few minutes, the men dismounted and were kneeling in the mud at the edge of the murky pools, some sucking up water through pursed lips, others lapping the water into their mouths by the palm-full. Some, already sated, sat wilted under the sun as the horses milled about, tearing up mouthfuls of grass where they could find them.

Boone felt Nooch stiffen beside him. He shifted his weight, wondering how the Ute knew it was time. From a nearby clump of willows he heard the hammer on Thompson's pistol ticking into position, muffled as if covered by a hand, and tensed up. Nooch started to rise before the gunshot, and Boone followed. When the pistol fired, the hidden men loosed shrieks and squawks as they leapt into their saddles, barreling out of the bushes like a flock of disturbed birds.

The attacking horde paid little attention to the unhorsed Mexicans, some shocked into inaction, others scrambling out of the way but unsure where to run. Instead, the attackers rode for the horses, stampeding the panicked animals away from the springs and into the desert, turning in a slow arc until the horses were aimed at the dusty arrow point that showed the way to the larger herd, now miles away across the Mojave.

CHAPTER ONE

Empty aguardiente bottles stood and lay on the table like casualties of war. From his seat in the dim corner of the stuffy cantina, its dirt floor and mud-plastered adobe walls and low *latilla* ceiling pressing in on him, Boone watched the circle of men around the table. From time to time, he sipped from the clay mug of pulque balanced with one hand on his knee.

The men were a motley assortment, their clothing a mix of Indian, Mexican, and American garb. He could not hear much of the conversation, but the accents and speech sounded like a polyglot of Yankee, Southern, Spanish, French, Creole, and more.

Despite the discomfort of feeling caged in after so much time in the open, Boone watched the men with interest. They were *hiverannos*. Trappers. Mountain Men. They were the reason he was here in the West. In Taos.

And Boone was determined to become one of them.

With another bottle emptied, the men quibbled and bickered amiably over who owed the next. After a time, a man with a wooden leg stood and stumped his way to the bar, returning with a bottle of the Taos whiskey in each hand.

The contents of those bottles must have been less agreeable than those that preceded it, as the conversation grew louder and more heated. One of the men—one with a French accent—jumped to his feet and pulled a Green River knife from its belted sheath, waving it toward the one-legged man. Spittle sprayed as he shouted, his words more French than any kind of English Boone could understand. The other men shoved away from the table, leaving the man with the wooden leg to answer the threat on his own.

Boone did not see or did not comprehend what happened next. But the Frenchman was on the floor, blood oozing from a head wound, his body flinching and shuddering from repeated blows to shoulders and chest and back. The man rolled out of the way, beyond the reach of the club in his attacker's hand. He hauled himself to his knees and touched his head wound, staring with wrinkled brow at the blood on his fingers. Wiping his hand across his already filthy shirtfront, the man made his way to his feet and walked away, casting angry looks at the one-legged man until he ducked out through the low doorway.

The one-legged man, breathing hard from the exertion, stayed in his chair, and Boone watched as he strapped his wooden leg back on—its duty as a club completed. The boy shook his head, wondering how the appendage had become a weapon in such a hurry. Despite looking on the entire time, he had not seen it happen.

"You had best keep your eyes peeled for that Canuck, Peg-leg," one of the men said, clapping the seated trapper on the shoulder.

"That I will, Bill. That, I will."

Others offered similar cautions as they readied to leave. The fracas—and the dark of night outside the door—signaled, it seemed, the end of the evening's entertainment.

"Care if I sit, mister?" Boone said to the one-legged man after the others had left.

"Suit yourself. Who be you?"

Boone dragged a chair back to the table as the man poured himself another glassful of aguardiente. "Whole name's Daniel Boone Trewick. I mostly go by Boone."

"I be Tom Smith. 'Pegleg' to most. Care for a drink, Boone?"

"No thank you, sir. I got this," Boone said, holding up the mug of pulque, still half full after an evening of nursing.

"Don't know how you can stomach that nasty stuff. Smells like it's already been in and out of somebody's belly." Pegleg swallowed off a glass of the Taos whiskey. "This stuff, now," he said, hefting the bottle, "this stuff tastes a damn sight better." He poured another glassful. "And it does its work a hell of a lot quicker." The refilled glass didn't stay full for long as it, too, was tossed off in a swallow or two.

"That fight—you did away with that feller in short order. 'Thout even gettin' out of your chair. I ain't never seen the like of it."

Smith lifted his wooden prosthesis and propped it on the opposite knee. "Damn thing's a nuisance, most times." He patted the peg leg as he would a lapdog. "Comes in handy, now and then, howsomever."

"How'd you come to have but the one leg? If you don't mind my askin'."

Pegleg Smith smiled. "Nah, I don't mind, son. Told the story, must be a hundred times." He swallowed some more of the aguardiente. "Back in '27, it was. We was a bunch of us up in the high Rockies a good ways north of here, place called North Park, when we got us into a scrape with a party of Indian braves. Most of 'em Arapaho, they was. They fell upon us as we was comin' across this little valley. We was ridin' hell for leather to get to somewhere we could find some cover when I took an arrow in the back of this here knee I ain't got no more. I stayed mounted, and we got to a stand of trees and fended them off, their arrows bein' no match for our rifles.

"We shaded up there to lick our wounds, mine bein' the worst of the lot. Leg swole up twice its size, it did, and turned black as the heart of whatever Arapaho it was that shot that ar-

11

row into it. When it took to stinkin' we knowed it was the leg or me, so we set to cuttin' it off."

Wide-eyed, Boone leaned forward across the rough table, the story reeling him in, ever closer to Smith. The mountain man slugged down more of the Taos whiskey and went on.

"I liquored m'self up much as I could and still wield a knife and went to whittlin'."

Boone's jaw dropped. "You? You cut your leg off your own-self?"

Smith smiled. "Oh, no, boy. Not all of it. By the time I'd sliced through all the meat I was getting' woozy, what with the whiskey and loss of blood and all. Then I passed out. I don't remember it happenin', but they said Milt Sublette cut through the bone whilst I was out. Then they stuck the barrel of my own rifle in the fire till it was glowin' red and seared off the end of my leg to stop it from bleeding any more. They could've warped the barrel of my rifle heatin' it up thataway. I'd a been madder'n hell and took it up with them boys if it had, I'm here to tell you. A good rifle don't come cheap."

Boone fidgeted while Smith emptied and refilled his glass. The boy's still half-full mug of pulque sat untouched on the table. "What happened then?"

"I don't recollect a whole lot of it, what with bein' sick as a gutshot buffalo. Them boys hauled me out of there on a travois. That ride was worse than gettin' shot and losin' your leg. Liked to killed me, bouncin' around on that damn thing over rocks and boulders and near gettin' tipped off the thing and whatnot.

"When finally I got to where I could tell up from down, I was a-layin' on a pile of buffalo robes in a tipi. My pards had left me with a band of Utes who promised to bury me when I died. Only they didn't, on account of I didn't. Did a damn fine job of lookin' after me, howsomever. There was this old woman who tended to my leg. She had some concoction of leaves and roots and who-knows-what all—buffalo dung, I suspect—she'd chew into a pulp and press it onto the stump. Took most all the winter, but it healed up right fine. Spent some of them winter months whittlin' this here peg leg and learnin' to hobble around on it."

Smith swallowed more whiskey and studied the worried look on Boone's face. "What's a-botherin' you, boy?"

Boone's look turned sheepish, and he squirmed in his seat. "Oh, nothin', really. Just wonderin' is all."

"Wonderin' what?"

The boy swallowed hard and squirmed some more. "Well . . . I was just thinkin' . . . just wonderin' . . . What did they do with that leg they cut off?"

Pegleg Smith laughed hard enough to shake dust out of the *latilla* ceiling. "Hell, son, I don't know. Never wondered about it, myself. I guess you'll have to ask Sublette or one of them boys should you see them. I reckon they just let it lay.

"Bein' diseased like it was, I doubt a wolf or bear would eat it. Wolverine might. Skunk, maybe." Smith laughed. "Could be some Indian come across it years after and made hisself a necklace out of the toe bones. Might be right handsome, that. I might wear it myself."

Smith laid the last aguardiente bottle on the table along with its fallen compadres. "Well, boy, I'm a-goin' to bed. Man my age can't sit up all night a-drinkin' no more, not like a youngster like you can do.'

"I'd like to talk to you again, if I could, mister Smith. Some things I'd like to ask you."

"You come find me tomorrow. I'll be around. You can ask me then. And tell me what the hell you're doin' in Taos."

Chapter Two

Morning sunlight dappled Pegleg Smith as he sat on a three-legged stool, contrived from sections of tree limbs bound together with rawhide, next to a coarse table beneath an aspen tree. Boone watched the mountain man shovel up chili stew with a tortilla. Steam wisped from a mug next to the wooden bowl.

Boone watched the slouching adobe hut and Pegleg at his breakfast for a few minutes before stepping out of the trees into the small clearing. "Mister Smith?"

Smith did not stop eating or raise his eyes. "Wondered when you'd get around to showin' yourself."

The boy said nothing. He shifted his weight back and forth from one foot to the other. He swallowed hard. "You knowed I was watching you?"

" 'Course I did. Heard you comin'. Saw you, too. Ain't like you was tryin' to catch me unawares. Or if you was, you was doin' a bad job of it."

"Sorry, sir. Just didn't want to disturb you, is all."

"Well, you may as well come on in. You et your breakfast yet?"

"No, sir."

"Hungry?"

"Yessir."

Smith turned toward the hut. "Rosa!"

A woman in a cotton shift with a rebozo draped around her

shoulders stepped into the hut's low, narrow doorway.

"*Qué?*"

"Scramble up some hen fruit and dump it into a bowl of chili for this boy."

The woman nodded and ducked back through the doorway.

"That your wife?"

Pegleg studied the boy as he chewed on a bite of tortilla. "My woman. We ain't married as such."

Boone nodded, still watching the hut. "Didn't think so."

"Why's that?"

Boone turned his attention to the man. "Can't see no white man marryin' no Mexican."

Pegleg stopped chewing. After a moment, he swallowed the bite, tore off another piece of tortilla, and scooped up more of the chili, watching the boy as he worked it over with his teeth. "Well, I'd marry Rosa if I could. Thing is, I've already got me a wife."

The boy said nothing.

"Her name's *Wici-ci*."

"Never heard no name like that before," Boone said, his voice so soft it was almost a whisper.

"Likely not. It's Ute. Means Song Bird. I just call her 'Song' most times."

"She an Indian, then?"

Pegleg nodded. Boone said nothing. He did not know what to do with his hands as he stood, weight shifting back and forth.

"Might as well sit down, boy."

Boone lowered himself onto the leather seat of a stool like the one Pegleg occupied.

Pegleg said, "What is it you want from me?"

The boy cleared his throat. "I want to learn the ways of the mountain man. Be a trapper. Like you-all last night is."

Much as he had done in the cantina the night before, Pegleg

tipped back his head and let loose a laugh that would rattle the ceiling, had there been one. Instead, four little gray birds flapped out of the aspen tree, whirring away across the clearing.

"I say somethin' wrong, mister?"

"Not wrong as such, boy. Wrong time, is what. Hell, son, you're ten years too late. Fur business's gone bust. What beaver there is left ain't worth skinnin' on account of there ain't nobody wantin' to buy the pelts no more. Silk hats. That's what them toffs wants on their noggins nowadays."

As Boone wilted and stared at the tabletop, Rosa set a clay mug of hot coffee in front of him, followed by a bowl of chili stew topped with scrambled eggs, and warm *tortillas* wrapped in a cloth.

"Eat your breakfast, boy. Then you can tell me how you come to be in Taos."

The food did not last long. It would have gone sooner, Boone thought, had he been given a proper spoon.

"Where is it you come from, young mister Boone?" Pegleg said as Boone licked the last of the chili off his fingers after having swiped them around the inside of the bowl, wishing he hadn't made such short work of the tortillas.

The boy wiped his fingers on a pant leg. "Clay County, Missouri. Family had a farm just outside Liberty."

"Been there," Pegleg said. "Leastways in the area. Nice place, if you've a mind to be a sodbuster. Why'd you leave?"

Boone's face flushed, and he ducked his head and mumbled. "It was on account of a girl."

"A girl?"

"Yessir."

"Must've been some girl to send a boy so far. What happened?"

"Well, sir, Mary—that's her name, Mary Elizabeth Thatcher—and me was caught cuddlin' in a buggy in her old man's carriage house. Reverend Thatcher—her daddy's a preacher—come upon us. He was right put out. Hauled me plumb out of that buggy. 'Daniel Boone Trewick,' he hollered. 'You shall not desecrate my daughter! You are pure evil, boy,' he yelled at me, 'to take advantage of a pure and undefiled virgin!' Well, that part of it weren't true—I wasn't the first boy to know Mary thataway—know her in the biblical meaning, if you catch my drift.

"Anyways, Reverend Thatcher flung me up against the wall of that there carriage house. 'Boy, I shall smite you hip and thigh!' he hollered and went to wailin' on me. Mary was screamin' and all. I grabbed aholt of a singletree that was hangin' on the wall and laid it upside the reverend's head a good solid lick.

"That made Mary squeal all the more. She bailed out of the buggy and knelt down by her daddy. 'Oh, Danny,' she wailed—Mary called me Danny, see. She's the only one that does. Everybody else calls me Boone. 'Cept my mom. She calls me Daniel. Anyways, Mary was whinin', sayin' 'I think you killed him, Danny!' I asked was he breathin', and she said he was, but his head was bleedin' somethin' awful. 'What if he dies?' she said. 'Oh, Danny! What if he dies?' Well, I figured if he didn't die he was likely to kill me. If not, he was sure to set the law on me. Or the family would, if he did die.

"Anyways, things didn't look so good for me in Clay County just then, so I lit out of there. Didn't even stop by the place to tell my folks I was goin'." Boone shook his head and took a long, slow breath. "I feel right bad about that. But I was so a-scared I could only think to get away from there quick as I could. Caught a ride on a delivery wagon on its way back to Independence. Got across the river and decided there weren't no goin' back."

"Rosa!" Pegleg hollered as Boone sat quiet, head bowed.

"Bring out some more of that coffee, would you/" He studied the boy as the woman came out with a battered tin coffeepot. She filled the two mugs, gathered Boone's bowl, and returned to the hut.

Pegleg tested the heat of the coffee and swallowed a slurpy sip. "Go on, boy. You've got as far as Independence with this tale of yours, but that's a hell of a long ways from Taos."

Boone sat upright, jolted out of whatever reverie he had fallen into. He scrubbed his face with the palms of his hands and resumed his story. "There in Independence was a freightin' outfit with an ox train settin' out for Santa Fe. The wagon master took me on as a herder for the spare cattle and what saddle mounts they had. He fitted me out with what I needed, on credit against my wages.

"When we got up there to Bent's Fort and laid over for a time, there was some trappers talkin' there, tellin' stories and such. What they was a-sayin' about livin' in the mountains and bein' free and all, well, it sounded good to me. Figured if the law come lookin' for me, there'd be no way they could find me in the mountains. Besides, havin' been named for Daniel Boone, seemed like I was born to be out there, somehow."

Pegleg's laugh wasn't as robust as his earlier outburst. "Don't know what them fellows at Bent's Fort was tellin' you, but most likely it was all tongue oil. Trappin' ain't no easy life. Besides which, like I told you, the mountain man's life is gone under. Every child I know what made his livin' off plews is lookin' for a new line of work."

The boy bowed his head again, as if the wood grain in the tabletop had something to reveal.

"You ain't the first pilgrim come to the mountains on account of a woman. Nor the first thinkin' the law was cuttin' his sign. Never mind that it's gettin' a mite populated for my taste out here, there's still plenty of country for a man to get lost in.

Go on with your story."

"There ain't much more. I knowed from what people said that Taos was where I'd likely run onto fur trappers in this country. So when we got to Santa Fe and I collected my pay, I come on up here to look for a start." Again, Boone's chin fell to his chest, and he shook his head with a sigh. "Guess I've been foolish with all my notions."

Pegleg and Boone sat in silence as the sun climbed. The mountain man's coffee was gone; Bonne's had gone cold in the cup. With a lengthy sigh, Boone stood. "Sorry for wastin' your time, Mister Smith. I best be gettin' on."

"Sit down, boy. We ain't done yet."

Boone dropped back onto the stool. Pegleg eyed him. "Can you ride?"

"Yessir."

"Good?"

"Yessir. My daddy had me ridin' the plow horse 'fore I could walk, even. Got around horseback most everywhere I went all my life."

"Mules?"

"Some. Horses, mostly. Why?"

Pegleg Smith said nothing for a time, instead scratching at the tabletop with a rough fingernail as he thought. Then, "You recall Old Bill Williams from last night?"

"Can't rightly say so. Don't know the names of any of them you was with."

"Well, Old Bill, he was one of 'em. That long, tall red-headed one. Him and me go back. You want to know a mountain man, you'd do right to look to him." After a moment, Pegleg said, "I told you about my wife, Song."

"The redskin woman?" Boone's eyes widened at Pegleg's sharp glare.

"That's right. And mind how you say that."

"Yessir."

"Well, she's got a cousin or half-brother or somesuch name of Wakara. Known him a good long time. Had all manner of dealin's with him."

Another pause, long enough to make Boone uncomfortable. "Me and Old Bill and Wakara and Jim Beckwourth is goin' partners on a business proposition. It's somethin' we've all done before, at one time or another, and if it works out there'll be plenty of money in it. But it ain't goin' to be easy. We'll be needin' lots of help to pull it off."

Another pause. "You want in?"

Boone swallowed hard. "I don't know what it is you're talkin' about." He swallowed again. "But I reckon I do, whatever it is. It ain't like I got any other prospects at present."

Pegleg nodded.

The boy said, "Can I ask what it is I'm a-signin' up for?"

Pegleg's cold stare turned to a smile. "We're goin' to California."

"California?"

"California."

Boone shook his head with furrowed brow and squinted eyes. "What we goin' to do in California?"

Pegleg held his smile as he stared at the boy. "Steal horses from the Mexicans."

The confusion on Boone's face deepened.

"That's all you need to know for now, boy. More, come to think of it. We'll be leavin' Taos in a couple days. Beckwourth's over in Abiquiu puttin' together a pack outfit. Wakara and his boys will meet up with us up the trail. You got all that?"

Boone nodded his understanding, although still unsure what he was getting into. Thinking himself dismissed, he stood again to leave.

"One more thing," Pegleg said.

"Yessir?"

"You recollect what I done to that Frenchie last night?"

Boone nodded.

"You breathe a word of this to anyone, and I'll unhitch this leg of mine and beat the livin' shit out of you before you can blink an eye."

CHAPTER THREE

Boone watched the five young Mexicans sitting, backs against the wall of Old Bill's adobe house, drinking what he assumed was coffee from steaming mugs, talking quietly. Two of them looked to be napping in the silver light of dawn. He knew the ground-tied horse not far from the door belonged to Pegleg, signified by the leather pouch attached to the left stirrup leather, built to accommodate his wooden leg in place of a stirrup. Old Bill's saddled mule stood tied to a sagging hitchrail. The boy assumed the saddled horse next to it, a rawboned *grulla* gelding, would be his mount. Five other saddled horses stood hip shot, tied outside a tumble-down corral where five mules nosed about in the dusty ground. In the dooryard lay a jumbled pile of packsaddles, camp equipment, and leather pouches of foodstuffs.

" 'Bout time you got here, boy," came Pegleg's voice through the open door. "Much longer, you'd be standin' alone wonderin' where the hell we was." The mountain man stepped out the doorway.

Boone walked to him, dropped his bedroll, and took the offered mug of coffee. "I ain't late, am I? You said we'd go at sunup."

Pegleg turned toward the east and nodded in the direction of the thin slice of the sun just peeking above the rim of shadowed mountain.

Blowing the steam off his coffee, Boone took a sip. "What's

with them Mexicans?" he said, pointing with his mug.

"Them's our *mozos. Muleros.* They'll handle the pack mules. These, and the ones Beckwourth's got rounded up in Abiquiu. And those boys'll ride with us when we get to them California ranchos."

Boone took another sip of coffee and shook his head. "Look like a lazy and shiftless lot to me."

Pegleg laughed. "Don't you worry none about them boys. They know what they're about. They'll have them mules packed 'fore you can swallow that coffee. Ever' one of them's been out to California and back on tradin' jaunts, tendin' to eight or ten mules in a train of a hundred. You'd do well to learn from them."

"Mexicans," Boone sniffed. "I don't trust a one of 'em."

Mere minutes later, Boone took a last long swallow to empty his mug and balanced it on the hitchrail post, slung his bedroll behind the cantle and tied it off, swung into the saddle, and heeled up the horse to catch up with the already departed company. He trotted past one of the *mozos* bringing up the rear, then the mules tied head-to-tail single file, then the cluster of the other four Mexicans ahead of the short train, and reined up to ride beside Pegleg. Old Bill Williams rode alone, a ways ahead. They would follow him west from Taos to strike and follow the Rio Grande for a time, then head cross country to Abiquiu.

Old Bill kept up a steady stream of talk throughout the morning ride, none of which the riders behind him could make out. His voice sounded as much like a clucking hen as a man.

Boone said, "What's he talkin' about?"

Pegleg laughed. "Nothin', most likely. Old Bill, he used to be a preacher. Probably preachin' hisself a sermon. Maybe givin' a lesson on religion to that mule. The man likes to be alone, mostly. Prefers the sound of his own voice for company."

23

"How come he rides thataway? All hunched over with his knees up?"

"Can't say. Always sits his mount like that since I knowed him."

"He always ride a mule?"

"When he can. He'll ride a horse now and then, but he prefers them long-eared hardtails. They can outdo a horse at some things, but me, I'd rather fork a horse."

It was still morning on the third day when the riders followed the Rio Chama through its canyon and into Abiquiu. The settlement sat on the floor of the river gorge, whose sandstone cliffs and walls showed all the colors of the sun, from the warm pinks of morning to the white-hot blaze of noon to sunset oranges and reds. Boone studied the village as they rode through, returning the stares of women and children peeking out the doorways of adobe huts clustered around the mission church.

"Everybody here looks Mexican," Boone said to Pegleg.

"Hell, boy, you're in Mexico. Who did you think would be here? Dutchmen?"

"But it ain't like this in Santa Fe. Or Taos. Plenty of white folks thereabouts."

"Well. That's on account of the Santa Fe Trail bringin' in all them traders to that place. Trappers been hanging around Taos for years—keeps us away from whatever government they got runnin' things in Santa Fe and their license fees and taxes and such. But now you're in New Mexico proper. Besides that, these folks ain't regular Mexicans. These is *Genizaros*. Times gone by, they was slaves—stole from Indian tribes up north and sold to the Spaniards and Mexicans."

"Slaves? Here on their own? Who oversees them?"

With a chuckle, Pegleg told Boone the *Genizaros* were no longer slaves but still considered a lower class of people, having descended from slaves. Long ago, military and political leaders had sent a group of them here to establish an outpost. "What they figured, I reckon, is that if Navajos or Utes or other Indians took a notion to raid, the *Genizaros* would get the worst of it. Leastways, slow down the raiders till the government could get the soldiers after 'em."

At the edge of town, the riders reined up outside a corral. A half-dozen horses and a few mules huddled in a corner of the pen built to hold many, many more animals—hundreds, Boone reckoned. Beside the corral was a long, low adobe building fronted by a row of uncovered doorways, each opening onto a small room where traders and their *mozos* could shelter as they outfitted a mule train bound for Los Angeles. A larger, sturdier stone building with a heavy wooden door kept their trade goods—mostly woolen blankets and serapes and silver—safe from plunder.

As the men dismounted, a black man ducked out of one of the doorways. He talked quietly with Old Bill and Pegleg as they stretched out the kinks from hours in the saddle. The *mozos* went to work unpacking the mules. Williams and Smith looped bridle reins around a corral rail and walked off toward the adobe building.

The black man walked over to where Boone sat horseback. The boy looked him over as the man patted the horse's neck. He said, "Pegleg and Old Bill have gone to get some grub. There is plenty for you. Unsaddle your horse and take care of it, and these other two, then come on over."

Boone sat upright. "I don't take orders from no darky."

Before he knew what happened, Boone found himself flat on his back in the dust, gasping to regain the breath forced from his lungs. The man stood over him, silhouetted against the mid-morning sun, a moccasined foot planted in the middle of the boy's chest. He bent low toward Boone until his smiling face came into the addled boy's focus. He pulled a heavy knife from a sheath on his belt and touched the tip to the tender spot under Boone's chin with enough pressure to make the boy wince.

"I don't know where you think you are, son, or who you think you are talking to. But you had best learn this, and know it right now. I am James Pierson Beckwourth, free trapper, man of these mountains, and a chief in the Crow nation. I take no sass from no one, let alone a fuzzy-faced boy such as yourself, barely old enough to make foam on his piss."

Beckwourth returned the knife to its sheath and grabbed Boone by his shirtfront and hoisted him to his feet, lifting him clear of the ground before dropping him to his feet. He pulled him close, ducking until his black face was inches from the boy's, pasty pale and whiter than usual. "Now, son, you tend to them horses straightaway. And if you have still got the stomach for it, come in and get yourself fed."

Later, Boone sat flat on the ground against the wall inside a dim room, lit only by light through the doorway and the orange glow of burned-down coals in the adobe fireplace, stuck like half a beehive in the corner. He spooned up mouthfuls from the bowl of beans, wondering if every dish in New Mexico was fired up with chili peppers. He stretched his neck, tipping it from side to side, and arched his back in an attempt to relieve the stiffness and ache from Beckwourth's slamming him to the ground. He eyed the black man's broad shoulders and back, rippling with muscles even through his buckskin shirt, as he squatted on the other side of the room talking with Old Bill and Pegleg in low voices.

No one else was in the room. The five *mozos* from Taos congregated out near the corral, laughing and talking and playing a knife-throwing game with their Abiquiu *compadres*. Three white men, who looked to be trappers and must have already been here with Beckwourth, walked among the horses and mules in the corral, checking teeth and hooves, massaging legs, and otherwise evaluating their readiness for the trail.

Rising from the conversation, Beckwourth walked out of the room, giving Boone a stern look as he left.

"He always this ornery?" Boone said to Pegleg and Old Bill.

"The man don't take kindly to insolence," Pegleg said.

"Where I come from, he'd have been whipped already for layin' hands on a white man."

"Well, boy, out here the man takin' the whippin' is the one whose mouth says things his fists—or knife or gun—can't back up. But I reckon Jim already taught you that lesson."

"Still, it don't seem right. A black man ought to know his place."

"Like I said, a man earns his place in these mountains. Don't matter where he come from or what he done before or what he looks like, he gets his due. I ain't been to Missouri for a time, but I don't guess there's as much respect due them Missouri Pukes by the dozen as what Jim Beckwourth has showed he's worth."

"Maybe so. But he best watch himself where I'm concerned."

Pegleg's braying laugh chorused with Old Bill's piercing cackle.

Boone finished eating in silence, chewing on what Pegleg said along with the beans. "What is it we do in the morning? Where do we go?"

"Head upriver, follow the Chama for a fair piece," Pegleg said. "Strike the San Juan River. The Animas, the Dolores. Follow the Spanish Valley northwest to the Grand River, on through more of that red rock country and desert to the Green River. That's some six hundred miles, they reckon."

Boone raised a hand. "Hold on—northwest, you say?"

"That's what I said."

"I thought California was out west of here. What for we goin' north?"

Pegleg mulled it over. "Go west out of here you find nothin' but trouble. Rough country—canyons deeper'n hell and harder to get out of. Miles of desert that don't grow enough grass to feed a jackass rabbit. Not much in the way of water—leastways water you can get to. And the Navajos out there don't want you around.

"Anyhow, not long after we ford the Green, the trail dips back toward the southwest and cuts through some hellacious mountains and long valleys and such and on through the Mojave Desert and on into California and all them big ranchos where we'll find the horses and mules we're a-goin' after."

"Only trail I ever seen is the one out from Missouri to Santa Fe. This don't sound much like it. Ain't no wagons out here?"

Pegleg chuckled. "Hell, no. Ain't been a wagon built can travel the country we'll be goin' through. Mule trains is how the traders go. But they been stringin' them mules out to Los Angeles for years, so the road is well used." The trapper watched the boy chew on his lip, looking to be lost inside his mind. "You havin' second thoughts, boy? Thinkin' of backin' out?"

Boone thought a while longer, then slowly shook his head. "No. I reckon not. It ain't like I got anywhere else to be at just now."

"Then you be ready to ride come the dawn."

CHAPTER FOUR

Along the banks of the San Juan River, the band of travelers from Taos and Abiquiu stirred in the gray light of dawn. The activity was sluggish, as there was nothing to do but wait. Thick coffee boiled in a battered pot, bacon swam in its own fat in a blackened skillet, and beans and chilies bubbled lazily in a Dutch oven never empty since the first camp. A weathered old packer named Manolo, veteran of several crossings to California, patted *masa* into tortillas and baked them two by two on a sandstone slab that served as a *comal* on his many trips.

Far away in the east, the sun flashed over the horizon, and, at the moment its ascending circle fully formed, freakish screams filled the air, the cacophony, combined with pounding hooves, drowning out the splash and spill of the river. Emanating from the direction of the sun, its source lost in the glare, the screeching and shrieking intensified, sending Boone and the *mozos* scrambling for cover and weapons. But the mountain men stood and faced the attack, yelling and yelping and adding to the clamor.

Dust stirred by drumming hooves filtered the blinding light, outlining a row of mounted, charging horses. At the verge of the camp, the row split, streaming past on either side, the riders then arcing and rejoining and sliding to a stop, reining around to line up and face the camp. Boone, knife in hand, watched the Indians, eyes shifting along the line, waiting for whatever threat would present itself. But the howling settled along with the dust.

The stone-faced rider near the center of the row of more than a dozen horses swung a leg over the neck of his mount and slid to the ground and with long strides approached Pegleg Smith. The scowling, one-legged man walked to meet him. They stopped an arm's length apart. Then, at a cue unnoticed by anyone else, the mountain man and Indian broke into smiles and embraced, Pegleg pounding the other man's back and laughing. The two men talked while the other Indians dismounted and stood watching, a near mirror image of the row of staring *mozos* and mountain men.

Boone sidled over to Philip Thompson, a trapper they had met at Abiquiu. "What the hell is going on?" Boone said.

"Oh, it ain't nothin'. It's just Wakara and his Utes showin' off. Plenty of Indian bands like to put on a show when they get to any kind of a gathering. I recollect one time at rendezvous on the Bear River, must've been two hundred Snake Indians come ridin' in thataway. Next day, a band of Crow near as big paraded in just the same. I reckon they do it for fun, is all. And if they can scare the bejeebers out of some pilgrim like yourself, well, that's all the more fun for 'em."

A flush rose up the boy's neck as he slid the knife back into its sheath. He took note of the Utes. Wakara, still a young man, looked to be one of the oldest. Two, maybe three, he thought to be near the same age as Wakara, and one, with gray-shot hair and deep lines in his face, was certainly the most aged. But there was no doubt Wakara was the leader. Others in the band Boone guessed to be about his own age, one even younger. Following a few minutes' palavering with Pegleg, Wakara said something to the Indians Boone could not understand, and they turned their mounts and led their packhorses a short distance away and went to setting up camp.

Boone bristled when the old man at the cook fire handed him a battered wooden bucket and sent him to fill it at the river. Intent in his anger, he did not at first notice the Ute boy squatted on an upstream boulder a few yards out in the river filling a skin bag. Boone dropped his bucket in the still, shallow water ponded at the riverbank and scooped it full as he hoisted it up. He jerked upright when the Ute boy spoke.

"That water is no good."

Boone dropped the pail into the shallows as he found the source of the words, then retrieved the bucket by the bail. Water dripped off the sides and bottom of the bucket onto his feet. "Why the hell not? It's comin' out of the same stream where yours is."

The Ute lifted the leather bag out of the river, bunged the spout with a wooden plug lashed to the neck with rawhide and slung it over his shoulder by its rope sling, then jumped from the boulder to the bank. He walked to where Boone stood and pointed at the bucket. "Look."

"I don't need to look. It's water in there."

"Yes. But there are also bugs. And mud."

"Them bugs won't hurt nothin'. And the mud'll settle."

"But the taste will still be there. If you fill from the flowing stream, the water is clear and sweet."

Before Boone could react, the boy grabbed the bucket without a word, dumped it, and jumped back onto the boulder. He swung the refilled bucket and used its momentum to help carry him back to the riverbank. "I am called Nooch," he said as he carried the dripping pail back to where Boone waited. "What is your name?"

The taken-aback boy hesitated before answering and swallowed hard. "I go by Boone. The rest of it is Daniel Boone Trewick."

"What does it mean?"

"What do you mean, 'what does it mean'?"

"Daniel Boone Trewick. What do the words mean?"

"I don't guess they mean nothin' 'cept for a name. Trewick, that's just our family name. My Pa, he was an admirer of Daniel Boone, so he give me that name. Ain't no more to it than that."

"Who is Daniel Boone?"

"Who? Hell, boy, ever'body knows who Daniel Boone is. Man's a hero back in America. Long hunter, pioneer. He opened up Kentucky 'most by hisself. Blazed trails all through that country."

Nooch thought that over for a moment, shook his head, and smiled. "I think you had better get this back to camp," he said, handing the bucket to Boone.

Boone followed the Ute back toward camp and dropped the bucket, sloshing out a wave of water that splashed Manolo's feet and earned a hard gaze for his effort. Pegleg Smith watched from where he sat on a rotting cottonwood log, stitching back together the torn edge of a panier with a string of rawhide.

"C'mon over here, boy," he said, and Boone folded himself to the ground next to the log. Pegleg poked a hole through the hide with a metal awl, worked the string through, and pulled it taut with his teeth. "Have you disremembered what I done to that Canuck back in Taos with my wood leg?"

"No, sir. I ain't forgot."

"You best practice better manners where the cook is concerned, or I will feel obligated to sharpen that memory."

"What do you care? He's just an old Mexican."

Pegleg did not answer until after pulling another stich tight. "One thing you'll learn in this country is to respect a man what can cook. That *concinero* you're talkin' about could make a right tasty stew out of a pair of worn-out moccasins. And them tortillas of his is the best I ever ate. Weren't for him, we'd be gnawin' on corn dodgers that'd likely bust a tooth." Another stitch drew tight between the mountain man's teeth. "If you was to upset ol' Manolo to where he quit cookin' for this outfit, I wouldn't have to kick your ass—there'd be men lined up to do it."

"All right, I guess. But tell me somethin'—why is it you're so all-fired concerned about me and my manners and such?"

Pegleg wiggled the rawhide string through another pair of holes. "It's like this, son. It was me as invited you to come along. I vouched for you by doin' that. You don't keep up your end, or aggravate the others by bein' a pain in the ass, well, that don't only make *you* look bad—makes me look bad, too. And I won't have it."

Boone sat silent for a time, watching the trapper's work while he watched the people in the camp as they sat in bunches and talked, or found odd jobs to keep themselves busy as Pegleg had done. He studied the Ute boy, Nooch, as he ran a willow stick back and forth through a handheld stone with a hole through it. He guessed the job had something to do with making an arrow.

Pegleg said, "Saw you talkin' to Nooch down by the river. Learn anything?"

The boy laughed. "Don't think there's much I could learn from an ignorant savage."

Pegleg's laugh outdid Boone's. "He talk to you in English, did he?"

Boone nodded.

"Unless I miss my guess, his English ain't no worse than yours or mine. He can also talk Spanish. Speaks Shoshoni, too, and can get by some in Navajo. And he speaks Ute, of course. Not so bad for an ignorant savage."

"Still, he didn't have no notion about who Daniel Boone is."

"Ain't no reason he should. Howsomever, I'd be willin' to

33

bet he knows more about white folks than what you know about Indians."

Head bowed, Boone scratched in the dirt with a twig. "How is it you know so much about him?"

Pegleg pulled another stitch tight through the leather with his teeth, then said, "He's my wife's brother, Nooch is. Him, and two of them other boys over there. Wakara's some kind of kin, too—Song's a cousin of his, or some such."

The mending complete, Pegleg cut off the remaining string and tossed the bag into Boone's lap. "Take that there panier over to where the supplies is piled so's the boys can get it packed." Boone rose to his feet and started away but stopped at Pegleg's voice. "One thing you'd do well to remember, son. You ain't in Missouri no more. Out here, a man's a man till he shows otherwise. We get out to California—hell, even on the way out and back—you may well find yourself needin' these men to save your bacon. You better hope to hell they'll bother to do it."

Boone started off again, and again Pegleg's voice stopped him. "We pull out at first light. If you're a-goin' with us, you'd best be ready. If you ain't, well, I reckon you can find your way back to Santa Fe—the States, so far as that goes."

It was still dark as Boone meandered through the herd of horses and mules by starlight seeking out his saddle horse. He had ridden some of the others at times, but looked for the mouse-colored gelding that fit him best. As he led the horse back to camp he passed a handful of the *muleros* on their way out to bring in the pack mules and saddle horses. Boone pulled taut the latigo and cinch as the gray ribbon of dawn stretched across the eastern sky, stepped into the stirrup, and swung into the saddle. Hands stacked atop the horn, he watched the packers hang panniers, stack and cover bundles, and throw diamond hitches. The work went fast, and the mules were strung out and ready to go long before the horses were saddled.

Old Bill Williams rode out first. Wakara and the Utes followed. Pegleg, Beckwourth, Thompson, and the rest of the Taos and Abiquiu trappers turned up the trail next, then the mule train with its *mozos* strung along in between.

Boone watched it all from his seat in the saddle, and, when the campsite was abandoned, he reined his horse around and heeled it into a long trot to catch up with Pegleg and find his place among the mountain men.

CHAPTER FIVE

One by one, lights winked off in the hacienda. From where he stood in the shadow of a pepper tree, Juan Medina followed the progress of the *hacendado*, Don Emiliano Peralta, along the wing of the house as he snuffed out candles and extinguished lanterns on the way to his bedchamber.

But Juan's interest was in the opposite wing, angling back toward the gardens, where the Don's daughter Magdalena shared a room with five of her sisters. The vaquero waited for a time after darkness settled in the house, then set out through the starlight toward the shutters, dark against the plastered adobe wall, behind which Magdalena waited.

He paused again at the window, listening. Hearing nothing, he reached out and scratched at the wooden shutter.

"*¿Quién es?*" came the whisper from within.

"*Soy yo.* Juan."

The boy stepped back as the shutter inched open. He sensed, but did not see, Magdalena through the crack. He inhaled sharply as starlight revealed the girl when the shutter swung wide. A thick, dark braid draped across her pale shoulder and lay over the whiteness of her shift. Dusky eyes glinted with flecks of reflected stars; dark lips—their redness lost in the dim light—framed a smile that seemed to glow.

Juan swallowed hard. "Your sisters?"

"*Dormido.*"

"*Bueno.* We must be careful not to wake them." He sighed. "I have missed you."

"As I have missed you. But I saw you today. The front doors stood open as we had dinner on the patio. You rode past, leading another horse."

"*Sí.* It was one of your father's favored brood mares. He expects special foals from her. It is her time, so I took her to *el semental.*"

Magdalena giggled.

Realizing too late what he had said, Juan slapped a hand to his mouth. The flush that colored his face did not show in the darkness, but the boy felt its heat. "Oh!" he said. *"Lo siento!"*

Again, the girl giggled. *"No es nada.* I am not an ignorant child, you know."

Juan had no answer, and, in the silence, he heard one of the other girls in the room stir. "I must go."

"Sí," Magdalena said, taking the boy's face in her hands. *"Te amo."* She kissed him lightly on the lips.

Again feeling a flush on his face—but, now, for a different reason—Juan turned to go. "Adios," he whispered over his shoulder as Magdalena pulled the shutter to.

The color in his face paled with the memory of his indiscretion. Shaking his head in chagrin, he berated himself under his breath for speaking to a young woman as if she were another vaquero. Such things were not mentioned in polite company. But seeing to the breeding of the Don's favored horses—albeit under the direction of the *Segundo,* the *mayordomo,* who oversaw work on the rancho, and his father—was second nature to the boy. And, while Magdalena did not seem offended with his rash behavior, he hoped she would forget it.

Reaching the pepper tree, Juan gathered the reins of the horse tethered there, stepped into the saddle, and rode the short distance to his hut in the workers' village. As a vaquero, Juan spent most of his waking hours in the saddle, mounting up to ride no matter the nearness of the destination. He had walked to Magdalena's window only for stealth. Horses wandered everywhere on the rancho, and Juan and the other vaqueros, as well as the Don's sons and other young gentlemen of the ranchos, simply saddled the nearest horse, rode it until it tired, then captured and saddled another. Even the humblest of the vaqueros considered walking beneath their station. Burros and mules, likewise, grazed the hills and valleys of the California ranchos in numbers beyond reckoning.

But, in addition to the common caballos populating his rancho, Don Emiliano kept a special herd, isolated in their own corrals and fenced pastures—horses of improved breeding and conformation. The Don was also particular about color. While his herd included sorrels and bays and browns and duns, he favored the palominos with their pale, golden hides and flaxen manes and tails.

Reaching home, Juan dismounted near the door of the hut he shared with his father, loosed the saddle cinch, and dropped the reins, ground-tying the horse where it would stand till morning in keeping with the custom of always having a horse at the ready. Juan pushed aside the hanging blanket that served as a door and slipped into the room, feeling his way toward the pallet in the corner where he slept.

"*¿Deseas morir?*"

Juan froze at the voice from the darkness. "No, father. I do not wish to die." The boy listened to rustling from his father's corner of the hut, and he watched the sparks that fell from striking flint on steel. From the glow in the tinderbox and gentle blowing, the wick on a candle flamed, illuminating the man's face and casting its glow into the hut. The man rose from where he reclined propped on an elbow to sit, and then scoured his eyes with the heels of his hands.

The senior Medina, like Juan, was a vaquero on the rancho

of Don Emiliano Peralta. And it was from his father that Juan learned horsemanship skills shared by few. Of all the vaqueros in his employ, only Miguel Medina—and, more and more, Juan—trained Don Emiliano's special horses. The expertise of the Medinas was of much renown among the Californio rancheros, and many brought their favored colts to Miguel to be turned into horses of distinction. Miguel also oversaw the breeding of mules for the rancho.

"Where have you been, my son?"

The question was asked, but Juan knew his father knew the answer. The boy only shrugged.

"I asked if you wanted to die. Perhaps you will not be killed when Don Emiliano discovers your attentions toward his daughter, but it will not go well for you."

Again, Juan shrugged.

"And the reputation of the girl will be compromised, if not destroyed. If you do not care for yourself, you should have concern for her."

"Magdalena knows her own mind. She does not shun my attentions. Rather, she welcomes them. Even returns them."

"That is of little note, my son. You know the *gente de razón* do not respect *indios* or *coyotes*. To them, we are but peons—good for nothing but work."

Juan lowered himself to his pallet and pulled off his poncho, which he folded and rolled to use as a pillow. "But father, we are more than *indios*. grandmother was *indio*, but our grandfather was *europeo*. And mother—God rest her soul—was from a Californio father!"

Miguel sighed. "This is all true, Juan. But parentage does not always equate with society. To the Don's way of thinking, even a stallion or mare of quality will on occasion throw a scrub foal. All that matters is that, in terms of society, we are of no consequence to Don Emiliano." Miguel blew out the candle.

"Sleep now, my son. There is work to do come the morning." He wormed back into his blanket. "And do not forget, Juan. That muchacha is not for you. Only trouble will come from it."

As much as Juan tried to sleep, his thoughts would not allow it. He finally drifted off, but it seemed that as soon as he fell asleep his father awakened him, shaking his shoulder.

"Arise, my son. Today, the horses we train will rest. Today, we work at the *calaveras.*"

Juan sat up on his bed and yawned. He did not look forward to the bloody work the day would bring, but the *Segundo* had so declared, and so it would be. Shaking out the poncho and sliding it overhead, he pulled his flat-brimmed hat—a castoff from one of the Don's sons—snug over his brow.

The flock of pigeons outside the doorway did little more than walk out of his way as Juan shuffled through them on the way to his saddled horse, standing just steps away from where he had dismounted the night before. After stretching the latigo to snug up the cinch, he grabbed the saddle horn with both hands, jumped, and swung a leg over the cantle, landing in the seat having never touched foot to stirrup. He slipped his feet into the stirrups, each carved from a solid block of oak, the front covered with *tapaderos,* and spurred the horse into motion.

Within minutes, Juan found horses grazing on the hillside behind the hacienda, built a loop in his rawhide reata, and with an easy backhand rolling throw landed it around a horse's neck. He stripped the saddle from last night's mount, threw it onto the back of the fresh horse and cinched it tight, pulled the bridle from one horse and hung it on the other, and swung into the saddle as before. As he coiled the reata, he turned and rode down the hill, where he would find a breakfast of tortillas and beans, stew, and whatever other food was in this morning's kettles at the workers' communal kitchen.

The sun had not yet risen when Juan joined the vaqueros

gathering in the yard in front of the hacienda. Horses snorted and pawed and pranced, tossing their heads, impatient with the waiting and eager to be on the go. The oversized wooden doors of the hacienda swung open, and Don Emiliano Peralta stepped out with his *Segundo,* Carlos Garcia, at his side.

Garcia wore working clothes, although in better repair than those of the mounted vaqueros, and even more so those of the workers afoot, the men who would do the bloody work of killing in the slaughter corrals, the *matanza,* the *calaveras,* or place of the skulls. The Don wore his usual finery: Knee-length pantaloons with silver lace at the cuffs were fastened at the waist with a wide, red sash, visible beneath the silver-buttoned vest and dark-blue cloth jacket. Shoes were topped with soft leather *botas,* embellished with tooled floral designs and tied below the knee with tasseled leather strings. His hat, similar in design to the hand-me-down Juan wore, lacked the vaquero's film of grease and powdering of dust. It was decorated with a ribbon around the edge of the flat brim, with a matching ribbon wrapped around the base of the crown.

Several of the Don's children followed the men out of the house, spreading in a row behind to witness the giving of the day's orders. Magdalena was among them, and Juan watched her as she pulled a colorful serape tight around her shoulders.

"Buenos dias," the Don said to the assembly. "There is much work to be done today. But if we bring many hands to the task it will go well." He turned and nodded to Garcia. The *Segundo* cleared his throat and instructed the vaqueros where to ride to gather cattle, adding, unnecessarily, descriptions of the age and kind and condition of animals to round up. The butchers were told to see to the sharpening of their broad-bladed knives. The women were to load *carretas* with water, food, *bolsas*—bags and pouches—and wooden stakes; and to hitch up burros to pull the loads to the *matanza.* The workers well knew their tasks,

having performed the same jobs countless times, but stood silent and respectful for the morning ritual.

Dust and the smell of blood were already in the air when Juan and the vaqueros he rode with arrived at the slaughter corrals with cattle gathered from their assigned hills and arroyos. A worker pulled the slip rails from the corral gate, and the riders pushed the cattle through. The gate poles were the only wood in the construction of the corral. A low adobe wall surrounded the enclosure, topped with a row of cattle skulls, their long horns interlaced and intertwined to form an impenetrable barrier.

Juan and the other vaqueros took their turns in the corral, roping cattle with their reatas and securing them for the men on the ground. The butchers and their knives went about the work of slaughter with sanguine efficiency, slitting throats and skinning animals, some still in the throes of death. Some blood filled *jarras* for use in cooking, but much more would be spilled than could be used, and soon dark puddles soaked into the dusty corral, creating slimy, malodorous bogs. Knives sliced the best meat from the carcasses for a time; the cuts wrapped in *bolsas* and loaded in the carts and carried to the kitchens, both for cooking and to make *carne seca* for storage and trade.

But today's cattle were not killed for their meat, but for their hides and tallow. And so, the men tossed most of the flesh and bones, along with offal, into a steep-sided arroyo adjacent to a corner of the killing pen. Tonight, the grizzly bears would feast.

As the day progressed, the grassy ground around the *matanza* was carpeted with hides, pinned hair side down to the ground with wooden stakes, roughly fleshed and left to dry in the sun. Carts laden with slabs of fat carved from the carcasses squealed their way to the rendering kettles, where the fat would be chopped up and cooked down to tallow over the days to come. They were beyond and downwind of the hacienda.

With the job nearly done in the late afternoon, workers staked out the last of the hides, and the butchers dumped the last carcasses into the ravine. Women stuffed the last of the fat into leather and cloth bags and loaded it into the carts, calling to the handful of playing children to get ready to go. Juan lay back in the saddle, one elbow propped on the horse's rump and a leg wrapped around the pommel, watching the dust settle. Screams jolted him upright.

Crashing through the scrub oak lining the arroyo, fast approaching the knot of playing children, came a grizzly bear. Despite the screams of the women, the children were slow to realize the danger. The bear was an old one, the hair on his hump and back silvered. Frowzy and thin, the bear looked sick, or perhaps diseased, which explained why he approached the humans in broad daylight. Still, despite his scruffy appearance, the bear's outsized front paws, paddling inward as he ran, and the teeth visible in a mouth stringing slobber offered more than enough danger.

In one fluid motion, Juan unwrapped his leg, found the stirrups, and spurred the horse into action even as he lifted the coiled reata and made a loop. He set his course to reach the edge of the ravine ahead of the charging bear, and the horse, though frightened, won the race. Standing in the stirrups, shouting and waving his arms overhead, using rein and spur to force his mount to rear, the rider and horse created enough of a distraction to stop the bear. The uncertain animal growled and stood on its hind legs, nose in the air, attempting to make sense of the interruption.

The instant the horse's front hooves hit the ground, Juan's already spinning loop snaked out. It dropped over the grizzly's head, tightening as Juan jerked the slack. The vaquero took two quick turns around the saddle horn as he spun the horse away from the bear. The frightened horse knew as well as the rider that their lives depended on keeping the rope taut. Each time the bear charged, Juan turned, jerking the bear. Soon, two other vaqueros had their ropes on the roaring animal, and the three strangling ropes were more than even a healthy grizzly could have overcome.

Now came four of the butchers, smiling at the prospect of dispatching the bear with their knives. In turn, they charged at the tethered grizzly, the reatas hindering his attempts to react quickly enough to their attacks. And then two of the men advanced at once, one on either side, and, as the bear turned to swat at the one, the other thrust his already bloody knife into the bear's throat. The enraged grizzly spun and raised a paw at the attacker, but the man had already retreated beyond reach. Blood poured from the slit throat, and the bear's struggles weakened until it fell on its side.

Showing no caution, Juan rode toward the bear, his reata going slack. He unwound the dallies from the horn and stepped out of the saddle, walked the few steps to the dying bear, and pulled his loop from its giant head. He marveled at the bulk of the animal—even in its wasted state and lying on its side, it made a sizable heap.

Grabbing the saddle horn, Juan swung into the saddle, turned his horse, and slowly coiled his reata as he rode away.

CHAPTER SIX

There were times Boone could see the trail they followed. When passing through canyons and along streams the route, beaten down by thousands of hooves over the years, showed the way as clearly as a city street. But at other times the boy saw no discernible path, and Old Bill or Wakara or Pegleg or whoever led the way seemed to wander at will over featureless plains.

The caravan skirted the San Juan Mountains and then, for what felt like endless days, crossed rolling prairies covered with grass and brush, cut with gorges and ravines. As they snaked to the northwest, sand blew unhindered at times, pelting man and animal alike, filling eyelids and nostrils and teeth with grit and saturating every crease and wrinkle in skin and clothing with irritating drifts of dust. The heat grew more intense and water increasingly scarce. Waves of shifting sand drifted into dunes, some solidified over ages past into wind-rippled rock. Outcrops and buttes and pinnacles of eerie, eroded shapes dotted the landscape, creating a world unfamiliar to Boone—similar to places he had passed before, but now on an unprecedented scale.

Near the end of a long, hot, dry day, the travelers piled up in a dry wash, progress stopped by a sandstone cliff no taller than a man standing on his saddle, but insurmountable for the horses and mules. Boone watched as the Utes and mountain men and *muleros* dismounted and tied their mounts to limbs on cedar trees or to the woody brush that sprouted from the sand.

Nooch and two other of the young Utes scrambled up the sandstone scarp, followed by a pair of *mozos,* one of which stopped to lend Old Bill a hand up. Pegleg signaled Boone to follow with a thrust of his chin. Meanwhile, the *mozos* had unpacked wooden pails from the mules and tossed them, followed by coiled reatas, to waiting hands above.

Boone, bucket in hand, paused to look around as most of the rest of the party climbed up and walked on by. They walked, and he stood, on what looked to be riverbed of solid rock, but there was no sign of water. Stunted cedar trees and scraggly brush clinging to cracks in the sandstone said water seldom coursed here. A mile, maybe less, ahead, a giant rock outcrop towered over the dry wash and surrounding plain, glowing in fiery reds and oranges in the low-hanging sun. Along a vertical wall beneath the dome above, a row of deep alcoves, like arched windows or doorways, cut into the mountain.

"*Casa Colorado,* that be," Old Bill said. "Means 'Red House' in Mex. I reckon you can see why."

Boone nodded, agreeing with the illusion. Looking around and seeing no sign of water, Boone held up the bucket. "Why we stoppin' here?"

Old Bill smiled. "Water." The mountain man laughed at the blank look on the boy's face. "C'mon. You'll see."

They walked up the sandstone riverbed a ways. Manolo knelt next to an oval hole in the solid rock, an opening maybe six feet across. Some four feet down inside the hole a pool of green water shimmered. The surface erupted into waves and splash when a bucket hit the surface. It tipped and filled and disappeared into the drink until it resurfaced as Manolo pulled it up by the reata tied to the bail. Other of the men did the same at a few smaller tanks nearby. Manolo scooped up a palmful of the thick water and drank. He winced at the taste but swallowed nonetheless.

"*La tinaja*," he said to Boone, pointing to the hole. "The jar."

"Indians have been using this place time out of mind," Old Bill squawked. "They say it has never been dry."

Monolo poured the water from his bucket into Boone's.

"Get at it, boys," Old Bill hollered. "*Mano a mano.*"

The men lined up, forming a bucket brigade, passing the filled buckets hand to hand down to the scarp, where the last man dumped the water over the edge. Down below, Pegleg and a few other men had scooped out a trough in the sand and lined it with the oiled canvas sheets that covered the loaded packsaddles. Two by two, as there was no room for more, *mozos* led the saddle horses, pack mules, and spare animals up to drink.

It was past dark when the watering finished. Boone washed down a plate of beans with a cup of the thick, green water and lapsed into a deep sleep on his bedroll. The sound of others stirring awakened him what seemed like minutes later, but the sky to the east was already graying. He sat and stretched his arms and shoulders, stiff and sore from working the bucket brigade.

The stiffness soon left, but the ache remained as he once again took his place in the line. With a day of travel ahead, the animals were given less water so as not to sicken them, making the work go faster. Shortly after the last animal drank, with the water bags and canteens filled, the mules packed and the horses saddled, the troop lined out in the usual northwesterly direction.

Boone heeled his horse into a trot and reined up next to Pegleg. "We goin' to be drinkin' that water for long?"

Pegleg chuckled. "What's the matter, son? It's a mite thick, but it's wet. Plenty of times I'd've cut off my other leg to have a drink of it." He rode on in silence for a bit. Then, "Howsomever, we'll camp by clear stream water tonight. Rinse that slime out of your innards. Next day, we'll strike the Grand. Plenty of water there—you'll be wishin' there was less of it by the time we get across."

Pegleg's prediction proved prophetic. For hours, the expedition followed a small stream down a valley confined by a sheer wall of red sandstone a thousand feet high or more on one side and rugged slopes on the other. It looked to Boone like the valley was a dead end, as the looming cliffs closed in, even as a wall of rock straight ahead looked to block any outlet.

Just before reaching the convergence of the walls, they met the Grand River. The deep, broad, swift stream flowed out of the east from between canyon walls no wider than the river and thousands of feet high, then looped around and into another gorge just as precarious less than two miles to the south. Stopping at the river's edge, the men studied the water.

"This be the only way across this river for miles," Pegleg said to the boy. "Most places you can't even get to the water on account of you bein' up on top there," he said, nodding toward the high cliffs, "and the river bein' down here. Find yourself rimrocked plenty of times. Nowhere to go but back the way you came. Don't know how the hell the Indians ever found this place."

As the *mozos* went to work unpacking the mules and setting up camp, the Utes and the mountain men cut willows from the stream's edge. Boone helped where he could but was at a loss to know what the job was. He watched as the men tied willow branches to form hoops and lashed together others, bending and tying the lengths to the hoop to form a bowl-like framework. With the bowl arching upward, the Utes threw on buffalo hides from their packs and bound them to the hoops. Come morning, he was told, the "bull boats" would carry the expedition's supplies across the river.

Come morning, that is just what happened. The strongest

swimmers held the edges of the bull boats to steady them from overturning in the current, while riders towed the conveyances across the river with reatas, reaching the opposite shore a considerable distance downstream.

Boone and the rest of the party urged the mules and spare saddle horses into the stream to ford on their own, to be gathered on the opposite bank. The crossing went off without a hitch until nearly all the stock was in the water. One of the saddle horses—a mount in Philip Thompson's string—refused to cross. No amount of driving, beating, pushing, or pulling could put the horse's hooves in the stream. Then a pair of the *mozos* folded and stretched a *reata* across the reluctant horse's backside just below the dock and told Boone and a Mexican rider to drop loops over the horse's head, dally up, and ride into the water. As the ropes drew taut, the *mozos* forced the horse from behind with the sling, as another slapped the fighting animal on the rump with a coiled reata.

Panicked, the horse leaped into the river. His hooves found a solid bottom, and he leapt again, striking Boone's *grulla* horse nearly broadside and unhorsing the boy. Boone hit the water and sank out of sight. He surfaced in an instant, the danger of the stream compounded by the thrashing hooves of the horses. The strength of the current soon had Boone and the horses in deep water, all struggling to stay afloat—the horses started swimming, but the boy had a worse time of it, weighed down by waterlogged clothing.

Downstream on the opposite shore, Nooch watched Boone bobbing along, sinking and surfacing as he went, the times under water growing longer than those above. The Ute boy urged his horse into the stream, calculating an angle that would intercept Boone. But he overshot the mark, or the current shifted the drifting boy, and Nooch forced the horse to turn about midstream. Boone bobbed to the surface and crashed into the swimming horse. Nooch grabbed Boone by the collar and dragged the boy across his mount's back as he slid over and off the rump and grabbed the horse's tail, hoping to be towed to shore.

The horse swam until he found footing and lunged toward the bank. Boone slid off and lay in the stream, disoriented. Nooch let go of the horse's tail, grabbed Boone under the arms, and dragged him to dry ground. Nooch sat beside the sodden boy, pounding him on the back as Boone coughed and gagged and retched up gouts of river water.

By the time the two boys made it back upstream along the bank, the bull boats were stripped down to their skeletal frames and the buffalo hides laid out to dry. The horses and mules were gathered, loose herded in the grass along the river. Boone, steady again on his legs, spied the unruly horse responsible for his dunking, head down and spraddle-legged. He picked up a limb of driftwood as thick and long as his arm and started for the animal.

But before he could put the club to work, Pegleg Smith stepped between the boy and the horse.

"Out of my way! I'll give that thick-headed horse a beatin' he won't forget."

Pegleg maneuvered to counter every one of Boone's attempts to pass. "You'll leave it alone, boy. That horse has had enough for one day."

Boone growled and threw the heavy stick aside. "Damn nag damn near killed me!"

"That is so. Howsomever, you ain't dead." Pegleg scratched at his beard. "But don't you worry, boy. The day may come we'll have to kill that horse. If that day comes, well, you can do the job—and that won't be all you can do to him."

"What do you mean?"

"Could be you'll have to eat him."

The day far enough gone, and wet saddles and blankets sure to cause sore backs and galls, the expedition set up camp on the narrow flood plain between the river and the cliff wall. As soon as the morning brought enough light, with Wakara in the lead, the band rode between high walls to the west. The trail was indistinct as the Ute leader guided the string around and through rock falls of blood-red boulders the size of houses. With a sheer wall to the left towering more than a thousand feet high, and steep, rocky slopes to the right, the gorge provided little room to maneuver. At times, the riders dismounted and led their horses through steep and narrow passages, encouraging reluctant, foam-flecked horses to jump to a higher ledge or slide down steep slopes as loose stones and solid sandstone bloodied hocks. The surefooted mules had an easier time of it, negotiating without pause passages the horses refused until forced.

Hours later up the rough trail, the boulder-littered slope to the right leveled out, offering an easier passage as the trail followed the cliff wall as it veered to the north. Late in the day, the trail maintained its northward course through the sand and sandstone as the broken cliffs turned again westward. A cottonwood grove surrounding a spring—more a seep—provided shade, water, and graze at the last waterhole for miles.

Boone stripped the saddle from his favored *grulla* mount, pulled a handful of coarse grass and scrubbed the animal's sweaty back, then rubbed down its legs and hoisted each hoof, checking for lodged-in stones, cracks in the hoof wall, or other damage. Nooch stepped up as Boone stood upright after examining the left hind hoof. The Ute carried a greasy leather pouch, which he offered to Boone. He took it, opened it, looked inside, then held it to his nose, grimacing at the smell.

Nooch retrieved the bag, reached inside, and came out with a wad of the thick grease in his fingers. He smeared the ointment on the cuts and scrapes on the horse's left foreleg. Boone got the idea and went to work on the horse's other limbs.

As the Ute boy walked away, Boone smelled his fingers but could not recognize anything familiar in the pungent unguent. He scrubbed away as much of the stink as possible with sand as he looked away to the northwest, following the faint trace of the trail as it climbed a low rise and disappeared into miles and miles of sand and dust.

He wondered at the future that waited out there, somewhere in the distance.

CHAPTER SEVEN

As the party continued northwest, Boone again found himself in an unfamiliar landscape. Under a dull, empty sky lay a world altogether dun in color. Variegated shades of pale and faded beige, buff, umber, and brown stretched away to the horizons. Even the occasional plants—bunch grass and spindly brush— were sun-bleached and powdered with dust.

To the north, an endless mesa drew a flat line between earth and sky, its fingers reaching out into the desert, step by step, as far as the eye could see. Bald cliffs fell from the top but soon flared outward in piles of bare, eroded scree. No matter how far they rode, the mesa maintained its distance, fluctuating in heat waves rising from the desert.

Again, Wakara led the way, a zig-zagging course through shallow swales and gullies in search of water. There was none to be found. The few shallow ponds held only dry, cracked mud—sad testimony to past water. Low spots in dry washes that held runoff from spring snowmelt and summer storms lacked any trace of moisture.

Heads hung low, the horses and mules walked on through the long day, the men who rode, led, and drove them determined to reach the Green River before stopping.

And so they did.

As if by magic, the river, as large—or nearly so—as the Grand, flowed out of the mesa. Cottonwoods and willows lined the banks, adding welcome color the drab land.

"Hard to believe this is the same water we trapped out away up north. Shoshoni called it 'Sisk-a-dee-agie,' but it's the same river," Old Bill Williams said as they reined up on its banks.

Said Boone, "Don't care who calls it what; I'm damn glad to see it."

Old Bill cackled and stuffed tobacco into a battered clay pipe. "Thirsty, are you, son? Best drink your fill whilst you can. We get out in that Mojave country, water's so scarce you'll forget what it tastes like." He would suck and gnaw on the pipe stem until fires were laid and struck in the camp.

As the *mozos* unloaded the pack mules and set out the camp equipment, the young Utes gathered driftwood.

"Best give them boys a hand," Pegleg said. But before Boone could dismount, the mountain man laid a hand on his thigh to stop him. "See that there rise off to the west, all them standing rocks?"

Boone nodded.

"Beyond that is a tangle of canyons and such that's near impassable. So we'll go on to the northwest to get around that mess for a day or two. From then on, we'll be a-goin' more or less southwest." He smiled at Boone. "That ought to be more to your likin' if memory serves."

"Least ways we'll be goin' toward where we're goin' 'stead of away from it. Only seems to make sense, you ask me."

Pegleg loosed one of his braying laughs. "That it does, son. Howsomever, the hell we been through these past few days don't hold a candle to what we avoided by comin' this-a-way."

Boone stepped out of the saddle, tied a rein to an upright limb on a fallen cottonwood log, and started gathering wood.

Later, that same wood snapped and popped in the cooking fire, built up after the meal as some of the men sat in its glow, resting from the day's ride. Others were already under blankets. The Utes, as they had since joining the caravan, kept their own camp nearby. It would be some days until they shared campfires with the Mexicans and mountain men.

Boone spat into the fire. "I been wonderin' something. How come it is we ain't seen no Indians, 'cept them?" he said with a nod toward the Utes.

Jim Beckwourth tossed the stick he had been whittling on into the fire and sheathed his knife. "This trail we have been on skirted the lands of the Navajos and Hopis—they live mostly west of the way we came. To my mind, it is best to avoid the Navajo when you can. They do not cotton too much to white folks like us—even black white men, which is how they see me and my kind. Cannot say as I blame them. Much of what we have come through of late is Ute country. They are spread all over these parts, all the way up to the Salt Lake, on over to the high Rockies, up into the Uintah Mountains—bands of them are everywhere."

"Then how come we ain't seen any?"

Beckwourth laughed. "Most Indians have better sense than to be down here in the desert in the heat of summer. They are, at present, already away up in the high country, where it is cool. They will be back down here when the snow flies up there—unlike white folks, who stay in one place like we are nailed down, no matter the season. If you ask me, Indians have got a lot better sense."

The mountain man stood. "I reckon I will be turning in now." He looked around at the few men still at the fire. "The rest of you-all would be advised to do the same. We cross at first light." Beckwourth turned to Boone. "Do not worry, young man. Once we get beyond the Rio Severo we will be in Paiute lands. Then, you may well get more than your fill of Indians."

Breakfast—cold, save for coffee—was over and camp struck before any hint of dawn. As at the crossing of the Grand River,

Pegleg assigned Boone to help shepherd the loose stock across the Green. On horseback, he sat on a rise above the riverbank as the newly built bull boats floated across, swimmers keeping them upright as mounted Utes towed the conveyances through the slow but powerful current that braided its way through sand bars and shallow, brushy islands.

With the rest of the party on the opposite bank, Boone, Manolo, Thompson, and two *mozos* whose names Boone did not know gathered the spare saddle stock and the pack mules into a tight bunch and pushed them to the water. This time, the drovers made certain to herd Thompson's hesitant horse into the middle of the pack, and the snorting animal had no choice but to enter the river. All the animals swam the stream without incident.

Within minutes, the mules were loaded and stringing out toward the northwest. A few miles beyond the river, the cliff wall took a hard-right turn, the sheer ledges now reaching toward the northern horizon. But the expedition followed its own, more northwesterly course across the barren, broken terrain as the jumbled red rock scarp to the west retreated slowly to the south.

Miles later, Pegleg Smith led the way into a broad, narrow, dry wash. Intermittent clumps of feeble cottonwood trees signified the presence of occasional water in the dusty stream bed. If any water was present that day, it hid beneath the surface. The dry wash pinched itself off in the shallow saddle between two low hills, and the trail clung to a side hill as it found its way around and between more outcropping hills and into a winding course through a shallow, narrow canyon.

The caravan stopped for a time to rest the animals, and Pegleg and Wakara rode to higher ground to study the route. Long past its zenith, the sun illuminated a gray wall of thunderclouds to the west, clinging to the top of the high plateau filling the horizon. As they listened carefully, thunder rolled slowly through the distant clouds. Curtains of rain reached out onto the desert. Most of those raindrops, the travelers knew, would evaporate before reaching ground. A rainstorm would offer respite from the heat, but the men agreed the storm would likely pass to the north, perhaps providing only a sprinkle where they were going.

But the Ute and the mountain man also knew that in desert country, even distant thunderstorms could mean danger. The sunbaked land absorbed little of the moisture, and it flowed off the surface, gathering force as it went, sending cascades of mud and debris roaring down otherwise dry ravines and arroyos, canyons and washes. The trail they followed would follow the winding canyon for miles yet, and so they agreed to send a scout out ahead to provide early warning should flash floods threaten.

Hours later, the sun still hot on the plodding mules and horses, a gunshot sounded, soon followed by high-pitched howling and warbling echoing down the canyon. Pounding hooves announced the coming of Quibets, the Ute scout, but before he arrived the horsemen were already scrambling up the steep sides of the canyon. *Mozos* guided mules, the strung-together animals both helping their mates out of the gorge and pulling one another back down in the scramble.

Boone turned down the canyon to avoid the chaos and spurred his mount up the side, rocks rolling and dirt sliding with every step. Reaching the top, he turned to look back up the canyon. Muddy water foamed over the floor, rolling rocks and stirring dust as it came. The water deepened, then raised up in a sudden wall, held nearly vertical by interlaced limbs and branches and uprooted brush. The roar of the surging stream drowned out the sound of the braying mules and whinnying horses and screaming men scrambling up the canyon walls to avoid the deluge.

Ahead of the flood, foam licking at his horse's heels, rode Nooch. Boone did not know why the Ute boy was yet in the bottom of the gulch, but it was clear he would not outrun the water for long.

Nooch jerked the rein, turning the horse onto the steep wall. The animal struggled, clawing at an impossible angle up and away from the flood. The lunge that would bring horse and rider to safety went wrong when a scratching front hoof dislodged a boulder, and its slide took the other front leg out from under the horse. It fell against the bank, and, as it slipped downward, Nooch grasped at a cluster of spindly brush, and the horse slid away, upended and rolled over and over downstream in the mud and debris.

Boone pulled a few coils from his reata as he rode along the rim. Sliding to a stop above where Nooch clung to the wall, he tossed the coils over the edge. The braided rawhide rope hit the wall just upstream of the boy, but with his face pressed into dirt, and watching his horse wash away, Nooch knew nothing of the rescue attempt. Boone recoiled the reata and tried again. This time, the *honda*, the knot through which the loop threaded, bounced off Nooch's head and fell into his line of sight. He let go of the brush and grabbed the rope but slid down the bank before Boone could take his dallies to secure the reata around the saddle horn.

But the rope drew taut, saving the boy from the flow of mud and debris, and Boone turned his horse away from the edge and rode up the hill as Nooch hurried the rescue by climbing hand over hand up the rope. Once he reached safety, Nooch turned on his back, gasping for breath. Boone rode to him, coiling the reata. The horse's shadow fell over the Ute boy, and he stood, grabbing Boone's outstretched arm to be pulled up behind the saddle to straddle the horse's rump.

In disarray, with horses and mules and men scattered on

both sides of the flooding canyon's irregular and rugged rim, the expedition was at a standstill at least until the floodwaters passed. The men worked their way to more secure ground and, once gathered, unloaded the mules to make what they could of a camp with the equipment and supplies on their side of the shallow but deadly gorge.

Boone, seated on a rock with reins in hand, uncorked his canteen and drank deeply. He wondered how a man could develop such a thirst in the presence of so much water.

Chapter Eight

Juan Medina squatted in the shade under the pepper tree watching the festivities at the hacienda. Long tables, knocked together for today's celebration, stood in a row outside the oversized, propped-open front doors. Their rough wood surfaces were covered with fabric and adorned with flower arrangements. Servants scurried in and out through the doors, carrying trays and chargers, platters and pots, and bowls filled with food. They brought out fresh fruit from the orchards—apricots and peaches, berries, figs, oranges—and garden vegetables—carrots and cucumbers, peas and beans, beets, corn, squash. Meats— beef, pork, goat, lamb, turkey—were served roasted, stewed, broiled, braised. Beans, rice, raisins, *huevos a la peruana*, tortillas, pastries, wines . . . It was a feast the likes of which the boy had never seen.

And it was a feast of which he would not partake, unless there were leftovers to distribute to the workers.

This was the wedding breakfast for Don Emiliano's eldest daughter, Rosa Maria—Magdalena's older sister—and today's celebration surpassed that of the previous three days. For today was the wedding day, and after the celebratory meal, the bride and groom and their legions of escorts would ride the ten miles to the mission church, where the marriage would be solemnized. And then the company would return to the hacienda for further celebration. Juan and his father, Miguel, as keepers of the Don's fine horses, would accompany them on the ride to and from the mission but were to remain inconspicuous.

A cheer went up among the celebrants when the groom, Vicenté Garcia, and his party arrived. Beside the groom rode the groomsman, who would present Rosa Maria with the traditional satin slippers, handmade by the groom. Next came Vicenté's father, Don Francisco, owner of a neighboring rancho much larger and richer than Don Emiliano's.

As the cavalcade approached, the Peralta family lined up to greet them. Juan's breath caught in his throat when Magdalena walked through the doorway to take her place in the long line after her parents and three older brothers and Rosa Maria. After Magdalena, a row of younger sisters and brothers stair-stepped all the way down to a toddler and a babe in the arms of a nurse.

The young vaquero had no doubt that of all the Peraltas, Magdalena was surely the most striking. She glowed in the mid-morning sunshine, and he was certain the effect was not only the result of reflected light from her white dress and rebozo.

Juan and several other of Don Emiliano's vaqueros led the Garcia horses away. They would unsaddle and wash the sweaty backs of the mounts before turning them out in a fenced pasture, where the animals would wait until readied for the ride to the mission church.

As the boys went about their work, the families mingled and talked for a few minutes before sitting down to heaping plates of the prepared foods. Afterward, in the interval before leaving for the ceremony, the women moved onto the patio to visit, while the men with their wine and cigarillos moved to the shade of a live oak tree near one of the barns.

The conversation, as it would among rancheros, soon turned to livestock. Don Francisco commented on the fine state of the cattle on the Peralta estate, mentioned the quality of the lambs and ewes scattered on the hillsides, and even admired the condition of the goats. But his highest praise he saved for the equine stock.

"Don Emiliano," Garcia said, "the excellence of your horses is to be much admired."

"You are too kind, Don Francisco."

"No, my friend. I speak in all sincerity. The superiority of your caballos is well known the length and breadth of the valley. I need not speak of your trained saddle horses, as their distinction is familiar to all. And, indeed, your brood mares are unsurpassed in all of *Alta California.*"

Don Emiliano said nothing. He believed the assessment to be correct, but humility forbad comment.

Don Francisco exhaled a stream of tobacco smoke. "I know whereof I speak, Don Emiliano, as I, too, have many excellent horses. In particular, I speak of the sires on our rancho. Their services are much sought after, and the foals they throw serve only to increase the demand for *los sementales de Garcia.*"

Again, Don Emiliano sat silent, head bowed as if studying the wine in his glass. Smoke streamed from Don Francisco's pursed lips. Then, "I speak of my stallions. But when it comes to *los machos* for the purpose of producing mules, once again it is Don Emiliano Peralta to whom I must bow. And, again, your brood mares . . . their preeminence once again comes to the fore when bred to your burros. The result is a mule without equal. My friend, I must have one of *tus machos* to stand at stud at my rancho so I, too, can produce such fine mules. It is imperative that we come to terms."

Again, the visiting Don drew smoke from his cigarillo, then tossed it into the dirt and ground it down with the sole of a glossy leather riding boot, the rowel of the spur scraping a track in the dust. "Ah, my friend. This is no time to discuss business. Today, we celebrate the wedding of your daughter to my son—and to a closer association between our families and *el rancho*

Garcia y el rancho Peralta."

"*Si, mi amigo,*" Don Peralta said. "Let us make ready for the procession to the church."

The young men of both families and their friends saddled their own horses. As with all boys raised on California ranches, they were introduced to the saddle even before they could walk, and riding was second nature to them. Young men took pride in their abilities as horsemen and tested their skills against one another at every opportunity, whether in match races, fancy riding and roping, or working cattle at rodeos.

But to Miguel and Juan fell the task of readying mounts for the Dons and the women. The Medinas took special care in selecting gentle horses for the women, but even they were at home when horseback, and many of the younger ladies were as adventurous in the saddle as their male counterparts.

As Miguel saddled Don Francisco's horse, Juan took special care with the palomino stallion on which Don Emiliano would carry Rosa Maria to the ceremony. The bride would sit in the Don's saddle, but, rather than riding astraddle, she would ride sidesaddle, cocking her right leg around the horn and securing her satin-slippered foot in a braided loop. For the occasion, a *mochila* covered the saddle, draped over like a leather blanket, with slits to fit over the pommel and cantle. Silver conchos and trim embellished the *mochila*. Behind the saddle rode the *anquera* upon which the Don would sit. Fashioned from the skin of a puma, tanned with the hair still on, the *anquera* draped over the horse's rump, hanging as low as the hocks, with thin silver tassels lining the bottom like fringe, jingling and tinkling with every movement of the horse.

Juan saddled a blood-bay gelding with four white socks and a blaze face for Magdalena. He fancied the horse's white markings and the girl's glowing white dress would showcase her beauty. And so they did. The boy and his father rode at the rear of the parade, but his eyes never left Magdalena. They remained locked on the girl on the return trip, as she laughed and talked with the Garcia girls and her sisters. The groomsman carried Rosa Maria on his horse for the ride back to the rancho, while the other young men raced up and down the hillsides, showing off their horsemanship. The padre who performed the wedding ritual rode beside Juan and Miguel at the rear, tapping his burro with a switch every step of the way to avoid falling behind.

Back at Don Emiliano's, the tables were laden with fresh food and flowers. As the day faded, bonfires were laid to illuminate the dooryard, and musicians provided music for dancing. Juan squatted under the pepper tree, watching the festivities. Her white gown traded for a more colorful dress, Magdalena mingled with the other young women, occasionally accepting an invitation to dance from a guest. The boys hung about at the fringes of the crowd, stepping back into the darkness now and then to partake of the free-flowing wine.

Juan caught Magdalena's eye as she strolled arm in arm with a Garcia girl near her age. He knew the meaning of the slight tip of her head in the direction of the barns and corrals. When, on the next circuit of the crowd, she stepped out of the firelight and into the darkness, Juan already awaited her under the large live oak tree where they had met on other dark nights. From beneath her rebozo she produced a flask of wine and they passed it back and forth, the effects of the drink calming fears and dulling senses.

And so it was a surprise when, wrapped in one another's arms while sharing a kiss, a strong hand gripped Juan's shoulder and ripped him away from Magdalena. Juan spun around with the attack, and, before his eyes could focus on his assailant, a fist landed in the middle of his face, flattening the nose and smashing a lip. Jerked upright from the ground where he lay gasping, yet another heavy blow from the fist slammed him back down.

"*¡Sal de aquí!*" a voice hissed through clenched teeth. "Go! Now!"

Magdalena's protest was cut short before voiced. In his stupor, Juan rolled to his stomach and pushed himself to hands and knees. His collar tightened as, again, he was hoisted to his feet, then spun around and slammed against the thick tree trunk. An open hand knocked all sound from one ear, and the back of the same hand knocked his jaw askew.

"What do you think you are doing, muchacho?" Another slap to his face rattled the boy's brains. "Don Emiliano will know of this," the voice said. "If he allows you to live, which is a matter open to question, take this as a warning: if ever again I see you in the presence of *mi hermana* I will kill you myself. If not for your father, I would do it this instant!"

The attacker landed several solid blows into the boy's midsection. He placed a palm against Juan's chest and pressed him against the tree trunk, squeezing what little breath he had out of him. His eyes, rolling in and out of focus, finally recognized the face inches from his own—it was that of Eduardo, the eldest of the Peralta sons.

Eduardo removed his hand, and Juan slid down the trunk, its bark abrading his back. He sat for several minutes, head pounding, drawing shallow breaths. He rose and made his way slowly home and collapsed on his pallet. The pain would not allow sleep, so he was still awake when his father stormed in, raising a candle to cast light on his son.

"*Estúpido!*" he said, dropping to his knees beside Juan's bed. "I have warned you to stay away from that girl! I have told you your infatuation would bring nothing but trouble to this house, and now you see that it is so! And who can say what Don Emiliano will do?"

Miguel shook his head, his ire spent. He fetched a bowl of

water and scrap of cloth, mopped the crusted blood from Juan's nose, lips, and chin, and wiped away the thin stream of blood below his ear.

Miguel held Juan's bruised face in his hands, staring into the glassy eyes. "Juan, *mi hijo.*" Again, he shook his head. "Try now to sleep. Tomorrow we must be ready for work. Don Emiliano may forbid it and send us away, but we will be ready to tend the horses and mules and hope for a miracle."

The *milagro* Miguel hoped for came to pass, for Don Emiliano said nothing to Juan or to his father. They went about their work with the horses as if the days following the wedding were like any other.

Or so it seemed to Miguel. It was not so for Juan. While feeding, while putting a horse through its paces in the corral, while riding through the hills, at any time, at any place, the boy might feel a tingle in his spine. At such times, he would stop what he was doing and search his surroundings to locate the source of the threat.

And, without fail, he would find Eduardo, or another of Magdalena's brothers, or, on occasion, one of the rancho's vaqueros, watching him from a distance.

CHAPTER NINE

Pegleg Smith led the expedition up a winding canyon through ever-higher mountains as the trail topped a high plateau, the highest ground yet crossed. The downhill ride followed a creek down a likewise long and winding canyon. The canyon narrowed in places to where the packs on the mules scraped the sides. But eventually it widened, opening into the valley of the Rio Severo, the river's green path a contrast to the bare hills skirting the higher mountains running north and south as far as Boone could see. The distance through and over the plateau would have made a day's good ride in more hospitable terrain but here necessitated a campsite in the mountains.

Upon striking the river, Boone wondered at its name. Small, it was, as rivers go, and "severe" could hardly describe its course through this valley. The stream meandered along the valley floor, cutting one lazy oxbow after another, adding miles to its journey. An early camp was made at the south end of the long valley, a few miles from where the river could be seen spilling out of a steep, narrow canyon.

Boone's saddle had just hit the ground when Nooch rode up. "Saddle a fresh horse, and come with me."

Boone followed his Ute guide westward, up a broad canyon leading to higher mountains. After an hour or so of travel, Nooch turned his horse uphill to the north. Boone followed him into a narrow box canyon, the irregular floor littered with cedar trees and brush and boulders fallen from outcropping cliffs.

Nooch rode near to a cliff wall and, when Boone reined up next to him, pointed to the sheer rock face. Boone's eyes widened at the sight of dozens of pictures scratched and pecked into the surface of the rock. Fantastic looking, but identifiable, animals. Geometric patterns of lines and circles. Strange human-like figures.

"Lord above," Boone said. "Who did this?"

Nooch shook his head. "I do not know. The Old People."

"Indians?"

Nooch shrugged. "Maybe. I do not know. My people know nothing of them."

"What does it mean?"

Again, Nooch shrugged. "No one knows. Some say the pictures tell stories—of hunts, of travels, of happenings. Others say they are records of the seasons, the sun and the moon and the stars. Maybe they tell of all these things. Or maybe they are just pictures and nothing more."

"How'd you know they was here?"

"I have been here before. A cousin showed them to me."

"How'd he know?"

Nooch shrugged yet again. "Someone showed him. Many of my people and those of other tribes know of these pictures—and of others like them in many other places."

The boys rode further into the small canyon, studying pictures inscribed on most every rock surface along the way. The sun fell to the crest of the mountains, casting long shadows.

"Come. We must go." Nooch turned his horse back toward the main canyon, dodging boulders and brush. Upon reaching the less restricted floor of the larger canyon, he heeled his horse into a trot toward the valley and camp. The boys raced the darkness and lost, but campfires in the dark valley served as a beacon to guide the last leg of the journey.

"Where you been, boy?" Pegleg said when Boone plopped down next to where the mountain man sat on a rock.

"Nooch, he showed me some pictures on the rocks up in the hills a ways. You ever seen 'em?"

"Not them. But I seen plenty of 'em. Some places maybe just one. Other places, there's lots of 'em."

Boone sat in silence for a few minutes. Then, "I ain't never seen nothin' like it. Don't know why anybody'd take the time to do such a thing."

"Aw, hell, boy, that ain't nothin'. They's places out here where them old Indians built whole cities of rock buildings, then just went off and left 'em. Up in the cliffs where a feller can't even figure how they got up there, they built houses the size of castles. Damndest thing you ever seen."

"What do you reckon happened to those people?"

"Far as I know, they ain't nobody knows."

Boone wondered at the mountain man's story. "Will we be seein' any of these places where we're a-goin'?

"Nah. Lots of them places is in Navajo country. A man takes his life in his hands to go there. But there's others. You stay out west long enough, you'll likely run across some." Pegleg scratched in the dirt at his feet with a twig. "Where we're headed, the Indians is a whole different breed. They don't build hardly nothin'. Make themselves a little hut out of sticks and brush and call it good. Don't hardly wear no clothes, neither— just a few rabbit skins pieced together, maybe. Some don't wear a stitch. How them people survive out in them deserts they live in is a wonder."

The mountain man stood and stretched his arms and yawned. "We best be gettin' to bed. Mornin's comin', and it won't wait."

Saddling up in the morning, Boone assumed the trail would take them into the river gorge. Instead, Wakara took the lead and left the stream to climb into the mountains east of the canyon. Boone wondered if there was something in that gorge that earned the river the severity of its name. Hours later, the caravan dropped down out of the hills to rejoin the river beyond where it cut into the canyon. A long valley stretched away to the south, carpeted with brush that occasionally gave way to grassy meadows.

The riders followed the river valley upstream to the south. Ahead, Boone could see a smaller stream flowing into the valley from the east, and a cluster of brush huts not far from the confluence. Indians scurried about the small village, shuttling children into the willows along the stream. The women followed them into the tangle, then the men, armed with bows, faded into the brush. Boone watched the riders ahead of and behind him, but no one paid the Indians any mind. He urged his horse into a trot and moved up the line to ride beside Jim Beckwourth.

"Don't nobody see them Indians up there?"

Beckwourth did not reply, only turned to stare at Boone.

"Well?"

"Of course we see them, boy."

"Then why don't somebody do somethin'?"

Beckwourth shook his head. "Son, those Indians are Paiutes. Panguitch band, unless I miss my guess. They'll steal you blind given a chance but represent no danger otherwise. As your eagle eyes no doubt have noticed, they have taken to hiding. Which is what one can expect of them whenever they see an outfit like ours."

"Why is that?"

"The Paiutes expect nothing but ill treatment from fur trappers and Mexicans. Or from Utes. They are often raided by the Utes, and their women and children taken into slavery. Sold to work down south in Mexico, or to the Navajos and Apaches."

"Indians get sold to other Indians? By Indians?"

Beckwourth chuckled. "White folks did not invent slavery. And one tribe of Indians is no more likely to get along with another than do the French and English."

"But—"

"The only thing you need to worry about right now, boy, is that these Paiutes—and others of their kind we will encounter along the way—are unlikely to give us any trouble. Oh, they will fight if pushed to it. But they will disappear into the hills when they see us coming and allow us to pass unmolested so long as we do not molest them. Still and all, it is best to keep a sharp eye."

Boone dropped back into line and studied the village as they passed. Other than smoke wisping from burned-down cooking fires, the place looked abandoned. Even the shoddy huts looked forsaken. They rode on beyond, and after a time Boone looked back to see the men with their bows materialize out of the brakes, a few women following them.

The next day, the trail abandoned the river valley and headed into the mountains, climbing toward the southwest. Foliage increased in thickness and height as they climbed, their course following the rim of a series of valleys drained by a small stream. They camped in the upper valley, surrounded by mountain peaks. A green meadow, carpeted with grass and boggy in places, allowed the horses and mules to spend a day of leisure grazing and rejuvenating. While all the riders now shared a camp, the groups tended to congregate with their own kind— Mexicans with Mexicans, the Utes in their own circle, while the mountain men kept their own company.

The men lazed around the campfires in the falling light, and Boone said, "This place got a name?"

Said Philip Thompson, "Bear Valley. This place be Bear Valley. Don't know what the Indians hereabouts calls it, but it's Bear Valley to me and my kind."

"Must be bears hereabouts," Boone said.

"Must be," Thompson said. "I ain't never seen one. 'Course I ain't never been here save to pass through. Them trappers that worked this here little creek must've seen some to give it the name. But I ain't seen no bears."

"Bears," Old Bill said. "You-all want to see bears, you just wait till we get to California. Bears there is thick as fleas in an Arapaho's buffalo robe. Grizzlies. Fat as a tick, they be."

"Why's there so many of them?" Boone said.

"Cows. The Mexicans have so damn many cows they don't know what to do with them. They eat as many as they can, but that doesn't even make a dent in the herds. So they kill them for their skins and fat and leave the rest to the bears and birds. The dried hides and rendered tallow, they cart to the sea and trade them to ships that come in. 'California Bank Notes' they call the flint hides.

"Anyway, all that meat makes them bears fat and sassy. The Mexicans use the bears for sport, too. The young vaqueros, they'll rope themselves a bear and drag him through town just for fun. They will let the dogs worry them some—if they don't care about losing a dog now and then, that is. And they'll bring in a big old bull with horns you couldn't span with the reach of your arms to fight the bears. Put them in a ring, tie them together, and let them at each other. The whole town turns out to watch. There will be wagering, too—though I don't hold with gambling myself."

Boone said, "Who'd win a fight like that?"

"Bear, most of the time. That's why they tie them together—they'll tie one of that bear's hind legs to the front leg of the bull as a means of evening up the odds somewhat. Don't know that it works."

Pegleg Smith said, "I saw one of them contests one time. Just like Ol' Bill here says. First thing, that big ol' black bull charged the grizz and knocked him ass over teakettle and went at him with his horns. Gored that bear pretty good. Howsomever, that bear swatted him on the snout a good one, then really got into him. They tussled around and around in the dust, both of 'em drawin' blood. Then the bear got his jaws around the bull's throat and started in to stranglin' him, pulled him right down to his knees. That ol' bull's tongue was a danglin' a foot out his mouth, and the grizz got his claws in it and dragged it out some more.

"Then, by damn, that bear let loose of the bull's throat and bit that tongue plumb off. That was all she wrote for the bull. He give up the fight and rolled to his side. Bear was mauled so bad he couldn't hardly get up hisself. Some of them Mexican boys waded in and cut the throats of both critters. The way the folks cheered and carried on you'd think it was the best fandango they ever saw. Could be it was."

The men sat in quiet, considering bulls and bears and California until Old Bill broke the silence. "Morning waits for no man. We had best sleep whilst we can."

Already, the fires at the Mexican and Ute fires were but glowing coals, and all was quiet save the incessant crickets chirping and locusts clicking.

"Boone, 'fore you turn in, fetch your reata from your saddle and take it with you to your bedroll," Pegleg said.

The boy's brow furrowed, and he stared at the mountain man. "What for?"

"If'n a bear should wander by in the night, I want for you to rope him."

Pegleg's laugh was loudest, bettering Old Bill's cackle, but only just. Boone did not laugh. But he could not stifle a smile.

CHAPTER TEN

For endless days, the riders chased water. Across high deserts, over low mountains, the horses and mules plodded through cedar and sagebrush, greasewood and shadscale, Joshua trees and creosote bushes, traveling from seep to spring, stream to pothole. At Las Vegas, an unlikely oasis surrounded by wide miles of Mojave Desert, Old Bill Williams declared a layover.

The livestock grazed the verdant meadows and watered at will in artesian springs. Old Bill, Wakara, Pegleg, and Beckwourth huddled together for hours at a time, talking and scratching at maps drawn in the dirt, occasionally involving Thompson or others in the discussions. Boone had no idea how the plans they were hatching would pan out but realized the tactics must be intricate.

Come the evening, Pegleg sat on a rock and unstrapped his wooden leg to massage the stump. Boone plopped down on the ground next to him. The mountain man kept up his rubbing and kneading and paid him no mind. The boy, transfixed by the puckered appendage, said nothing. Pegleg finished the rubdown and slipped back into the wooden leg.

"You'd think a man would be used to it all these years later," Pegleg said. "Oh, I get around all right. Howsomever, it pains me sometimes." He arched his back and rubbed at his hip. "Ridin' ain't so bad. But walkin' around throws ever'thing else off kilter, and I get crampy. Hell of a thing to lose a limb, boy. Pray it don't happen to you."

Boone said nothing for a time. Then, "You and them others've been right busy. What are you-all fixin' to do?"

Pegleg scratched at his whiskers as he considered a reply. "All of us men, we been on these raids to California before." He laughed. "Wakara, now, that man's stole more horses than any man alive—if it weren't so, I wouldn't say it. Me and Old Bill, we know what we're about as well. And Beckwourth, he's stole horses aplenty from the Sioux when he was runnin' with the Crow. Howsomever, this here little party we been plannin' ain't like nothin' any of us ever done before."

Pegleg wondered how much to tell the boy, then decided he'd have to hear it all sooner or later, and now was as good a time as any.

"Here's the deal. We get to California, each of us men—and maybe Thompson, too—will take a few of you young'uns along and set out for different ranchos and missions, all the way from San Bernardino and San Gabriel and out toward San Juan Capistrano. We wait, and all strike the same time, or as near to it as we can, roundin' up stock on all the ranchos and missions 'round about as we head back to the gatherin' place. We'll be out of there almost 'fore them Mexicans knows it. Doin' it this-away, we figure we can get away with a whole hell of a lot more horses and mules."

Boone thought about the plan. "Won't they come after us?"

"Oh, them Californios will generally make a show of it, but they don't never follow very far. Thing is, they got so damn may horses and mules, losin' a few don't matter much."

"Sounds like you-all are figurin' to make off with more'n a few."

Pegleg nodded. "True enough. But we don't reckon there'll be much trouble. Leastways, not for long. If them Mexis chase us much beyond Cajon Pass, I'll be right surprised."

Man and boy were on their feet in an instant with the screaming and snorting of a horse. Off at the edge of the remuda, two unfamiliar Indians were horseback, one pushing other mounts out of the herd, the other straining to stay mounted as a horse hanging back on a lead rope he held reared and fought.

A shot from Old Bill's pistol ended the struggle, the Indian dropping the lead rope and lighting out into the desert. Just before the Indian disappeared into the dust cloud left by his companion and the driven horses, a second shot—this one from Jim Beckwourth's rifle—rolled the rider off the rump of the horse.

Before the horse thief hit the ground, Nooch was mounted and in pursuit of the other one driving the stolen stock. Without saddle or bridle, he controlled the Ute horse with pressure from his knees, clinging to its back like spots on a pinto. By the time Nooch faded into the receding dust trail, Wakara, Old Bill, Manolo, Boone, and a few others were away on hastily saddled horses. Pegleg organized those left behind to protect the horse herd from lingering thieves, should there be any, while Beckwourth rode out to examine his kill.

By now far out into the desert, Nooch urged his horse onward, gaining on the small bunch of stolen horses with every stride. The thief rode among the panicked, running animals, riding low and using the horses as a shield. But the Ute was the better rider, working his way ever closer to his prey. He guided his mount past the left hip of the stolen horse, then eased up, and the two ran side by side, stride for stride, as if hitched together.

The horse thief looked wide-eyed at Nooch but got only a glimpse of the young Ute before the stone head of an arcing war club shattered his forehead and knocked him off the horse. He did not feel the pounding hooves that drove his already dead body into the dry desert dirt.

Nooch pushed ahead to the leaders of the stampede and

turned them, keeping up the pressure until the small band circled, then slowed to a trot, then followed Nooch back toward the meadows. He leaned back and tugged gently on his horse's mane to stop when he met the other riders where they clustered around the dead horse thief. The rescued horses pawed and tossed their heads and milled about but did not stray far, content to catch their breath after the long run.

The Ute boy rode close and looked down at his victim. He looked at Wakara, who nodded. Nooch slid off his horse, pulled a knife from its sheath, lifted the dead Indian's head by a hank of hair, sliced till the blade ticked against the skull, and yanked the scalp free.

Boone turned away, swallowing hard to keep the contents of his heaving stomach down. The men remounted and trotted away toward Las Vegas, bringing the recovered horses along. Utes, Mexicans, and mountain men alike were gathered around Jim Beckwourth when they reached the camp, admiring the scalp hanging from his belt. Beyond that trophy, the mountain man had taken the dead Indian's ears, the leather string on which he'd threaded them dangling from his neck. A cheer went up when Nooch held aloft the bloody scalp he had taken.

"Stop!" Pegleg Smith hollered. "Stop, I say!"

The cheer shut off as if a blanket were thrown over it.

Pegleg talked on. "Lettin' horse thieves in amongst us ain't no cause for celebration! Hell's fire! We ought to all be ashamed. Here we be, a bunch of horse thieves ourselves, and we can't even keep our own horses from bein' taken! What the hell happened?"

No one spoke up, the men looking sheepish, searching the dirt between their feet for an answer, toes of boots and moccasins alike scratching to uncover it.

Then, Beckwourth said, "The one I shot was Paiute. No more than a boy. I reckon the other one was as well." He looked to Wakara, who nodded his assent.

Old Bill said, "They have probably been following us since the Muddy River. Belong to one of those villages back there, I'd say. Out to prove themselves."

"That is likely," Beckwourth said. "I took a little stroll and did not see evidence of any more of their kind."

"Mayhap we should post a guard," Pegleg said. "We can't count on the next bunch of thieves to try and drag off that contrary bangtail of Thompson's. We be damn lucky they did, this time. Had not that useless horse pitched a fit, them Paiutes would've got out of here slick."

"Oh, that horse ain't so bad," Thompson said.

"Like hell!" Boone said. "He damn near got me killed me back there when we was crossin' the Grand River."

"He does get notional now and then. But all in all, he ain't a bad horse."

Pegleg held up a hand, and the laughter died down. "We're all happy your horse decided to get 'notional' today, Philip. Howsomever, the question is, had we ought to be postin' a guard?"

"Nah," Old Bill said. "Like I said, those Paiute boys were just out on a frolic of their own, trying to make a name for themselves. That's my way of thinking. I don't believe there are any more of them hereabouts."

Wakara did not disagree but offered to have two of his young men spend the night out with the remuda just in case more Paiutes arrived. Then he and Old Bill, Pegleg, and Beckwourth huddled and decided to stay on at the meadows one more day as planned, even in light of the Paiute attack, and move on the day after tomorrow.

The night passed without incident. Still, Boone's sleep proved fitful and shallow, and he rolled out in the morning unrested. Only Manolo was up and about readying breakfast when the boy shuffled to the fire. The Mexican offered Boone a cup of coffee. He took it and sipped at it slowly, but it went cold as he cradled it in his hands as he stared into the glowing coals.

"You're up mighty early, boy," Pegleg said.

The voice startled Boone.

The mountain man sat on his favored rock and adjusted the straps on his wooden leg. "You look out of sorts. You ain't gettin' notional on us, like that horse of Thompson's, are you?"

"Nah. Just didn't sleep much, that's all."

"Spit it out, son. What is it that's a-botherin' you?"

Boone squirmed, noticed the tin cup in his hands, took a sip, and spat out the mouthful of coffee gone cold. He tossed the rest into the fire, listening to the hiss and watching the steam rise. "Why is it Nooch and Jim scalped them Indian boys? Jim cut off that one's ears, too."

"You've heard of scalpin' ain't you? Folks in Missouri ain't so civilized these days they forgot about it, have they?"

"No. I've heard about it plenty. But I ain't never seen it done before."

"Been so long since I see'd my first scalp taken I don't recollect how it was for me."

"Why do they do it?"

Pegleg considered the question. "They's all kinds of reasons, I reckon. Proof of the kill, for one. Sign of bravery. Indians believe it's an insult to the enemy to lose their hair. Collectin' scalps brings a man honor. White men, I guess they take hair for the same reason. Push comes to shove, if a foe sees scalps hangin' from your belt, well, he might decide to leave you be."

"What about them ears Jim strung onto a necklace?"

"Same thing, I suppose. I ain't never taken no man's ears, but I don't reckon it's no different than takin' hair, to them that does it."

"Don't seem right, somehow."

"Might not be right, was you back in the States," Pegleg said. "But out here there's whole different notions of what's right and what ain't. Anything helps a man stay alive is right to my way of thinkin'. And when you're dealin' with Indians, your notion of what's right don't matter to them. Most of 'em would as soon lift your hair as look at you."

"But Beckwourth ain't no Indian."

Pegleg laughed. "Don't tell that to the Crows. They reckon he's Indian enough they made him a chief. 'Course that don't matter none to other tribes. Far as they're concerned he's a white man." He laughed again. "White folks, though, they don't see ol' Jim as a white man. He is a puzzle, Jim is."

The two sat in silence for a time, mulling over the conversation. Pegleg stood and clapped a hand to the boy's shoulder. "Was I you, son, I wouldn't worry over much about takin' a man's scalp. What matters is bein' ready to take a man's life should it be required of you. That way, you won't have to worry about him liftin' *your* hair."

Pegleg walked away. Boone sat at the fire and watched the camp come to life around him.

CHAPTER ELEVEN

Juan Medina squatted beneath the pepper tree, watching, from across the dooryard, night fall on the hacienda. He knew Magdalena was inside . . . knew the very window behind which she could be found lying in her bed sleeping, perhaps dreaming.

He had not seen Magdalena for days, weeks even, their mismatch forbidden by her family. As he rose to his feet, he felt yet the lingering pain in his ribs, pain left there by a beating at the hands of Eduardo, Magdalena's brother, to reinforce the fact that he, a mere vaquero, was not fit company for a daughter of Don Emiliano Peralta, owner of the rancho where Juan worked.

Following his moon shadow across the yard, making his way home to the hut he shared with his father, Juan watched Magdalena's window, hoping against hope the shutters might swing wide, offering a glimpse of the girl.

It did not happen.

But Juan did not pass the hacienda unseen. For behind the house, near the barns, beneath the live oak tree where last Juan had held Magdalena, a man in the shadows watched the boy. Under Eduardo's—and Don Emiliano's—orders, the watcher, who tended the rancho's goat herds, would spy on Juan until relieved of the task at midnight by another.

No sooner had Juan closed his eyes than his father jostled his shoulder. The gray dawn visible through the adobe hut's window said he had been asleep for some time, but rest had eluded him, and he arose as weary as when he had retired. After breakfast, Miguel told him, they would ride to where the rancho's best brood mares were pastured and, with the *Segundo,* choose several of the stoutest for breeding to *los machos,* the jacks that threw the mules Don Emiliano's rancho was known for.

"Si, *Papá.*" Juan sat on his pallet and stretched, wincing at the pain it caused. After breakfast, Juan saddled a horse from the corral and rode up the hill behind the barn to bring in mounts for his father and the *Segundo.*

The pasture was a few miles away in a barranca, where a small stream of clear water kept the grass carpeting the canyon floor lush and the horses fat. Riding up a gentle sidehill, the men studied the mares, Juan listening as Miguel and the *Segundo* discussed their breeding history and the quality of foals and mules they produced. How they remembered so much about so many was a mystery to the boy.

They agreed on some two dozen mares and rode down into the shallow canyon to cut them from the herd. That job was given to Juan, as the horse between his knees, in the early stages of training, would benefit from the experience. The two men sat horseback down canyon, holding the cut and watching the boy at work, Miguel offering quiet advice when Juan brought in one of the mares and pointing out another to cut from the herd.

Rancho headquarters was abuzz with activity when the riders trotted in with *manada de yeguas.* Eduardo stepped out, signaling Miguel, riding ahead of the herd, to turn the mares into the corrals out back rather than continuing on. He called the *Segundo* aside, leaving the penning to Juan and his father.

The *Segundo* and Eduardo were still talking when Juan and Miguel returned. When Eduardo left, Miguel asked what all the excitement was about.

"Someone has stolen a bag of coins from the hacienda. It was left last evening on a table, as the Don and Doña were to go to

Los Angeles today and required the cash for their business there."

"But who could have done such a thing?"

"It is not yet evident, Miguel. But Eduardo is asking questions and conducting a search."

The men talked some more as Juan stood by. Several of Don Emiliano's children and house servants milled about in front of the hacienda, talking quietly. Juan did not see Magdalena among them, but his breath caught when she walked through the doorway. Their eyes met, and Magdalena smiled. Afraid his father and the *Segundo* would hear his pounding heart, Juan felt a flush rise from his neck to his face.

"Juan Medina!" came the shout.

The boy looked around and found the source of the sound—Eduardo, with the Don, calling from beside the house. He looked at his father, who shooed him toward the beckoning men and followed behind as he went. Several others were gathered around when they arrived; others drifted that way. But Eduardo and another man walked away, long strides taking them in the direction of the workers' huts.

"Juan Medina," the Don said softly. "I have been given a report that you were seen in the vicinity of the hacienda last night. Is this so?"

Juan swallowed hard and looked around at the faces surrounding him. He sought Magdalena's eyes, but she stood with bowed head, grasping her rebozo about her.

"Is it so?"

Juan swallowed again. His father, standing behind, poked a finger into his back. *"Hablar!"* he whispered.

"Who has told you this thing?" Juan said.

"El pastor de cabras," the Don said. "He saw you sitting beneath that tree over there, watching the hacienda. When all was quiet and the lights were extinguished, he saw you walk

toward the house. Is this so?"

Juan said nothing.

Don Emiliano studied the boy's wan face, the flush that had colored it moments ago gone. "Tell me. Is it so?"

"If I may, Don Emiliano," Miguel said. "What was the goat herder doing at the time? Should not he be suspected, as well as my son?"

"Señor Medina, I have been assured by my son Eduardo that such a thing is not possible. That man was performing an errand for Eduardo himself. Now, muchacho, answer my question. Is it true that you were lurking about the hacienda last night?"

"It is true, Don Emiliano."

A gasp followed on the heels of the reply.

"But I can assure you, sir, I did nothing wrong. I did not enter the house—I only walked past it to reach my home and bed."

The Don grasped his hands behind his back, watching the boy's face. "And what, may I ask, were you doing watching my house at such a late hour?"

Juan hung his head. Again, he felt his father's finger in his back. He cleared his throat, hesitated, then, "It was my hope to see Magdalena."

Again, the people gasped.

"Father!" Eduardo shouted as he hurried toward the crowd, a hand held aloft, clutching a leather pouch. *"La bolsa de monedas de plata!"* He stepped through the circle of onlookers to reach his father, opened the pouch, and spilled a few of the silver coins into his hand.

"Muy bueno," the Don said. "And where did you find my little bag of money?"

"It was in that one's hut," Eduardo said, nodding toward Juan. "Hidden beneath his bed."

Juan's face paled even further. "No! *No soy un ladrón!*"

Eduardo sneered. "But you are, Juan Medina! You are a thief!"

No one spoke. No one moved, save Magdalena, who turned and rushed away.

Don Emiliano was saddened at the apparent transgression of a talented young horseman but did not object when Eduardo shackled Juan's wrists and ankles and chained him to the live oak tree between the barns and house.

"The day is too far gone for travel. Tomorrow, I will accompany you to Los Angeles to conduct your business," Eduardo said to his father. "I will take this thief to the authorities and prefer charges against him. I trust the *alcalde* will lock him up. Perhaps imprisonment will teach him a lesson." Then, to Juan: "You will come to know your place, boy. You must learn to keep your filthy hands off things belonging to the Peralta family. *All* things! *Todo!*"

The next day, they started early for Los Angeles. Don and Doña Peralta, with three of their younger children, rode in a carriage. Don Emiliano himself took the lines, driving a team of matched mules. Eduardo and a brother rode horseback behind. Eduardo hurled a nearly continuous stream of taunts at Juan. The verbal insults stung, but the greatest insult of all was that Eduardo had mounted Juan bareback on a burro tied by a lead to the back of the carriage, his wrists shackled and ankles hobbled below the burro's belly.

Juan's appearance before the *alcalde* in the city went much as Eduardo predicted. The boy was pronounced guilty of theft based on Eduardo's evidence. Juan sensed the futility of a person of his station refuting the charges and so stood silent, offering no defense. He wondered if Magdalena—or his father, for that matter—believed him innocent.

And so, he found himself locked in a filthy jail that lacked even the barest necessities, forced to share the squalor with hardened criminals. Smugglers, road agents, murderers, thieves, deserters, even foreigners locked up after abandoning trading ships, wasted away without hope in the wretched *cárcel.*

On the rare occasion when tortured sleep allowed dreams, Juan dreamed the same dream. In the dream, he rode free and easy on a fine horse, across golden hills and green valleys beneath a cloudless *cielo azul,* with Magdalena riding beside. The greatest pain of incarceration was the despair he suffered upon waking from the dream.

CHAPTER TWELVE

Boone turned in the saddle for a last look at the green slash of Las Vegas in the dun-colored desert. The trail wound around hills and outcrops that rose from the desert like ships from the sea. Off to the west, red rock glowed in the low light of a morning sun creeping up the sky, pushing temperatures ever higher as it rose.

By now, Boone was accustomed to the trail meandering from water hole to water hole rather than following a more direct path toward its destination. But as they waded into shallow catchments to allow the horses and mules to suck up refreshment, he wondered how a herd of horses of a size they intended to steal could find enough to drink in these murky ponds surrounded by dry, cracked mud flats. Few of the springs had any depth or supported plant growth more than stirrup high.

The trail dropped lower into a desert basin and then started a long, slow climb toward higher mountains on the horizon, some still snowcapped above blue skirts. Upon reaching those skirts, the horses and mules climbed into the heart of the mountains, trending southward along a rugged trail that reached its summit and then the downslope, weaving in and around hills and ridges and intersecting canyons. The long, winding pass occasionally spread into valleys, and on one such brushy plain the outfit set up camp.

"Almost there, boy," Pegleg said to Boone as they unsaddled.

Boone looked around at mountains hemming them in in

every direction. "Where the hell's 'there'? Ain't seen no sign of us bein' anywhere for longer'n I can remember."

Pegleg chuckled. "It's a far piece between places out here, for certain. But you wanted to come west, boy. You're in it."

"I reckon so. But where are we?"

"This pass we're a-followin' cuts between the San Bernardino Mountains there to the east; them to the west is the San Gabriels. When we come out of these mountains we'll be about where we're a-goin'—dependin' on who gets sent where in the valleys below. Won't be many days now till you'll be up to your ass in stolen ponies and runnin' for your life."

"Well, at least it'll be a change. I'm growin' old doin' nothin'."

Pegleg laughed, his bray drawing the attention of many of the men. "Old? Good hell, boy, you ain't even old enough to grow whiskers. You ain't seen old." He pulled off his hat and swiped his forehead with a shirtsleeve, then raked his fingers through tangled hair. "Howsomever—and bear this in mind—if you don't stay sharp these next days, you won't live to see old."

Again that evening, the leaders huddled, their sticks scratching in the dirt, the marks wiped away to be replaced by new ones as plans evolved. With supper underway, Old Bill climbed atop a small rock outcrop to address the assembly.

"Here's what's going to happen, fellers. Each one of you-all will be meted out to ride with Wakara or Pegleg or Jim or Thompson. I will get to that presently. Each one of them knows where they're going, and you're to follow along and take their orders as they see fit to give them. You're to stay out of sight as much as you can. Some of you will hide out in camp somewhere for a few days until those riding farther out have time to get to where they're going.

"In three days' time—three days from morning, that is—you strike. Go in hard and fast and push as many horses and mules as you can, from as many ranches and missions as you can.

There's stock aplenty out there, so don't worry overmuch if some get away from you. Just keep pushing, and round up more as you go. Don't stop till you get back to where we are right now. We'll gather here and push on through the pass as soon as everyone shows up."

Old Bill went on with the assignments, putting Boone under Pegleg Smith's command along with Nooch, one of Pegleg's Ute brothers-in-law named Ankatash, and Julio, one of the Mexicans from Taos.

Pegleg gathered them about, and they squatted in a circle as the mountain man put his stick to work in the soil, sketching in the mountains, scratching the rough course they would follow, skirting the San Gabriel range as they moved west.

"We'll get us out beyond Mission San Gabriel a fair piece and lay over there in some out-of-the-way canyon. We come down out of the hills on the appointed day and hit a couple of big ranches I know of thereabouts where they got some damn fine horses and mules. We hit those two, the San Gabriel Mission, and everything else in the way of small ranches we find within strikin' range as we come back.

"Now, each one of you-all will be more or less on your own once we strike up the band and this ball gets underway. So pay attention to where the hell you are and where you been so's you-all can find your way back should you get separated. We'll be movin' fast, so it ain't likely we'll be able to save your bacon should you wind up in a jackpot. Understand?"

The men all nodded.

"Say, I got a question," Boone said. "What'll Old Bill be doin' in all this? He didn't say nothin' 'bout where he was goin', and he ain't got but two Mexicans with him."

Pegleg said, "Whilst the rest of us is skulkin' around avoidin' bein' seen, Old Bill and them two Mexicans and a string of pack mules will ride in plain sight, pretty as you please, right on in to Los Angeles. He'll load up on such supplies as he can get. Anybody asks—and somebody will, as the Mexicans is mighty suspicious of any Americans what come into California—he'll tell 'em he's headin' north up the coast to the Oregon country, maybe do a little trappin' for beaver and otter as he goes. 'Course they'll deny him a permit to take peltries and order him to go back home the same way he came." Pegleg chuckled, as if some memory intruded into his story. "Old Bill'll head back this way, all right. Howsomever, them Mexicans will be watchin' for him to steal a march on them and go north. That's what Jed Smith did years back.

"If it works out like Ol' Bill thinks, them Mexis'll be lookin' the other way while we're a-runnin' off the stock. By the time they see what's happenin' we'll be gone, or near to it. They'll make a show of comin' after us, I reckon, like they always do. But they ain't never had the heart to follow us once we reach the desert."

Boone slept little that night. By moonlight he checked and double-checked and rechecked the latigos and cinches on his saddle, adjusted the stirrups, and then returned them to their original position. He refolded his saddle blanket. He sharpened his knife and checked his powder flask and shot pouch, and stuffed a few extra grains of powder and balls into each. He stitched up a tear on his shirtsleeve and rerolled his bandana and retied it around his neck. Then he checked the edge on his knife blade and decided to touch it up with a bit more whetting.

"Lord amighty, boy!" Pegleg grumbled from his bedroll, propping himself on an elbow. "Get to bed! You're a-goin' to wear that knife plumb out."

"Sorry. Can't sleep."

"Well, I can! Leastways I could if you'd quiet down." Pegleg lay back down. "You scared?"

Boone swallowed. "Sort of. Not scared so much as skittish, I guess."

"Just as well relax. Ain't nobody goin' to be tryin' to kill you for a few days yet."

"One thing does worry me, kind of."

"And what might that be?"

"It's that Mexican ridin' with us. Julio? I don't know as he can be trusted to hold up his end."

"Hmmm. And how 'bout Nooch and Ankatash? You worried 'bout them?"

"Nooch, no. He's showed his mettle pullin' me out of that river. I reckon he's got sand aplenty. That other Indian probably does, too. Leastways I hope so."

Pegleg let it lie for a time. "You're right about Nooch. And Ankatash . . . well, he's my woman Song's brother. And I'll make it as plain as I can. I'd trust him a hell of a lot sooner'n I would you, no matter what comes up."

It pleased the boy that darkness prevented Pegleg from seeing the flush that colored his face.

Pegleg went on. "As for Julio, he's as good a man as there is."

"But he ain't nothin' but a muleskinner."

A long sigh preceded the mountain man's answer. "He's a *mulero*, all right. And there ain't a better one. He's just as handy with horses, maybe more so. Hell, I seen him ride at a dead run, reach to the ground and pluck a chicken out of a hole without his mount breakin' stride or losin' balance."

Boone laughed. "What the hell would anyone want to grab a chicken for?"

"Oh, it's a game them Mexicans play. Shows off how well they sit a saddle. They's other contests, too—ropin' cattle, racin' horses, and such like. Besides all that, Julio has rode with me thievin' horses before." Pegleg paused to let the boy absorb what he'd said. Then, "Point is, you needn't concern yourself about Julio holdin' up his end. He'll do that—and likely hold up some of yours, as well."

Boone lay on his back atop his bedroll and, using his forearm as a pillow, stared into the stars. He held the same position hours later when Pegleg kicked out with his wooden leg, the blow landing in his ribs. He opened his eyes, unaware they had ever been closed, but saw only a few faded stars in a sky turning gray.

"Off your ass and on your feet, boy. We're the first ones ridin' out of here this morning. Better get your fill of hot coffee and grub, 'cause there'll be no fire in our camp tonight."

The pass opened into a long, wide valley broken here and there with hills and low mountains, and cut by ravines and arroyos. Before entering the valley proper, Pegleg turned to the west, following what Boone assumed to be cattle or game trails up and down the coarse ridges that reached out into the valley, staying as concealed as terrain and thickets of trees and brush allowed.

They holed up the first night short of their destination, loosening cinches but leaving the horses saddled, bridle reins tied to a wrist as they slept, or tried to. As they rode the next day, Pegleg stopped to point out the Mission San Gabriel out in the valley, then, farther along, the two big ranches he had in mind to raid. Boone and the others marveled at the numbers of cattle they passed in the hills and saw in the valleys, and the big herds of horses grazing here and there.

For the next two nights, a deep arroyo branching off from a rugged, narrow canyon unmarked by any distinctive trail concealed the thieves as they waited. Toward sunset, they scrambled up a steep southwest-facing ridge to catch the cooling breeze.

Pegleg drew a long, slow breath. "Smell that, boys?"

All three young men tilted noses to the sky and inhaled.

"I smell something," Boone said. "What is it?"

"That'd be the Pacific Ocean. Ain't but about twenty, thirty miles from here."

Nooch said, "Have you seen it, the ocean?"

"That I have."

"I cannot imagine such a thing. I am not even sure I believe the stories I have heard. The salt lake in the mountains, and the water you call Bear Lake—I have seen those, and they are beyond reckoning. But so much water to reach beyond the horizon—I cannot see such a thing in my mind."

"I'm with him," Boone said. "How come you to see the ocean?"

Pegleg squirmed around until his backside found a more comfortable seat in the rocky soil of the ridge. "Years ago, we was trappin' the Gila River, me and Ewing Young and some others. We decided to come on to California and try our luck, but the Mexicans wasn't havin' none of it. It were winter time, so we decides to just hang around till spring. So we sold our packs and done just that.

"We wandered up and down the coast, down to San Diego and on up to Mission San Luis Obispo. Saw plenty of the ocean, for sure. Watched 'em load hides onto sailin' ships one time. Them hides is dried in the sun and stiff as a board, and folded in half, longways. They haul 'em down to the shores in donkey carts, then carry 'em on their heads out into the water to meet boats that row in from the ship anchored out there a ways. Trade them hides for cloth and shoes and all manner of goods.

"A man could live a fine life in this country if the Mexicans'd let him. But they don't cotton much to Americans. I fancy I could live like they do, howsomever. They don't never have to work too hard, seein' as most everything you need is there for the taking."

Pegleg slid out of his seat and sidestepped down the hill

toward the makeshift camp. "Best come on along. The sun won't yet be up in the morning when we ride out of here and commence stealin' horses."

CHAPTER THIRTEEN

Pegleg Smith roused his men early. They squatted in a circle on the ground, bridle reins in hand, horses circled around them, awaiting the dawn and enough light to launch the raid. The leader relayed last-minute instructions.

"Most all them horses run loose. They'll be in bunches all up and down these hills. We'll gather all we can. But closer in to the ranch buildings there'll be pens and corrals and fenced pastures. That's where the best critters'll be. No matter if they's stud horses, brood mares, jacks, mules—get 'em out the gates or knock down the fences or whatever you can do to get them animals. Got it?"

Boone, Nooch, Ankatash, and Julio nodded in assent.

"Howsomever, I don't need to tell you that gettin' them out of them pens near them haciendas will be the most dangerous. If we're to get shot at or otherwise come under attack, that's where it'll be. So, you-all move fast and keep movin'. Once we get the horses on the run they'll keep runnin' so long as the rest of the bunch does. I'll ride up front and keep 'em movin' in the way we want to go. You got any questions, now'd be the time to ask 'em."

The boys looked at one another, faces pale and drawn but with eyes glowing, and shook their heads. Pegleg stood, snugged up the cinch on his saddle, and turned his horse in a tight circle before stepping into the stirrup, swinging his peg leg across the saddle and sliding it into its sleeve. The others followed suit, and Pegleg rode over the top of the ridge that concealed them and stopped below the skyline. In the near distance, straddling the road that bisected the valley, spread the headquarters buildings of the ranch of Don Francisco Garcia.

Lantern light glowed, and smoke rose from the chimneys where food preparation was underway, but all else was dark, and there was no sign of activity. Pegleg pointed out bunches of horses on the hills and in the valley with cattle scattered nearby. He assigned Nooch and Boone to the hills on one side of the valley, Julio to the other side, and said he and Ankatash would take the valley floor and the corrals at the ranch buildings.

Boone spurred the *grulla* gelding, his favored horse since leaving Taos, into a gentle lope, urging more speed as they neared the first band of grazing horses. He unlatched his reata from the saddle and unfurled several feet from the coils to use as a lash to frighten the curious horses into action. With the first bunch on the run, Boone pushed them at an angle down toward the valley floor as Nooch veered off to ride herd on another band. Across the valley, he saw Julio likewise stirring horses into motion, turning the running horses away from cattle gathered near a stream.

Turning hard up a ridge to reach a bunch of mares and foals standing with heads up and ears alert, watching the chase below, Boone rode past them as they turned to watch, the mares pawing and snorting, then circled toward them and aimed for the middle of the bunch, hollering and swinging the reata overhead. As he neared, the boss mare trumpeted a shrill whinny, nipped at her foal, and started the herd toward the valley. The panicked horses barely slowed upon reaching a deep arroyo cut into the hillside. Sliding down the bank on their hocks, the frightened mares lost track of their foals, some of which tumbled down the side. All but one regained their feet to resume the chase; that filly neighed and snorted as it struggled to rise.

Boone reined up some and leaned back against the cantle as his horse slid down through the loosened dirt. As they bottomed out, he caught a glimpse of the injured foal, its right foreleg dangling uselessly. He ducked away from the sight and the clouds of dust and leaned into the slant as his horse clawed its way up the slope to clear the arroyo.

The sun spilled light over the tops of the mountains to the east, illuminating the hills to the west, the glow crawling its way eastward across the valley floor, chasing the running horses. The ranch buildings were still in shadow when Pegleg and Ankatash arrived, running the captured horses ahead of them, others joining the stampede at the rear.

Barking dogs appeared out of nowhere, further stirring up the horses as the snapping curs darted in and out of the herd. Now and then a yelp rose above the rumble of hoofbeats as a slashing kick spun a menacing dog out of the way.

Pegleg stopped at a corral gate and, leaning out of the saddle, pulled the rails down. His horse leaped over the lowest rail into the big pen, and Pegleg circled the mares and young mules in the pen and pushed them through the gap. Ankatash used his knife to slash the bridle reins tethering five saddled night horses to a corral rail and shooed them into the running herd.

Once past ranch headquarters, Pegleg slowed the pace some but kept the horses moving at a deliberate speed. The riders on the side hills pushed more small bunches of horses into the herd as it moved along the valley floor and pushed the drove from the rear when time allowed. Boone guessed there to be well more than a hundred and fifty animals on the run—maybe as many as two hundred.

The day was well underway when the herd reached Don Emiliano's ranch. Vaqueros, servants, ranch hands—most every person at headquarters—stood with their backs to the sun, lured by the approaching thunder of pounding hooves. The crowd scattered, along with flocks of strolling pigeons and scratching chickens, when the leaders, Pegleg in their midst, charged into the yards.

Some realized in an instant what was happening, and vaqueros rushed for their mounts, some already saddled. Eduardo ran to the corral, shoved aside a vaquero, and mounted the man's horse. He and a couple of others already mounted rode into the streaming horses attempting to stem the flow, but their shouting and waving only served to push the horses harder.

Miguel Medina charged out of his hut and ran toward the hacienda, wielding an ancient flintlock pistol. He was almost run down as Ankatash pushed saddle mounts and young horses in training out of a large corral. Seeing the armed man coming, the Ute slipped his bow off his shoulder and nocked an arrow. His aim proved true, even from the back of a prancing horse, and the arrow pierced the horse trainer's chest. But the man did not fall, and Ankatash lunged his horse in an attempt to ride over him. Miguel stepped aside and fired, the lead ball trailing smoke as it struck the Ute in the cheek and obliterated his brain. The Indian slid from the saddle and fell into the cloud of powder smoke and dust as his horse raced away to rejoin the herd.

Through the dust and confusion, Pegleg saw the old man go after Anakatash and heard the shot, but he did not see the result.

On the hillside above the buildings, Boone pulled the rails from the entry into an adobe corral. He looked in wonder at the white skulls topping the wall, the horns tangling into one another like tree branches. He rode into the herd of jackasses in the pen, hollering and swinging his reata lash overhead, slapping the *honda* onto the rumps of any burros within reach. The jacks were big, obviously mature males used for breeding for mules. The jacks brayed and milled and finally streamed out the gate, following the edge of a deep ravine downhill to join the running herd.

Eduardo, cursing and yelling, spun his horse in useless circles, trying to stir the people to action. *"¡Apurate! ¡Detenerlos! ¡Vamos!"* He watched Boone push the rancho's prized jacks into the herd and spurred his horse after them.

Boone saw him coming through the dust. When only the length of a horse separated him from the onrushing Mexican, Boone turned in the saddle, whipped his reata in a circle, and laid the rawhide rope across Eduardo's shoulder, the stinging end wrapping around his back, nearly knocking the man off his horse. Boone spun the reata again; this time the end whipped around the Mexican's head, cutting deep into the flesh of his cheek, barely missing his eye, and splitting his scalp.

Knocked nearly unconscious and sagging, Eduardo managed to keep his seat as his mount slowed and veered away from the stampede, then turned and trotted back toward home. The horse stopped, snorting and pawing, near the corral where a crowd gathered around the fallen Miguel. He still breathed, but with every breath, bloody foam bubbled out of the hole left by the arrow, since withdrawn and lying in the dirt. And then he breathed no more.

Don Emiliano stood and grasped the cheek piece on the skittering horse, speaking softly to the frightened animal as two vaqueros slid Eduardo from the saddle and sat him on the ground, propped against a corral rail. Handing the reins to one of the men, the Don squatted in front of his son, then barked orders to one of his daughters to fetch a bowl of water and towels from the hacienda, and to bring her mother. As they waited, the Don unsheathed his knife, leaned his son forward and sliced up the back of his shirt, then stripped it off him. He cursed between his teeth at the bloody welt across Eduardo's back and used the wadded shirt to mop blood from his son's neck and shoulders, then dabbed gently at the blood around the gaping wound on his face and head.

The Doña arrived, skirts gathered in her hands, and knelt before her son. Squeezing water from a rag in the bowl her daughter held, she sponged at Eduardo's wounds, studying their severity. Over the years, through her experience doctoring injured workers on the rancho, as well as nursing her own family's ills, the matron of Rancho de Peralta had developed considerable skill as a healer and nurse. She stood and hiked her skirts, firing off orders to another daughter to fetch a certain leather bundle from a certain shelf in a certain room in the hacienda, along with some other necessary items. Then she instructed her husband and the vaqueros standing by to carry Eduardo to the shade of the big live oak tree, while other men fetched a table from the workers' communal dining area.

Eduardo stirred back to consciousness when laid on the table, attempting to rise. "*Quédate quieto, mi hijo,*" his mother said.

He blinked, trying to focus on his parents' faces looming above. "*Papá,*" he said, barely above a whisper. "*Los caballos . . . los machos . . .*"

Don Emiliano told his son not to worry. Horses and burros could be replaced. Sons, not so easily. The Doña wiped sweat from Eduardo's brow, encouraging him to stay quiet. She lifted his head and told him to drink. He coughed at the burn of the liquor, but the next swallow, and the next, and the one after, went down easily, and he drifted into shallow sleep. His mother ordered her son's horse brought nearby, and she yanked a hair from its tail and threaded it through the eye of a curved needle.

Eduardo winced when she bathed the wound on his cheek with the whiskey but lay silent and still as she pierced his skin with the needle and drew the horsehair through, pulling the edges of the cut together, knotting the thread, snipping it off, and repeating the stitching along the length of the gash. She did not sew up the wound in his scalp, rather wrapping his head tightly with a strip of muslin. The winding continued to cover the stitched cut on his cheek, leaving only a narrow gap through which Eduardo would see, once he opened his eyes.

As the Doña worked on their son, the Don instructed the men hanging about to carry Miguel's body to his hut. He would send some women to prepare him for burial. The men were to dig a grave in the rancho's *cementerio.*

"*¿Y el indio?*" one of the men said.

Don Emiliano looked toward the dead Ute lying in the dirt of the corral and spat on the ground. He was not to be buried, the Don said. Rather, the men were to drag the body to the corral used for killing, the *calaveras,* where he would be dumped in the arroyo there and left for *los osos grizzly.*

Well beyond the Peralta ranch, Pegleg again slackened the pace. He took down his reata and dropped a loop over the head of a likely looking horse and led it off to the side of the herd, dismounted, pulled the saddle and bridle from his tired mount, and placed them on the relatively fresh Peralta horse. Nooch rode down a hillside driving a few horses, caught a fresh mount for himself, and joined Pegleg.

"Pretty good morning's work," the mountain man said.

Nooch nodded. "There are some fine horses here. They will bring much money in trade." He tightened the cinch and tied off the latigo. "Where is Ankatash?"

"Don't know. Last I saw him, he was ridin' into a big corral back at that ranch. Heard a gunshot. Don't know if he made it out of there." Pegleg rocked his saddle to check its security on the horse's back, then turned the animal in a tight circle before swinging onto its back. "Boone up there?" he said, pointing up the hill with his chin.

"Yes. He was circling around some horses when I came with these."

"Watch for him to come down and tell him to swap mounts.

Julio'll know to do it. Let's keep pushin'."

"I am worried for Ankatash."

"So am I. Howsomever, there ain't nothin' to be done. Mayhap he'll be along. If not . . ." Pegleg shrugged, reined his horse around, and spurred him into a lope alongside the trotting herd, hollering and slapping his coiled reata against his wooden leg to hurry them along.

The raiders again created chaos upon reaching Mission San Gabriel. The mission covered extensive territory, with some two dozen villages and *rancherias* scattered throughout the valley. Some years earlier, the Mexican government had taken control of the mission from the Franciscan fathers, and management of the fields and herds had been slapdash ever since. Stock wandered freely through the valley as fences fell down. Cattle and horses reproduced unchecked, resulting in increased numbers, but reduced quality in the herds.

Pegleg Smith and his raiders cared not, for a horse was a horse to some buyers, and all would result in a profit, no matter the price, when the purchase cost involved no money. The well-bred, high-priced animals rustled from the ranches earlier in the day would offset the scrubs in the final tally.

The raiding continued through the night under the co-operative light of a horse-thief moon. By morning, Pegleg and his party and their herd of jaded animals were into the mountains and on the trail to Cajon Pass and a rendezvous with the other raiding parties. Horse tracks beyond measure cut into the trail, even widening it as it climbed, but there was no knowing how many stolen horses had already passed. Pegleg's rough estimate said his herd numbered near six hundred head; most were horses, but with a goodly number of mules and jacks in the mix.

He calculated it a fair trade for the life of one brother-in-law.

CHAPTER FOURTEEN

Old Bill Williams, Wakara, and Pegleg stood atop a low, rocky ridge in the early morning light.

"I make it near about twenty-five hundred head," Williams said.

Wakara nodded in agreement.

Pegleg kept up his count of the horse herd spread across the mountain valley, mumbling to himself as he wiggled and waggled his fingers in some form of computation sensible only to himself. "I'd say that's about right," he said when finished. "Give or take a hundred head or thereabouts."

"If Beckwourth brings in a good herd, we have made a good trip," Wakara said.

"Damn right. I don't reckon anybody's ever taken this many horses from them Californios," Old Bill said.

"That's likely so," Pegleg said. "Howsomever, we still got to get 'em home. That ain't goin' to be easy with this many."

"Aah, we'll do all right. We'll just take it slow and easy. Make sure we keep 'em watered. They'll get a mite hungry, but we'll feed 'em up good here and lay over where there's grass—"

"—Listen!"

"What is it, Wakara?"

"Listen."

Pegleg furrowed his brow and cocked his head. "I hear it. You hear that, Bill?"

"I do. Must be Beckwourth."

Wakara said, "It sounds like he is in a hurry."

The men watched down the canyon where the trail would round a low ridge and enter the valley. Soon, horses streamed into sight, running hard, but labored. Jim Beckwourth rode among the leaders, lather winging from his horse's shoulders and ribs and mouth. He recognized the three men on the ridge and veered away from the herd and rode toward them. The men in the camp came to life, waving saddle blankets, slowing the rushing horses and turning them into the valley where the other animals grazed. Only two other riders came in with the horses.

Beckwourth pushed his horse up the ridge, reining up a few yards from the men, and stepped out of the saddle. The horse, head hanging, struggled to breathe, sucking in air that appeared to have no effect.

Beckwourth, too, was out of breath. "We had best break camp and get on the trail," he said between gasps.

"Looks like you-all had trouble down there," Williams said. "What happened?"

"We had trouble, all right. The last ranch we hit last night. It was as if, somehow, they knew we were coming."

"Couldn't have. Not unless you-all doubled back or something."

"If they did not know, they had a goodly number of men mounted and armed for some other reason. They came out of the hills like a swarm of hornets."

"How many?"

"Perhaps a dozen. We were fortunate they chose not to press the attack after we retaliated. I shot one. Quintero put arrows into two others. Quintero fell. As did Flaco."

Pegleg said, "Quintero! They got Quintero?"

"I am afraid so, my friend."

The mountain man shook his head. "Them Mexicans must've killed Ankatash, too. Now Quintero. Them's both Song's brothers—she ain't goin' to be none too happy with me. She'll reckon I should've been lookin' after them boys."

Wakara said, "They were fine young men. Strong and brave. We will speak their names no more."

"Well, there is nothing to be done for it," Old Bill said. "They knew what might happen." Then, after a moment, "Looks like you got away with most of the horses, Jim."

Beckwourth nodded. "I would guess there are some six hundred head there. We lost a few in the melee at that ranch. A few more tired and quit the herd along the way, as we lacked enough riders to keep them in line. But there is no time to rest. I do not think pursuit will be long in coming."

Williams pursed his lips and furrowed his brow, looked to the sky, and scratched the whiskers on his neck. "I reckon you're right. We'll push on through the pass and see how things look when we hit the desert. They have never chased us any beyond these mountains before." He looked at each of the others in turn. "What do you think, gentlemen?"

All agreed. The men worked their way down the rocky ridge toward camp. Beckwourth led his tired mount, the breathing of both horse and rider back to near normal.

Old Bill broke up the circle of men in the camp, gathered round the riders who had just come in, and listened to their reports. "Best saddle up, boys," he said. "We're leaving now so as to get ahead of them Californios."

The *mozos* went to work, and the mules were packed in a matter of minutes. Boone's rested *grulla* was already saddled, so he and Nooch cut the cinches and latigos on the saddles that came in empty on some of stolen Mexican horses, to render them useless in any pursuit. The leaders gathered for a short meeting to outline assignments. Wakara would lead them out of the pass. He assigned two of his men to stay behind: one to find a high place from which to watch as much of the back trail as possible, the other to watch for his signal, then hurry to catch up the herd with a warning.

The *muleros* with their strung-together pack mules were to follow Wakara. Riders would be dispersed along the three- to four-mile length of the herd to keep the animals moving in good order as they long-trotted through the pass toward the high desert. Pegleg, with Philip Thompson and one of the Abiquiu men, would eat dust at the rear, ready to fend off any attack that might come until the other riders could rally to the fight.

But no pursuit arrived that day. The men pushed the rustled horses out of the mountains and onto the desert, and kept pushing until reaching Rabbit Springs. Boone and the other riders struggled against the thirsty horses and mules, cutting the herd into smaller bunches so as not to overrun the water hole. After drinking, the animals were allowed to seek out a meal among the brush and bunch grass, while several of the men rode herd to keep them from roaming too far.

Before sunrise, the low light illuminated a wispy dust trail on the desert between the water hole and the mountain pass. An identical plume followed it a mile or so behind.

"I don't know who that is," Beckwourth said, "but they are coming fast."

Pegleg watched the riders coming closer. "No way to tell who's chasin' who."

"It is not a chase," Wakara said. "The first rider is Patnish. The other is Toquana. Their coming can mean only one thing— someone is pursuing us."

"Damn!" Pegleg said, then spat in disgust. "Best get Bill and talk this out."

By the time the Ute lookouts arrived at the spring, their horses breathing hard and quivering in exhaustion, the leaders of the raid were well into a debate to determine a course of action.

"I tell you we got no choice. We push on and don't stop till we hit Resting Spring. They won't chase us that far," Williams said.

"Damn it, Bill, that's a good hundred and fifty miles from here. Every inch of it dry as a bone if we don't follow the trail to what little bit of water there is out there," Pegleg said.

"I know that, Pegleg. But hellfire! You know as well as I do that there ain't enough water at some of those springs to quench as many horses as we've got. We just plain don't have time to wait for the seeps to fill the water holes so they can all drink."

"But you don't know as them Mexicans'll keep after us. They ain't never done it before."

"We've never stolen this many horses before! Was I them, I'd chase us to hell and back."

"Howsomever," Pegleg said, "you ain't them, and they ain't you. They ain't nothin' but a bunch of easy-livin' Mexicans who ain't got the stomach for the kind of fight like we'd give 'em. No matter how many horses and mules we got, there's still more'n you can count wanderin' them California hills."

"I don't know, Pegleg . . . These critters have already cost us blood enough. I'd hate like hell to lose them now."

"Good hell, Bill! We drive 'em all the way to Resting Spring we could lose most of 'em anyway! They'll die tired and thirsty out in that desert—so will we, most likely."

Williams shook his head. "What do you think, Beckwourth?"

Before Beckwourth could answer, Wakara rejoined the deliberations, returning after hearing the report of the lookouts.

"Toquana says they are coming, as we thought."

"How many?" Beckwourth said.

"He says thirty riders—no more than that."

"Thirty!" Pegleg said. "Hell, there's near that many of us. I say we stay right here and give 'em a fight."

"You would risk losing more men?" Old Bill said. "We don't have enough to handle this stock as it is."

Pegleg turned and spat. "Who says we'd lose anyone? We've most likely got 'em outgunned. And there sure as hell ain't a man among 'em can shoot like me or you, Bill—or Jim or Thompson, neither. Hell, most of Wakara's boys can shoot the eyeball out of a lizard at half a mile. Them Mexicans ain't no match for us!"

"You willing to bet your life on it? And the lives of others?"

"Damn right!"

Williams thought for a minute. "What do you think, Jim? Philip? Wakara?"

"I believe Pegleg is right that we could best them in battle," Beckwourth said. "In spite of that, I do not believe it worth shedding any more of our blood."

"Not only that," Thompson said, "There could be more of 'em comin'. We could be in for more'n we bargained for. I say we get the hell out of here."

"And risk killin' these horses?" Pegleg said.

"Better'n gettin' more of us killed."

Again, Pegleg spat. Eyes burning, he looked from one man to the other. "What d'you think, Wakara? You ain't said nothin' yet."

"I have an idea," the Ute said.

"Let's hear it."

"I say we do as he says," Wakara said with a nod toward Old Bill.

"Damn!" Pegleg said.

"But," Wakara said, "I say we leave some men here—say nine or ten of our number. The Californios will be tired and thirsty, as we were on reaching this place. Our people will conceal themselves. When the others have watered their horses, and are dismounted and distracted with quenching their own thirst, our men will steal their horses."

The men said nothing for a moment. Then, almost in unison, they laughed.

"Hell of a fine idea!" Pegleg said.

Old Bill nodded. "You-all agree?"

Thompson and Beckwourth did.

"There'll be some risk, but I'm of a mind we could pull it off without losing anyone," Williams said. "Philip, you want to run this little show of Wakara's?"

"Why, sure. It'll be a pleasure."

Pegleg said, "Phil, was I you, I'd take Nooch and young Boone out of my bunch. I believe they'd both do you proud."

"I'll do that. Wakara, pick out a couple of your boys, if you will. Beckwourth, send me one or two of them that rode with you. I've got a couple or three of my own in mind." Thompson smiled. "I do believe this'll be right fun!"

Old Bill climbed aboard his horse and called the men to gather round. He explained the plan, and the men agreed that it should work. He said that the leader of each raiding party would call out the men who would stay behind to meet the Mexicans. He told the rest to pack up, saddle up, and be ready to ride, as the herd would be on the trail as soon as possible.

He did not say there was a possibility that one hundred and fifty long, hot, dry miles would be behind them before they would next stop.

CHAPTER FIFTEEN

Eduardo Peralta's head throbbed with his horse's every hoof fall. The white bandage around his head and face showed scarlet splotches where blood from his wounds seeped through, drying to rusty brown at the edges of the stains. Too uncomfortable to sit on his head, Eduardo's hat hung at his back, dangling from a thong around his neck.

Riding with him were three vaqueros from the Peralta rancho, accompanied by four men from the Garcia rancho riding with Vicenté Garcia, the young man recently wed to Rosa Maria Peralta. Four others, gathered from the Mission San Gabriel *rancherias*, rode with them. With Los Angeles as their destination, the armed men—their arms of various quality and condition—intended to demand the *alcalde* there assemble a posse to pursue the horse thieves, a posse for which they would be the first volunteers. The riders had followed the trail of the stolen horses toward Cajon Pass but gave up the chase in favor of gathering reinforcements, and so turned back toward Los Angeles. It would be well into the night before they would reach the city.

Although it was now near sunset, the morning's injury, the blood loss, and the whiskey that accompanied his mother's stitches still had Eduardo addled, and he struggled to keep his seat in the saddle. But he sat upright when he topped a rise overlooking the rancho of Don Ygnacio Palomeras. A herd of horses hundreds strong streamed through the valley, driven by mounted riders—a mirror of the morning's raid on his family's stock. An Indian drove brood mares out of a large corral while a black man gathered mules from a pasture.

"*¡A las armas!*" Eduardo shouted. "Attack! Shoot them!" he yelled as he spurred his horse to action.

The men followed, racing down the hill. Someone of the party fired a useless shot on the run and from a distance, serving only to alert the raiders of their presence.

The black man in the mule pasture reined up his horse and watched the men come. He stepped out of the saddle, drawing his rifle from its scabbard as he did so. Resting the weapon over the seat of the vacated saddle, he drew a bead on one of the approaching men and fired. The ball from the heavy rifle punched a hole in Vicenté Garcia's chest, tipping him out of the saddle and rolling him off the horse's rump.

The Indian unleashed two arrows in quick succession, one piercing the thigh of a San Gabriel rider, who turned his horse around and started back up the hill. The second arrow sliced through the throat of one of Eduardo's vaqueros, unleashing a fountain of blood.

The attackers now in chaos, Eduardo was barely able to make his horse stand long enough for a shot at the Indian raider. His aim proved true, and the man slouched over the neck of his mount but slipped off the side and to the ground as the horse ran away. Another of Eduardo's men killed a skinny Mexican raider chousing the stolen mares away, but he did not know who fired the shot.

Dust and powder smoke filled the air. The attackers watched through the haze as the rustlers and their stolen herd raced off toward the mountains, leaving behind two of their dead. Eduardo leaned over and expelled the contents of his stomach into the dirt. He spat away the residue, wiped his mouth on the sleeve of his shirt, then rinsed his mouth with a swig from his canteen and spat out the soured water.

Eduardo ordered the surviving men to load Garcia and the dead vaquero from his rancho onto their horses, and they rode on to the Palomares hacienda. Don Ygnacio Palomares, with several of his family, vaqueros, workers, and servants, met them in the yard, and some of the men lifted the bodies from the horses and laid them on plank tables carried out from the workers' *comedor*. The wounded San Gabriel vaquero had said nothing, and, in the confusion, no one had paid attention to him until he fell from the saddle, bled out and dead from the wound in his thigh. His body joined the others on the tables.

"Your losses are unfortunate," the Don said. "Still, we are fortunate you happened by, or our losses would be much worse. *¿A dónde vas?*"

Eduardo explained that they were on the way to Los Angeles to alert the authorities of the raids on their ranches, and to encourage pursuit of the thieves.

"How much stock did you lose?"

Eduardo sighed. "The animals taken from the Peralta and Gracia ranchos and Mission San Gabriel numbered five, perhaps six, hundred. Maybe more. *¿Quién puede decir?* The herd here tonight looked to be much the same in number. The losses are significant. Our best brood mares are gone. Our stallions. *Los machos. Nuestras mulas.* The *ladrones* swept up everything in their path, from the best animals to the ordinary. Such thievery cannot be allowed to stand unpunished. We must gather our forces and retrieve *los caballos* and jail the thieves. Or kill them."

"You are right, of course. Let us hasten on to Los Angeles. The prefect, or the *alcalde*, will give us the necessary authority to assemble a posse. I, myself, will lead the pursuit," Don Palomares said.

The Don left instructions for his people to carry the bodies of the dead to Mission San Gabriel, the Rancho de Don Peralta, and the Rancho de Don Garcia for proper burial among their own people. He assembled a handful of his trusted vaqueros to ride with the posse and left his *Segundo* in charge of operations at the rancho. Powder and shot issued from his own stores ensured that every rider would take to the trail with sufficient ammunition should a fight ensue.

Darkness had fallen by the time the riders left the ranch. The early hours of morning would arrive in Los Angeles with the nascent posse.

But when they arrived in the city, the city was not asleep. Nor had it been. The *alcalde* and prefect and other officials were out and about, taking reports and fending off demands for justice from men from ranchos and *rancherias* and missions throughout the valley whose livestock had been driven off in the widespread raids.

Eduardo made his report. "When the *ladrones* struck my family's rancho, they swept everything before them—our breeding stock, for both horses and mules; horses of every age and description, trained and unbroken; mules; foals. They took it all, save those animals grazing in out-of-the-way places and the few who escaped."

"And who were these thieves, these *ladrones?*"

"*Americano. Mexicano. Indio. Negro.*"

"*Si. Si*—reports from the others are the same. *Chaguanosos.* Thieves of many nations." The official scribbled notes with a stub of a pencil on a scrap of foolscap. "*Muertes?*"

Eduardo reported the deaths he knew of firsthand—Miguel Medina at his family rancho, and Vicenté Garcia and the two vaqueros from the fight at the Palomares rancho. He did not bother to mention the *chaguanosos* killed, whose deaths were of no consequence. The official asked about his wounded head, and Eduardo dismissed it with, "*No es nada.*"

113

Anxiety rose with the sun. The representatives of the rancheros and missions whose stock had been stolen demanded a posse take to the trail immediately. With every passing hour, they entreated, the *ladrones* and their plunder traveled farther and farther away, increasing the difficulty of overtaking and recovering the lost herds. The *oficials* feared the consequences of an uncertain strategy, the dangers of imperfect preparation, the hazards of hasty pursuit.

The rancheros drew up lists of *ganaderos* and vaqueros in the valley whose participation in the posse should be demanded at risk of a fine for noncompliance. They suggested emptying the *cárcel* to impress into service able-bodied prisoners for the mission.

Then, some thirty of their number mounted fresh horses, packed such supplies as were at hand, and rode off toward the mountain pass with Don Ygnacio Palomares at their head. In their impatience, the men did not spare the horses. And so, upon reaching San Bernardino de Sena Estancia, the party was forced to commandeer the few mounts available there, going so far as to scour the surrounding hills for *remontas.*

Into the mountains toward Cajon Pass they rode, following a trail cut by innumerable hooves. With intentions noble and firearms primed, the riders, more eager than observant, did not see the Ute watching them from high above, nor did they detect his signal to his accomplice below, nor witness the dust stirred by Indians as they retreated out of the mountain pass and into the Mojave Desert.

Juan Medina sat slumped against the wall in the jail cell, studying the wall opposite. From every vantage point, from every angle, he had memorized every crack in its plaster, every stain in its whitewash from the grime and slime of human contact, every intrusion of adobe where the coating had escaped its bond, all the names and dates and misery and hatred etched into its surface by prisoners confined by the walls over the years and decades.

Others in the cell coped with the interminable hours and days through amusements of their own. Some muttered endlessly, rehashing, perhaps, their lives and the wrongs done them, the injustice of their confinement, and vengeance in various forms. Some sat in a daze, or a doze, with their fellow inmates unable to determine which. Some of a musical bent sang songs, their repetitive monotony continuing until stifled by threats of bodily harm. The contribution of these time-consuming activities to the sanity of the convicts, in every case, was questionable.

Juan came alert at the sound of a key in the lock on the heavy wooden door. The hinges squealed, and a guard and some other man stepped into the stink of the cell. The *guarda* stood, back to the wall, hands clasped behind his back, watching the ceiling as the other man looked over the prisoners.

After a moment, the man cleared his throat to attract the attention of the guard. He pointed out prisoners of interest to his purpose. "Him. That one. The one over there. Those two. And him."

The man stood back as the guard summoned each of the six men called out to stand. The man looked them over again, nodded, and left the cell. With a thrust of his chin, the guard directed the chosen ones out the door. Last in the line, Juan noted that those left behind were older, sickly, or otherwise more feeble than those called out.

The prisoners, herded into an empty yard within the outer walls, joined with convicts from other buildings. Three men— one, the man who called them out of the cell—stood watching the prisoners as guards assembled them in untidy ranks. The man nodded at the captain of the guards, who clapped his hands for attention.

The man said, *"Mi nombre es* José Antonio Carrillo. I have a question. You must answer honestly, or there will be consequences for your lack of candor. I ask each of you, *¿Quién puede montar a caballo?"*

Confused by the simplicity of the inquiry, the prisoners turned, one to the other, and looked with bewilderment at the questioner.

Then, Juan stepped forward. "I can, señor. I can ride. I ride well."

Juan's confession unleashed a flood of similar responses. All but a few of the assembled convicts claimed the ability to ride horseback. Some, like Juan, were vaqueros, and riding was for them as ordinary as walking. If one were to measure their experience as riders, whether in terms of hours spent or distance covered, going horseback would prove more commonplace than being afoot.

"It is as I told you, Señor Carrillo," the *carcelero* said. "Most of our inmates are from the countryside. Many work as vaqueros on the ranchos. I am confident these *presidiarios* will suit your purpose well."

Carrillo stepped forward. "Our valley has been infested with a pestilence," he said. *"Chaguanosos* have plundered our ranchos. These *ladrones* have made off with horses beyond number. They have stolen mules. They have destroyed property." Carrillo paused.

"And, they have killed."

The prisoners mumbled, wondering if their ranchos, their families, had suffered at the hands of the raiders.

Raising his hand for silence, Carrillo said, "We will have our revenge. A party of Californios is already in pursuit of these evil thieves and murderers. But they are small in number. Today, we raise a posse of a hundred men. And you—you men—will be released from your cells to ride with us. Take heart, *mis amigos. Alta California* will never accept abuse of this kind. We will seek out, and we will destroy, those who exploit us. We will recover that which has been pilfered from our midst. We will have revenge! *Y ustedes—ustedes hombres—*will take a hand in our vengeance. We ride at first light!"

A cheer rose among the incarcerated men, echoing off the walls.

CHAPTER SIXTEEN

Boone swatted a swarm of biting, stinging bugs away from his face and used a shirtsleeve to wipe sweat from his forehead. He watched as the tail end of the horse herd faded into the cloud of dust stirred in its wake.

"Gather 'round, boys," Philip Thompson said. "Here's how this here little fandango is goin' to happen."

Nooch and three other Utes huddled around Thompson, joined by three Abiquiu Mexicans. Boone stood at the edge of the circle.

"Wakara's scouts has said there's a band of Californios on our tail. 'Bout thirty of 'em, best as they could count. They'll be stoppin' here for water 'fore long, and we'll be waitin' for 'em."

The man named Ortega said, "But they are thirty! We are only nine."

"Don't you worry none about that. Won't be but one shot fired if things go how we figure they will."

No one of the men could summon a response.

"See, we ain't goin' to fight 'em," Thompson said.

The men looked from one to another, unsure of what he meant.

"We're goin' to steal their horses."

Still, the men could make no sense of what they were hearing. Thompson let them stew for a bit, then outlined the plan hatched by Wakara.

The men would conceal themselves in the mesquite and

118

willows bordering the water hole, muzzling their horses. The Californians would expect that the *ladrones* they were chasing had moved on with the stolen horses, whose dust trail in the desert was visible for many miles. Tired and thirsty, as the raiders themselves had been when reaching Rabbit Springs, the posse would water their horses, then quench their own thirst.

When the time was right, Thompson said, he would fire a shot. On that signal, they were to whoop and holler and shriek and squeal, ride out of the brakes, and drive off the California horses. With luck, the surprise would be so sudden, and the theft accomplished so soon, that the victims would have no time to react or respond.

"So find a hole and crawl in it," Thompson said, "and wait for my signal."

Boone and Nooch sat in the scrub, sweating and swatting and talking.

"*¡Aquí vienen!*" Ortega yelled from the other side of the thicket.

Boone stood and looked toward the mountains. A cloud of dust rose above their back trail. Soon, he heard the drumming of hooves.

"All right, boys, quiet down!" Thompson said. "Grab your horses by the snout so's they don't whinny out a welcome."

The only sounds were hoofbeats, buzzing insects, and breathing. The breaths Boone drew were so heavy he feared the oncoming riders might hear them. He cleared his throat. His horse waggled its head, rattling the headstall. Nooch hissed a warning. Boone nudged him, drew a long breath, and squeezed his horse's nostrils a little tighter.

The Californians rode up to the spring and watered their horses, one rider stirring up the mud as he rode into the water, drawing a rebuke from the leader.

Boone noticed a hatless man, his head wrapped in a bloody

bandage and with black stitches across his cheek, and thought he recognized him from one of the raids. He tried to control his breathing, but it echoed inside his head as its rate increased, and he feared it was audible to the men now lazing around the spring pond.

Then, he felt, sensed maybe, Nooch stiffen beside him. He heard the muffled ratcheting of the hammer on Thompson's pistol. By the time the report sounded, Boone was already in the saddle, and with the shot he rode screaming for all he was worth, spurring his horse out of the willows and into the open. He saw frightened men scramble out of his way; others only stared in shock.

It was over almost before it started. The California horses, still under saddle and as frightened as their now-afoot riders, raced into the desert. Boone and the others pushed them into a bunch and eased the stolen horses into an arc ending in the direction of the curtain of dust left hanging by the larger herd.

Boone chanced a look back at the spring. The unhorsed posse stood in a row like so many pigeons on a wall, watching. Powder smoke rose from a few useless shots from the Californians.

After a few miles, Thompson, in the lead, slowed to a trot, then a walk. He fell back to ride beside one of the posse horses, withdrew his heavy knife, and sliced through the latigo and tipped the saddle off into the dirt and brush to lighten the load on the captured horse. The others followed suit, taking time as they rode to pilfer anything of value from saddlebags and bedrolls before spilling the refuse to the ground. One of the Mexican riders took a shine to a California saddle and dismounted long enough to switch it to his mount.

Through the day, the riders stopped now and then to throw their saddles onto a relatively fresh horse and then pushed along, following the hoofprints of the thousands of horses ahead of them and the distant dust cloud they lifted. As the day faded to evening, the horses, clawing their way across the desert in a mile-eating trot, waned. Boone rode up beside Thompson.

"Say, Philip—ought not we to be findin' water pretty soon? We been pushin' these horses plenty hard."

Thompson eyed the boy, his eyes blank. "There won't be any water. Not till we reach Resting Spring. We ain't stoppin' for nothin' till we get there."

"How far?"

Scratching his jaw whiskers, Thompson said, "Oh, hundred miles or so, I reckon. Maybe more."

Boone's eyes widened. "And we ain't stoppin' till then? Why the hell not? There was other water holes we hit on the way out here."

"True enough. But there ain't many of 'em could water three thousand head. And we're followin' the herd till we catch up to 'em. Besides, it's best to put some distance between us and them Californios."

"But they ain't comin'—we got their horses, didn't we?"

Thompson nodded. "These. But there could be more a-comin', and, if there is, we don't aim to be where they can get to us."

Boone rode along in seething silence for a time. "Damn it, Philip, we'll kill these horses if they don't get some water and feed and rest!"

Thompson only nodded.

And they rode on into the darkening night.

Boone saw the first carcass not long after sunrise. He stopped and looked down at the foal lying in the brush, ribs and hip bones clearly visible against its brittle hide.

And there were more and more as the miles and hours passed, the hulks swelling in the heat. At first, the dead were the young and old. But then there were fallen horses and mules in what should be the prime of life rather than death. Boone surmised they were mostly from the band Beckwourth brought in, as those animals had not gotten any rest in the mountains but were driven on in a rush soon after arrival. As the day lengthened, it was no longer necessary to see the carcasses littering the plain—the smell betrayed the presence of death. Rolling slowly toward their backs as they bloated, the dead horses raised hooves and legs skyward as if in surrender. Horses from their own small herd staggered, stumbled, and fell.

As he had the evening before, Boone rode up beside Thompson.

"Damn it, Philip! What the hell for did we ride all the way to California to steal these horses for if we was only goin' to kill 'em?"

Thompson offered no explanation, no excuse, no answer at all. He did not even look at the boy. He rode on, chin on chest, weary from long hours and miles in the saddle. His canteen, like all the rest, was empty, his throat parched beyond useless talk. With no food, no water, there was nothing to do but ride.

In the night, they started passing horses still on their feet. Some stood, legs splayed and heads down, as if somehow their muzzles might find sustenance in the dust. Others plodded along, step after slow step, their heads, too, hanging low. When the tougher, heartier mules appeared among the fallen, Boone understood the situation was more precarious than he had realized.

And then the horse he rode raised its head. He looked around and saw others doing the same. A snort. A weak whinny. The smell of water on faint breeze called up some hidden reserve in the animals, and they pressed on. Boone and the others rode right through the larger herd, or what was left of it, rustling for forage in the moonlight. The herd thickened as they neared the spring and the greener, thicker grass that bordered it.

When they jostled their way through bunches of horses and

reached the verge of the water hole, Boone did not stop but spurred his mount on into the pond and kept riding until it wet his boots. Sliding his feet from the stirrups, he rolled to the side and fell with a splash, sinking under the surface, and felt the liquid seep into his every pore. He raised his head out of the water and filled the crown of his hat again and again, pouring water over his head and sinking just enough to suck in draughts of the pond water.

Had it been daylight, Boone and the others in his party, likewise relishing the refreshment, might have noticed that the water swirled with mud, and insect hulls and leaf litter floated on the surface. Had they noticed, they might not have cared.

The late-arriving thieves stumbled through their sleeping partners, making way to a campfire burned down to coals. A coffeepot contained thick coffee boiled bitter; breaking through the scum in a blackened pot revealed a mess of beans, some in the mix cooked to mush and others with a decided crunch. Tortillas stacked stiff and cold on a sandstone *comal*. Corn dodgers lay heaped on a cloth beside a batch of their mates, held captive by congealed bacon grease in a heavy skillet. Rough-cut slabs of bacon curled and twisted cold in another pan.

Giving no thought to the palatability of the fare in normal circumstances, the men poked and prodded in the darkness, filling and refilling plates already used. They gorged themselves, washing half-chewed mouthfuls down their gullets with water and more water.

And then Boone unfurled his bedroll, damp in places and drenched in others from his ride into the water hole, and plopped his own still-soggy body atop it and fell into fitful sleep, his abused stomach rebelling through the remainder of the night. The coming day was already washing the stars out of the eastern sky when deep sleep finally came upon the boy.

He did not awaken with the stirring of the camp come morning. His hat propped over his face kept the light from waking him. But with the light from the sun came heat, and, when he sat up and scoured his eyes with his knuckles, a film of sweat covered him, binding his clothing to uncomfortable parts of his body. Boone sat for a few minutes, scratching and stretching and spitting, gathering his wits. He looked around, seeing hundreds and hundreds and hundreds more horses scattered around the springs and into the surrounding desert, tearing at the scant grass. Even with all the dead animals left lying along the trail—approaching half the herd, he estimated—the number of living horses was still sizeable, with a goodly number of mules and burros in the bunch. But the sight and smell of those killed by indifference and, to him, a rash decision, roiled his thoughts.

Boone stood, arched his back to stretch out the kinks, and stepped into a clump of willows to relieve himself. The breakfast leftovers at the campfire were a reprise of the leftover supper he'd gorged on the night before. He picked at what he put on his plate and dumped what was left into a waste hole dug for such a purpose, then knelt at the edge of the pond and laved water over his face to wash the remnants of sleep away.

Old Bill, Pegleg, Beckwourth, Wakara, and Thompson sat in council in the shade of a cottonwood tree. Boone walked over, stepping between where Pegleg sat on a rotting log and Wakara perched on a rock. The conversation stopped with his arrival, the men staring at the boy standing amidst them as if he had earned a place among the leaders in council.

Pegleg spoke. "Well, boy, I see you're back amongst the living."

Boone nodded. "I am." He swallowed hard. "Wish I could say the same for all them dead horses back there."

"We did lose a fair number, that's for certain."

"What I want to know is, why?"

Pegleg chuckled. "Why? What the hell do you mean, why? You know damn good and well why."

"I know they died of thirst, and from bein' driven too hard. What I don't know is why we—you-all—done that."

The other men looked on as Pegleg chewed on his lip, staring at the boy. "That's just the way of it. We lost some of 'em, and that's a damn shame. Howsomever, it's better to lose some of 'em than lose 'em all."

"Some of 'em? We must've lost damn near half the herd! For what? There's water out there. There weren't no need to bypass them springs just to avoid a bunch of dirty damn Mexicans! It just ain't right. I never rode all this way to steal dead horses. You-all ain't nothin' but a bunch of damn fools!"

Pegleg stood in an instant and spun to face the boy. Without a word, he backhanded Boone, knocking him to the ground. Boone looked up at Pegleg standing over him, felt a trickle from the corner of his mouth, wiped it away, and saw it was blood. He started to rise, but Pegleg's wooden leg in the middle of his chest pushed him back down and pinned him to the ground.

"You done runnin' your mouth, boy?"

Boone nodded.

"Good. Now, you listen to me. You don't know one damn thing about stealin' horses. Fact is, you don't know one damn thing about much of anything. You was invited along for no other reason than I took a shine to you back in Taos. I see now I was mistook in that. Here's the deal. Either you shut up and do as you're told by those of us who's earned the right to talk, or you cinch your saddle onto the back of one of these horses and ride on out of here. You can have your pick of the horses—don't care a damn which one you take. So that's it. You either ride with us, or you ride away."

Pegleg stepped off the boy. Boone picked up his hat, stood,

swiped again at the trickle on his chin, dusted off the seat of his pants, and walked away.

CHAPTER SEVENTEEN

Juan Medina rode along the twists and turns of the trail through Cajon Pass, savoring the freedom of fresh air and walls made only of mountains. The horse the authorities provided was serviceable, but not trained as well as could be. The means and methods of training Juan learned from his father on the Peralta rancho had spoiled him for ordinary horses. Still, he would rather ride a burro bareback than fester in jail.

The posse was a mixture of vaqueros pressed into service from the ranchos, citizens drawn from the more than two thousand residents of the city, a few civic authorities, and the prisoners. Juan's attempts to count the riders spread along the trail proved difficult, but he estimated there were as many as seventy, or even eighty. A few others followed several hours behind, bringing along spare horses and supplies. The boy was unsure how the posse, under the command of José Antonio Carrillo, would fare in an engagement with the *chaguanosos*. While the Californios were superior in numbers, they were poorly armed. The convicts were unarmed, and many of the others carried only pistols, some nothing but swords or spears. A few dozen rifles rode across saddle bows, in saddle scabbards, or propped on thighs.

The procession halted in a narrow part of the canyon. Juan could see Carrillo standing in his stirrups, looking ahead. Soon, a scout riding in advance of the posse came racing back down the trail and slid to a stop beside the leader. Juan could hear nothing of what he said, but the man flailed his arms wildly, pointing up the trail. The scout calmed, and he and Carrillo kept talking as bits and pieces of their conversation passed down the line.

"He has said someone is coming . . .

"He has said he does not know who they are . . .

"He has said he does not think it is *indios* . . .

"He has said he does not believe they are the *ladrones* . . .

"He has said they are *ambulante—¡están sin caballos!*"

Juan, like the others, could not imagine why a group of men would be afoot rather than mounted this far from the settlements.

Carrillo raised his hand and signaled the posse forward. They rode on a short distance to where the canyon opened into a small valley, and Carrillo signaled the men to form abreast across its width, dismount, and prepare to engage whoever was coming. Several minutes passed as the men fidgeted. And then, around a bend in the trail, the walking men appeared. Strung out, staggering, some stumbling every few steps, they limped into the opening, unaware of the reception awaiting them.

One by one at first, the walking men noticed the posse. Some fell to their knees, some hurried, some stood and stared. And then, here and there along the line of the posse, men recognized someone among the sore-footed *caminantes*. Realization spread that these men were from the first posse to go out after the thieves and the stolen horses.

Tired, hungry, and thirsty, no man among them offered any explanation. They begged for water, gratefully gnawed at any bit of food offered, and embraced acquaintances. A man with a bloody and soiled bandage around his head approached Juan, and he recognized Eduardo Peralta.

"I will have your horse, Juan Medina," Eduardo said, his voice gravelly and weak.

Juan took a step back and gripped the bridle reins tighter. "No."

"Hand me *los riñones*. I will not ask you again."

"And again, I tell you no."

Eduardo grabbed the front of Juan's shirt and twisted, jerking the boy toward him. Juan lashed out with a fist, striking Eduardo's injured cheek. The blow burst one of the stitches, and Eduardo ducked, grabbing at his face, seeing the blood.

"*¡Te mataré!*" he said.

Carrillo appeared as if from nowhere, forcing his mount between the man and the boy. "There will be no killing here! Step back, both of you."

The posse leader asked Juan what was happening.

"This man demanded my horse."

"Do you know this man?"

"*Sí.* He is Eduardo Peralta."

Carrillo turned to Eduardo. "And you, Señor Peralta. What gives you leave to demand another's horse?"

"This boy is a thief. Only recently I had him jailed for stealing from my family. He was a worker at the Rancho de Don Emiliano Peralta. The Don is my father. This boy, this thief, assisted his father, who trained horses there. But that is in the past." Eduardo turned to Juan and fixed him with a cold stare. "Now, Miguel Medina sleeps with his fathers."

A gasp escaped Juan, and he stepped backward.

Eduardo smiled, then said to Carrillo, "As I said, this boy should even now be imprisoned. He has most likely escaped and lied to you about his situation."

Juan said, "My father—how did he die?"

Eduardo said, "The *chaguanosos* killed him as they stole horses from the rancho. He died from an arrow from an Indian's bow when we resisted and put up a fight." Then, to Carrillo, "I, myself, was wounded *en la pelea,* as you can plainly see. We have been in pursuit of the *ladrones,* and I require this boy's horse, or another, to continue the chase. And I shall have it."

"You will have no such thing. This is my expedition, and I give the orders. Return to *tu grupo* and await my instructions, which I shall convey once I have sorted out with Señor Palomares what transpired to bring his posse to such a sorry state." Carrillo rode away.

Eduardo touched his face, studied the blood on his fingers, and again fixed Juan with a stare before walking away.

As the former skirmish line unraveled, Juan did not move. His father was dead. Eduardo had threatened his own life. He feared what was to come, for he thought it unlikely that Carrillo, or anyone else in a position of authority, would favor a simple vaquero—and *un prisionero* at that—over the son of a wealthy ranchero, a *gente de razon.* His throat tight, he blinked away tears. Juan draped an arm over the saddle, leaned into the horse, tucked his face into the crook of his elbow, and the world around him faded away.

How much time passed before laughter roused him from his musing, Juan did not know. He looked around, his mind focusing on his whereabouts. Most of the members of his posse stood circled around the walking men, now seated on boulders or on the ground, many with boots and shoes removed, massaging their feet. Juan knew not the reason for the laughter, but the footsore hombres did not appear to appreciate it. He wiped his eyes with his shirtsleeve and led his horse toward the assemblage.

"*¿Que esta pasando?*" he said to a vaquero at the edge of the circle.

"*Silencio,*" the man said. "*Escucha.*"

Juan listened as the parties exchanged barbs. Members of his posse mocked the walkers for losing their horses to the *chaguanosos.* In return came excuses and explanations, which were dismissed with laughter. He learned from other conversations that Carrillo had likewise upbraided Palomares and assumed overall command of the operation for himself.

Unhorsed posse members were invited to select mounts from the remuda expected to catch up soon. But Carrillo could offer nothing in the way of saddles or bridles to replace those lost at the water hole. Makeshift hackamores, to be fashioned from cut-apart reatas, would be the only thing available in the way of gear. Carrillo had also made it clear that no man was entitled to one of the horses unless he accompanied the posse on its mission—those wishing to return home to the valley could continue walking.

The posse awaited the arrival of the *remonta* before pressing on. The only relief from the discomfort and chafing in store for those mounted bareback came in the form of bedroll *mantas* offered by some sympathetic posse members, and halved saddle blankets from under the saddles of others. Eduardo Peralta, stiff and sore from the walk, used a boulder for a mounting block to climb aboard his borrowed horse. And as he did so, he again glared at Juan Medina—a look sharp enough to cut. The boy did not respond, only turned his horse and spurred it ahead to join the line of the posse nearer the front.

Carrillo led the men out of the pass at a brisk pace. He surveyed the desert when they cleared the mountains but saw only the faintest trace of dust, if that, in the far distance. A mile or so from Rabbit Spring, the posse halted. A dozen men, those with the best arms, rode ahead on Carrillo's orders to ensure that none of the horse thieves lay in wait as they had for the Palomares posse. When no hostiles were found, the horses and men took on water and followed the trail of the stolen horses deeper into the Mojave Desert.

Another halt was called upon sighting something unexpected in the distance, huddled on the desert floor among clumps of spindly brush and bunchgrass. After watching for some time and sensing no movement, the scouts again rode forward, spreading themselves across the plain. Slowly forward they went, stopping and going, watching and waiting. At last, the scouts waved the others onward.

Exclamations erupted into cheers when the scattered objects became saddles. Men with sweat-stiffened trousers and skin rubbed raw rode among the *monturas* seeking their own. The search proved successful for most; others gathered gear not their own but discarded in trade by the *chaguanosos* in favor of a better California rig. With unsheathed knives the men went to work stripping leather thongs and punching holes and stitching together cut latigos and mending cinches. The saddles could prove unsteady under the cobbled repairs but still offered improvement over riding bareback.

Carrillo pushed the posse even harder after the delay, fearing the thieves would escape beyond his reach.

First came the smell. Men hiked up ponchos to cover their noses and wrapped *pañuelos* around mouth and nose. But there was no escaping the stink that permeated the air. Then, like the discarded saddles, carcasses appeared on the plain—few at first, then in numbers. The decaying horses and mules provided a feast for scavengers that would be the envy even of California grizzly bears on cow-killing day. *Lobos*, coyotes, *zopilotes*, *águilas*, *cuervos*, and other carrion eaters had been at the dead animals. Even as the riders approached, buzzards hopped away and took flight, coyotes slunk away, and ravens squawked displeasure at the interruption.

"*¡Madre de Dios!*" Juan mouthed for perhaps the hundredth time as he rode through the *animales muertos*. He turned to the man riding beside him. "*¿Por qué?* Why would these *ladrones* take the trouble to steal our horses if only to kill them? Why?"

The man shrugged.

Juan rode on, ashen-faced. The posse's horses were tired and thirsty, but travel at a slower pace kept them from falling. The boy's stomach roiled, more at the callousness and cruelty than the stench. "There must be a thousand dead horses." Again, but now with resignation rather than surprise, *"Madre de Dios."*

And again, the man beside him shrugged.

Miles ahead, Carrillo's scout thought he saw faint traces of wispy smoke in a sky lit by a sun nearly horizontal. And he believed he detected the weak odor of the smoke, infringing on the smell of death in the warm breeze. He turned from the trail to climb a ridge extending from one of the many bald desert mountains. Near the crest, he dismounted and dropped the bridle reins, securing them with a stone, and scrambled to the skyline. In the distance, a slash of green betrayed the presence of water. Surrounding the *prado* he imagined, almost as much as he saw, hundreds and hundreds of dots that did not appear attached to the landscape. And he imagined, more than he saw, some of the dots moving.

But he did not have to imagine, for he knew he could see, the pinpricks of orange that two campfires seared into the scene. The scout slid down the slope, displacing stones as he went, their rattling down the hill causing the horse to prick its ears and lean against its tether. But the rock held the reins fast until the rider retrieved them to mount up and urge the horse straight down the hillside on his hocks. When the horse's front hooves reached the desert floor, the scout leaned forward, tapped the animal's belly sharply with his spurs, and with a slap of reins on the horse's rump, hurried back to rejoin the posse.

After hearing the scout's report as night fell, the *commandante* directed the men to turn aside from the trail to make a cold camp behind the concealment of a hill.

"There are to be no fires. There is to be quiet, if not silence. Our prey is miles away, but they may send scouts along the back trail to discover our presence," Carrillo said. "We will retain our baggage and remuda at this place and ride swiftly from here with the rise of the sun. The capture of the thieves and the recovery of the stolen horses are within our grasp. Speed is of the essence, and surprise will prove our most effective weapon. Select now a fresh horse, and secure it nearby. Make fast your riding gear, and see to your weapons. There will be no time to waste come *salida del sol*. Take heart, *mis amigos*. For tomorrow, we ride to glory."

Juan stepped out of his saddle. Someone approached and stood close as he loosened the cinch. He turned and in the low light recognized the bandaged head of Eduardo Peralta, the wrappings no longer white but still visible in the darkening night.

"Ride with eyes in the back of your head tomorrow, Juan Medina," Eduardo said. "One can never know from which direction danger may come."

CHAPTER EIGHTEEN

Wakara sent Nooch out at dawn with instructions to ride a wide arc through the desert. If the Californios are to come, the leader said, they may depart from the trail proper in an attempt at surprise. The boy rode to a ridge top and stopped, watching light from the rising sun crawl across the desert. A faint stirring of dust beyond a low hill a mile or so away caught the sunbeams, so he rode down to investigate. As he reached the desert floor, a string of riders rounded the base of the hill.

The horsemen spotted Nooch almost as soon as he saw them. As he wheeled his horse and raced toward the camp at the spring, the lead rider sent two of his men in pursuit of the fleeing Ute. But Nooch, riding a well-bred and now rested mount stolen from the Californios, outran the scrub horses in the chase, and the riders turned back when they came within sight of the camp.

Nooch rode in shouting a warning that trouble was but minutes away, and already rising dust from the California column hung in the morning air. Old Bill, Pegleg, Wakara, and Beckwourth spouted orders for their men to saddle up, pack up the camp, round up the horses, load the mules—orders often confusing and sometimes contradictory, as men were sent here then there, to do this and that.

"To hell with it!" Pegleg Smith hollered in a voice that drowned out all others. "Get your sorry asses mounted, and get these horses on the move!"

The onrushing Californios were within sight, whipping up their horses and coming at a run. Bringing rifles to bear, the mountain men fired into the still-distant attackers. Old Bill saw a rider spilled with his shot. A horse died midstride, cartwheeling over its rider, when Pegleg's bullet shattered its forehead. Other bullets wounded riders and panicked horses.

The leader of the posse waved at his men to spread out. Some, armed with rifles, sent puffs of powder smoke streaming as they fired hopeful but useless shots from running horses. Bullets shot from pistols, even more ineffective, further reduced the firepower of the posse.

Another volley from reloaded rifles from the camp took more lives, caused more wounds, and spilled more horses. By then the mountain men could see sabers and spears in the upraised hands of some of the riders. Even with their superior firepower, with pistols primed and ready, Old Bill could see they would be overwhelmed by sheer numbers and ordered a retreat. The men were quickly in the saddle and on the move, save Pegleg. With his left foot in the stirrup, he hopped and hopped on his wooden leg, attempting to stay upright as his frightened horse shied and spun in the confusion.

Beckwourth looked back, saw his partner's predicament, and turned around. After three failed attempts, he got a hand on the bridle and jerked the panicked animal to a stop. Pegleg, out of breath from the struggle, managed to swing his wooden leg over the cantle. Beckwourth slapped the horse on the rump, and, as it raced away after the others, Pegleg hung onto the saddle horn as he struggled to find the stirrup sheath for his appendage.

His posse in disarray and men armed with guns wasting any chance of using their bullets to effect, Carrillo shouted unheard—or ignored—orders to hold fire. He watched helplessly as the long-distance rifles of the *chaguanosos* felled men and horses around him and instilled fear into his followers, some peeling away from the charge. But there was nothing to be done but attack, with the aim of using their greater numbers to overrun and overpower the thieves.

Juan Medina, among the many unarmed members of the posse, rode low on his horse, his position near the front of the charge offering a prime target. No bullet found Juan or his horse. But, all the same, he was taken out of the attack when a horse beside and slightly ahead of him went down—whether from a stumble or bullet he did not know—and rolled in front of his horse, upsetting it and sending Juan rolling.

Stunned by the tumble, barely conscious, and with the breath forced out of him, Juan instinctively curled in a ball with arms wrapped around his head, hoping the horses running past would, could, avoid stomping him into the desert soil.

The posse reached the hastily abandoned camp at the spring and found nothing but disarray. The men pilfered the deserted packs, finding food but little else of value. Pots and pans still propped above fires gone cold were passed from hand to hand, the men sampling the cooking of the horse thieves. The few horses and mules left behind in the confusion were gathered and started back down the trail that had taken the lives of so many of their kind.

But all that remained of the thieves themselves and the stolen herds was a cloud of dust, by now miles away and getting farther away by the minute. Carrillo threw up his hands. With horses jaded from the hurried attack, and fresh mounts miles away, he called off the chase. He would report their efforts to retrieve the stolen animals and punish the thieves as a brave and valiant attempt but ultimately ineffective owing to circumstances beyond his control.

Juan neither saw nor heard any of this. After the charge, the dust long since settled, he managed to sit up, leaning against a fallen horse for support. And there he sat, still addled, when Eduardo Peralta rode up, his horse covering the boy with its shadow. Silhouetted in the sun, the man laughed at Juan. The boy squinted into the sun, barely able to recognize Eduardo.

But there was no doubt of his identity when he stepped out of the saddle. Smiling, sneering, rather, Eduardo pulled a ceremonial sword from its sheath and a dueling pistol from his sash. Juan knew both belonged to Don Emiliano, keepsakes from his long-ago service in the Spanish military.

"With which of these weapons shall I take your life, Juan Medina?" He held up the sword, eyeing its blade as it sparkled in the sunlight. "*La espada*, perhaps? Or *la pistola?*" he said, ratcheting back the hammer. He looked from one to the other, then to Juan, and back to the weapons. But it was all for effect, for Eduardo believed a gunshot would attract notice and betray the murder.

But his taunting had the desired effect, for the fear played on Juan's mind. At the same time, it energized him, brushing the cobwebs from his brain and sharpening his senses.

He was ready when Eduardo shrugged and tucked the pistol back into his sash. Again eyeing the blade, Eduardo swished the steel back and forth, enjoying the glint of the sun on its polished surface. His eyes betrayed his next move, and Juan rolled aside when the sword came slashing down, striking only the saddle on the dead horse against which Juan had been leaning.

As he rolled, he swept his legs around Eduardo's, scissoring him off his feet. The attacker lost his hold on the sword as he fell, and Juan's hand found the grip. He leapt to his feet, and, as Eduardo rolled over and then attempted to roll away, Juan stopped him with a prick of the blade. He shifted the sword to his other hand and reached down and pulled the pistol from Eduardo's sash, cocked the hammer, and without ceremony shot Eduardo in the chest.

Juan slid the sword back into its sheath and from Eduardo's saddle found a powder horn and shot pouch, which he slung over his shoulder under his poncho and likewise concealed the pistol in his waistband. Kneeling beside the bleeding body, he unlatched the silver-mounted spurs from the boots and concealed them, as well, under his poncho. He left Eduardo's horse where it stood and picked up the reins of another likely looking horse standing nearby, climbed aboard, and rode to the *ladrone*'s campsite.

"I heard a shot fired," Carrillo said. "What is the reason for that?"

"A horse with a broken leg. I merely relieved him of his misery. The pistol, it was damaged. I discarded it after the shot as no longer serviceable."

Carrillo nodded.

Juan watched the men wandering through the camp and, when he saw an opportunity, led his horse into the willow brakes surrounding the spring to wait. And there he waited until Carrillo ordered the posse members still in the camp to mount up and start the long ride home.

Once the retreating posse was out of sight, Juan led the horse out of the thicket, mounted, and turned the horse toward the dust cloud raised by the horse thieves and their stolen herd.

Boone, riding near the front of the herd, spat in disgust as he pushed the horses across the desert at an easy lope—or what would have been easy for properly fed and rested horses. Although somewhat rehabilitated by the sojourn at Resting Spring, the horses and mules were far from fit enough to maintain the pace set by Wakara. Soon, Boone feared—knew—animals would fall by the wayside, dead or dying.

But when a lookout hurried to ride beside Wakara, the Ute leader slowed his horse to a trot, then a walk, as the slowing worked its way back through the herd. Leaving the lookout to lead the procession, Wakara turned aside to await the arrival of the mountain men. Boone rode over to the waiting Ute and asked what had happened.

"The Californios have turned back. They are no longer after us."

Boone looked confused.

Wakara shrugged. "It would seem their bravery has its limits. I am not surprised. Except to say that I am surprised we were pursued this far. Never before have they followed us beyond the Cajon Pass."

"We left behind most of our gear back there. And grub. We goin' back to fetch it?"

The Ute shook his head.

"We ain't? Why the hell not? What we goin' to eat now?"

Wakara looked at the boy. Then, he inclined his head toward the horse herd streaming past.

At a loss for words, Boone could only stare at the Ute, who returned his stare. And then Boone turned away to ride alongside the horses.

They pushed the herd through the day and deep into the night, stopping only upon reaching Las Vegas. Boone spent the remainder of the night riding around the herd, even though there was little danger that any of the worn-out horses would wander far from the water or grass in the meadows. Come sunrise, he rode into the campsite and stripped the saddle from his horse—the fourth to carry the saddle since the Californios chased them out of the previous camp.

Boone walked, stiff and sore, to the fire and lowered himself gingerly to the ground. Pegleg, Old Bill, and Jim Beckwourth, faces still smeared from sleep, squatted around the fire, gnawing at handfuls of meat. Beckwourth pulled a willow stake from the

140

ground with a slab of meat sizzling on its end and offered it to the boy.

"What is it?"

"Breakfast," Beckwourth said.

"I mean, what was it?"

Old Bill said, "When we got here in the night it was a scrawny sorrel mare—leastways I think 'twere a sorrel, bein' as it was dark and all."

"I ain't eatin' no horse."

Pegleg laughed. "The hell you say! You're likely to get damn hungry, boy. This here is a mite tough and stringy, but generally speakin' horse meat ain't bad. Howsomever, I prefer a nice fat mule, myself."

"I just don't get you-all," Boone said with a shake of his head.

The mountain men looked from one to another, then Pegleg said, "What do you mean?"

"We rode all the way out to California to get these horses. We had men die gettin' 'em. Now there's at least a thousand of 'em dead out in the desert on account of thirst and you-all runnin' 'em to death. And now you're killin' more and eatin' 'em!"

"They ain't but horses, boy," Pegleg said.

"But if they 'ain't but horses' why go to all the trouble of goin' after 'em? 'Specially when near half of 'em's goin' to end up dead?"

This time Old Bill answered. "It's like this, Boone. The half that makes it back to Santa Fe amounts to a whole lot of money."

"It'd be a whole lot more money if you-all didn't kill so many of 'em, wouldn't it?"

Pegleg said, "You're right. It would be. Howsomever, if we took it slow back there and let them Mexis catch us, we might not've got away with any horses at all."

"The way it adds up is this," Beckwourth said. "Half of

141

something is a whole lot more than all of nothing." He took a bite off the hunk of meat in his hand. "As for this particular animal," he said as he chewed, "I would much prefer that it be dead than for me to starve to death."

"We're a long way from starvin'," Boone said.

Beckwourth belched. "Not as far as you might think. Spend much time in this country—meaning most anywhere out west, where help might be hundreds of miles away—you will learn to eat when and what you can, for there will be times you will not know if you will ever eat again."

"Or you could just sidle on in to one of them eatin' houses," Pegleg said. "I hear they got plenty of 'em back there in Missouri."

Old Bill said, "If you read your Bible, son, you'll see where God told old Noah, 'Every moving thing that liveth shall be meat for you.' I never read anywhere in scripture that said that doesn't include horses. The Gospel according to Old Bill Williams on the subject is this: eat, or go hungry."

Boone rose to his feet and walked away.

"I guess your young friend will go hungry," Beckwourth said.

Pegleg smiled. "Not for long . . . not for long."

Late that afternoon, Nooch rode into camp.

"What is it, Nooch? Ain't you supposed to be on lookout?" Pegleg said.

"There is someone out there. A man on a horse."

"Is he comin' this way?"

Nooch shook his head.

"Well? What the hell is he doin' then?"

"He is just sitting there. He rode to where he is, and he stopped. I have watched him for some time, and he has not moved. He just waits."

"What d'you reckon he wants?"

"I do not know. He knows I have seen him, but he did not ride away when I showed myself. He only sits, watching."

"Well, hell. Round up Boone, and we'll go see what the hell he wants."

Chapter Nineteen

Juan Medina watched the *chaguanosos* ride toward him. He was tired. The horse under him was tired. Both dripped sweat—the boy from the heat of sitting in the desert sun, his mount from exertion. It had taken time to catch up to the *ladrones,* and now that he had done so he was unsure of his next move. So he sat, watching the riders approach—one, a bearded white man, another *Americano* who looked to be about his own age, the third an *indio* of similar years.

They separated as they approached and stopped a few yards away. They watched him. He watched them. The bearded man spoke.

"Who are you?"

Juan had no reply.

"What do you want?"

Again, he could not respond.

The man looked to the Ute and nodded.

Nooch spat out the question in a voice louder than necessary. "*¿Quién eres tú?*"

"*Mi nombre es* Juan Medina."

Before Nooch spoke again, he rode up beside Juan, lifted the hem of his poncho, saw the butt of the pistol, and pulled it from the waistband of the boy's trousers. He reined his horse around and passed the flintlock handgun, with its fancy engraved metal and carved grips, to Pegleg, who noted the pistol too fine for one such as the boy before them.

The conversation between Nooch and Juan continued in Spanish. Pegleg understood most all of it but chose not to betray his understanding. Boone caught not a word of it. From time to time, Nooch passed along the essentials in English.

"*¿Eres de California?*"

"*Sí.*"

"Why are you here?"

"I am no longer welcome in *Alta California.*"

"Why?"

Juan swallowed hard, looked from one of his captors to the other, and swallowed again. "I will be counted as an escapee from the jail. I am riding a horse that does not belong to me." Another hard swallow. "And . . . and . . . I have killed a man."

The story of the killing unfolded, Juan backtracking to the beating by Eduardo for the dalliance with Magdalena, Eduardo's false accusation and frame-up for theft from the Peralta hacienda, the dispute over a horse while with the posse, Eduardo's attack in the desert—which resulted in the man's death—and, finally, Juan's hiding and stealing away from the posse.

"And so you see," Juan said, "I cannot return to California. Nor do I wish to do so."

Pegleg said, "Tell the boy he can come on in to camp. I don't reckon he means us any harm. Tell him we'll talk more later."

As they rode to the camp, passing through scattered grazing horses as they went, Juan watched the animals carefully. From time to time he stopped, paying close attention to certain animals. At the camp, he unsaddled his horse, and Nooch told him to turn it loose to join the herd. Then Juan drank his fill of spring water and, using his saddle for a pillow, curled up in the shade of a mesquite tree and slept.

"Keep an eye on that boy," Pegleg told Boone. "I don't expect he'll be any trouble. Howsomever, it don't hurt none to be careful. Watch him."

Juan slept for hours and did not so much as twitch the entire time, at least not that Boone saw. He awakened past sundown but before dark, sat up, and rubbed his eyes and cheeks with his knuckles and fingers. Boone walked over and squatted next to him, and Juan started talking. Holding up both hands, Boone stopped him. "I don't know much Mex talk outside of 'adios,' so you're wastin' your time talkin' to me."

Juan looked confused and shook his head.

"Hungry?" Boone said, pantomiming eating.

Juan nodded and followed Boone to a fire where horse meat steaks sizzled on willow stakes bent over low flames and glowing coals.

"There it is, if you want it," Boone said, gesturing toward the cooking meat.

Pulling up a stake, Juan studied the seared flesh, sniffing at it. *"¿Qué es?"*

Boone threw up his hands. A Ute, sitting by the fire, nibbling bits of dripping meat from the stick in his hands, looked at Juan and said, "Caballo."

"¿Qué?"

"Es carne de caballo," the Ute said.

Juan let go of the willow stick as if it burned his hands.

Boone chuckled. "Guess he ain't no more inclined to eat a horse than what I am."

A *mozo* sitting at the fire snatched up the stake, eyed the meat, and brushed dirt and litter from it before stabbing the stake back into the ground so the horse meat again dangled over the flames.

Boone tugged at Juan's sleeve and with a tilt of his head invited him to follow. He led the way to another small fire some yards away, where Philip Thompson hunched over the coals. But, rather than slabs of horse meat, the flames of his fire flared up from juices dripping from four rabbit carcasses stretched lengthwise along willow spits held up by forked sticks planted on either side of the fire.

"Thompson and me, we snared these jackass rabbits out in the brush yonder," Boone said. "Leastways I set the traps accordin' to how he said to do it."

Juan's look at Boone was blank, but there was no question in the way he eyed the skewered rabbits.

"*Sentarse,*" Thompson said. "*Comer.*" He lifted one of the sticks from its props and, with a knife oversized for the job, slit the rabbit up the center of its ribcage, did the same along the spine, and, with a hand oblivious to the heat, handed half to Juan and the other half to Boone. He then sliced a hindquarter off another carcass and took as big a bite as bone would allow from the haunch of meat.

"I've et horse aplenty," Thompson said, "but it was purely starvin' times when I did it. I prefer rattlesnake." He repeated the explanation in Spanish. He continued talking with Juan as they ate, Juan holding up his end of the conversation and Boone interrupting from time to time to know what they were talking about.

"You need to learn some of the lingo, you intend to stay out here," the mountain man said.

Boone snorted. "Like hell I will. I ain't learnin' no Mex talk. Nor Indian jabber, neither. They-all can learn to talk American, they want to talk to me."

Now it was Thompson's turn to snort. "You'd do well to remember you ain't in America no more."

"Don't make no never mind to me."

Thompson eyed the boy through his eyebrows as he scraped remnants of meat from a leg bone with his teeth, then picked up the conversation with Juan. "What about family? Ain't you got family back where you come from?"

"*Ya no más,*" Not anymore. He told the mountain man that his mother died long ago. The boy choked up when relating Eduardo's report that his father had been killed by the horse thieves.

"Damn," Thompson said. He looked around the camp, saying it was likely one of the men here had done it. Juan shrugged. All he knew was that his father had been killed by an arrow from an Indian's bow.

"Say, Boone. Anybody in your outfit kill a man? One of the Utes, maybe?"

"Ankatash could've. Pegleg said he put an arrow in some old Mexican's ribs. Then the old man shot at him. Don't know as they died, but they'd've killed Ankatash for sure if the old man's bullet didn't do him in." Boone sucked on a bone, then said, "I larruped a fellow on the noggin with my reata, but he was still horseback last I seen him."

Thompson relayed the report to Juan. A tear dripped off the boy's jaw. He contended Boone's story told of his father's death. "*Eso fue Eduardo,*" he said. The man whose face was slashed was his nemesis, Eduardo, son of Don Emiliano, owner of the rancho where he had lived and worked. With another hopeless shrug, Juan walked back to his saddle and lay down, and, if he did not sleep, he was still the rest of the night.

Boone and Thompson talked on into the night, nibbling at the jackrabbit meat until only slick bones remained. They tossed those away to scorch in the coals of the fire.

"You think that boy will cause trouble on account of all that?" Boone said.

Thompson mulled it over. "I reckon it's possible. Once it sinks in what happened, there ain't no tellin' what he might do. Losin' your pa ain't no little thing—'specially for a boy 'bout to be a man. On the other hand, the boy might come to think highly of you for whompin' that Californio like that. Eduardo, he said he was. He didn't like him none at all." Thompson stood. "I'll talk to Old Bill and Pegleg and them, see what they say. Best you keep an eye on the boy tonight."

Boone stretched out near Juan, watching the boy but dozing off from time to time. Toward morning, he fell asleep for good and did not stir until Juan jiggled his foot. His eyes snapped open to see the boy standing over him, and Boone scrambled to his feet. He looked around the camp, scrubbing sleep from his face with the palms of his hands.

"*Buenos días,*" Juan said. Boone's only response was a wrinkled brow and shake of the head. Juan mimicked eating, and Boone followed him to Thompson's fire.

The mountain man laughed when he saw Boone. "Fine job of keepin' watch on ol' Juan, here. Good thing he didn't slit your gullet whilst you slept."

"Sorry 'bout that," Boone said, shaking his head. "Guess I was tuckered out."

Three fresh jackrabbits sizzled over the fire, the flesh seared to a deep brown shade that made Boone's mouth water.

"I checked your snares," Thompson said. Boone and Juan sat on the ground, and Thompson handed each one of the skewers. "These don't fill you up, there's horse meat aplenty over yonder to finish the job."

The men ate in silence, again cleaning the bones. Thompson licked his fingers clean and wiped them across his shirtfront, which showed evidence of many such wipings. "Had a word with Old Bill and Wakara. They don't reckon Juan is up to anything untoward. Still and all, they say for you to keep an eye on him. And make sure he knows it—they figure if he sees he's bein' watched he won't take any notions to get up to somethin' he oughtn't."

And so Boone kept close to Juan throughout the day. Whenever the boy walked to another part of the camp, Boone followed. But all Juan did was study the herd. He would walk to one edge of the camp and then the other, occasionally walking out to the fringes of the herd to walk among the grazing animals as they cropped grass to recover from the hard drive across the Mojave.

From time to time Juan would launch into a discourse, speaking rapid-fire Spanish, pointing out particular animals. Boone understood none of it, or little enough of it to tally as none. He knew *caballo* meant horse and fathomed that *mula* and *mulo* must mean mule. But other words meant nothing—he heard *machos* and *yeguas* and *cria* and *entrenador* and *jinete* and *semental* and what must have been hundreds of other words spew from Juan's mouth, sometimes running like a rushing river when the boy was excited. Boone gave up his attempts to dissuade the boy from talking.

That evening, Pegleg Smith called the camp to gather. He climbed atop a boulder, unsteady until finding a secure spot on the irregular rock for his peg, and told the thieves to be ready to move on tomorrow. "Wakara's scouts say there ain't no sign of that posse that came after us, so there ain't no danger on that account. Howsomever, it don't take long for this many critters to eat up ever'thing in sight, and any fool can see the grass here's all but used up. So we'll be pushin' on up toward the Muddy River come the mornin'."

Again, Boone spread his bedroll close to Juan's nest, but he made no attempt to stay awake to watch the boy. Daylight would find them horseback, and the day would be a lot longer than the night.

CHAPTER TWENTY

Las Vegas, the lonesome green puddle in the desert, gave way straight away to endless stretches of beige and gray, white and tan, buff and umber. Rock piles, rugged ridges, and arid mountains protruded from plains and playas. The herd, spread rods wide and miles long, trudged along hour after hour, stirring dust in the wake of every footfall. The herders rode loosely along its length with little to do but blink mud from their eyes, spit grit from their teeth, and hack slime from their throats.

Boone and Juan rode side by side at the rear of the herd through the morning with nothing to say. Boone spat out a gob of barely wet mud from all the dust he had inhaled and uncorked his canteen. He took a sip and swished it around in his mouth before swallowing, and followed it with another drink. He fixed the stopper and shook the canteen in Juan's direction until it sloshed. "Water?"

Juan nodded and quenched his parched mouth and throat much as Boone had done. He handed the canteen back to Boone. *"Agua."*

"Augwah?"

"Sí. Agua."

"Water," Boone said.

"Water."

"Right. Water."

"Agua."

They rode on in silence for a while. Juan pulled off his hat and wiped sweat from his forehead and scalp with a shirtsleeve. He put his hat back on and pointed at the sun and said, *"Sol."*

Boone squinted into the sky. "Sole. Sun."

"Sun."

Boone swept a pointed finger along the rugged mountains off to the right. "Mountains," he said. "Mountains."

Juan smiled. "Mountains. *Montañas.*"

"Montonyas."

Juan nodded. *"Si. Montañas.* Mountains."

They rode on for hours, exchanging words. Rocks. Brush. Cactus. Sky. Saddle. Bridle. Bit. Reins. Cinch. Eyes. Nose. Mouth. Ears. Hoof. Leg. Mane.

Along toward evening, Old Bill Williams, hunched in his saddle ahead of the herd, spouting a squeaky sermon to no one but the mule between his hefted knees, turned the mule around and raised a hand, signaling a halt. The lead horses stopped, and the reaction spread back through the herd as the horses and mules crowded into a more compact bunch.

One by one and two by two the riders gathered, dismounted, and stretched backs and shoulders and legs, stiff from hours in the saddle. Old Bill allowed that they should let the herd rest awhile, and the men should eat what horse meat they carried from the cook fires at Las Vegas. Then, they would saddle fresh horses for the rest of the ride to water at the Muddy River and its confluence with the Rio Virgin.

The thought of cold horse meat held even less attraction for Boone than a steak hot from the fire. So he dropped his saddle, scraped stones out of the way with the side of his boot, and sprawled flat on his back, hat propped over his face to block the light from the low-hanging sun, and slept.

The sun was long gone and with it most of the light when Old Bill hollered out orders to saddle up and mount up. But this time it was Pegleg Smith who took the lead. Boone and

Juan rode the back trail through the fading light until reaching the last of the herd. They put the stragglers into motion, chousing the reluctant horses, the weakest of the bunch, to keep up with the rest of the herd. The animals lined out after a few miles, finding a pace that kept them in sight of the horses ahead of them through the darkening night.

It was still night when Pegleg rode down off the bluffs and into the shallow, meandering waters of the Muddy River a ways above its joining the Virgin. He rode on across without stopping and crossed the short distance to the Rio Virgin, which, while still a slow-moving stream, ran clearer than the Muddy. There he stopped, watching as the horses passed on either side to wade into the river and drink, burying muzzles in water just deep enough to cover them. Riders who reached the river drove the drinking horses back from the water as much as they could so they would not drink too much and sicken.

By the time the drinking was over, Wakara, Nooch, and another of the Utes had fires built from deadfall from cottonwood trees along the stream, the twin blazes guiding the thieves to the camp, a ways upstream and away from the river. One of the weaker horses lay just outside the campsite, blood puddled around its head from the knife slit across its throat. The carcass, still warm, was already carved up, hide peeled back, and slabs of bloody meat cut from loins and hindquarters stacked on the shoulder.

Old Bill encouraged the men to eat and sleep as quickly as possible. They would not linger here beyond morning. Horse meat steaks soon dangled from willow sticks over the fire. The smell of the cooking meat filled Boone's mouth with saliva, the temptation to eat proved almost more than he could resist. But, at least for one more night, disgust and revulsion held sway, and he went to sleep hungry.

When the herd moved out in the morning, the riders kept

busy pushing the tired and hungry horses along. Rather than walk, the horses wanted to graze the grassy banks along the Rio Virgin's braided course. Whooping and hollering, cussing and cursing filled the air, along with the snap and pop of reatas working as whips to keep the herd moving upstream.

The long day's drive ended a few miles west of where the river disappeared into a sheer cliff wall hundreds, perhaps thousands, of feet high. Tangled sand streams in the bottom of a wide, dry, wash meandered into the river from the north. Scrub brush and willows between the ravels and along the banks showed evidence of water under the surface, but no water wet the bed save backflow from the river at the junction. Here, the trail would leave the river and set off across the plain to the north, paralleling the dry wash until, miles later, it climbed a long incline into the Beaver Dam Mountains.

Horse was the only thing on the menu again that night, and again Boone rolled into his blanket hungry. Hunger awakened him before dawn, and he watched as Beckwourth, Thompson, and Manolo rode out of camp headed north, each with a mule on the lead.

"They've gone on ahead to hunt meat," Pegleg said in answer to the boy's question. "They get up into them mountains, they're likely to find some deer—maybe bag a nice fat doe or two. Might get a bighorn sheep, even. Leavin' early, they are, on account of us getting' up there with this herd will scare off every critter with feet and wings. Even snakes'll run for cover from this mob."

Boone took a long drink from his canteen and shuffled off to the river to refill it, hoping for success for the hunters as it gurgled full. He did not know how much longer he could survive on a diet of water. If the hunters did not succeed, he would have to surrender and eat horse meat. His stomach roiled, whether from emptiness, or the thought of filling it, he did not know.

Come morning, the trail threaded its way up the plain through a scattered forest of spindly trees, or cactus, with scaly, twisted, trunks and branches ending with tufts of long green spikes at the ends. Even the tallest of the trees, thirty feet and more, did not cast enough shade to provide relief from the desert sun. Summiting as it wound around a jagged cliff, the trail followed yet another dry wash into an irregular valley flanked by high peaks to the east, red mesas to the southeast, and rugged mountains to the north and south.

The smell of smoke and, Boone imagined, cooking meat signaled the presence of others. Those others turned out to be the hunting party, already in camp along the banks of the Rio Santa Clara. Letting the horse herd find their own way to water and grass, the riders, tired and hungry from another long day on the trail, rode into camp in turn, unsaddled, and collapsed. Boone's mouth watered with the realization that the smell of cooking meat he imagined was not imagined at all—Manolo had quarters of deer skewered over cook fires and sliced meat sizzling on stakes over the flames. He saw three other deer carcasses hanging in cottonwood trees near the camp.

He held himself back from running to the fires. Manolo smiled at the hunger in the boy's eyes and took his time examining in great detail the meat on each of the stakes, seeming to choose one for him, then shaking his head and turning his attention to another, finally making a show of selecting the finest of the sizzling steaks and offering it to Boone with great ceremony. The boy bit into the meat, tearing loose mouthfuls, ignoring the heat that seared his tongue.

Licking the drip from his lips and wiping greasy hands on his pant legs, Boone eyed the other stakes dangling over the fire.

"What's that?" he said, pointing to slices of white flesh surrounded with green rinds.

Manolo pulled up one of the stakes and held it out toward Boone, who fingered a slice, singing his fingers and pulling them away, then pulled his shirt cuffs over his fingers and slid the slice off the stake. He looked it over, then looked at Manolo.

"*Calabaza*. Eat."

Boone nibbled at the squash, then wolfed it down, ripping another chunk from the stake.

"That's good, Manolo."

Beckwourth, squatting by the fire and watching, said, "You have eaten squash before, haven't you, boy?"

"Squash? Sure. Ma grew it in the garden back home. But it didn't taste like this. Came in different colors, too—yellow and orange and such."

"Well, these particular squashes are not altogether ripe. They will turn all manner of colors as they grow."

Manolo offered Boone another slab of venison, which he took time to savor as he ate it. "Squash grow on its own out here?" he said as he chewed.

"No. Paiutes grow them. There is a village upstream a distance."

Boone kept chewing. "They give you these?"

Beckwourth laughed. "Not at all. I guess you could say we seized them in our need. There were no Paiutes about save an old man and two old women. The rest of them must be hiding out. They do not trust strangers. And with good reason. People like us—Americans, Mexicans, Utes alike—steal their children and keep or sell them as slaves."

Boone nodded. "I heard tell 'bout it. You ever done that?"

Beckwourth shook his head. "Not I." He looked at Boone. "You, being from Missouri, can imagine why a man of my complexion might not hold with slavery."

Old Bill spared Boone from a response when he shouted out

an order for attention in the camp. The men gathered round in the deepening twilight. "By now you've et your fill, and now there's work to do. There are Paiutes hereabout, and seeing as how we've been eating plunder from their gardens, they ain't likely to be too happy with us. So circle up the horses and close herd them tonight. Five men riding herd at once, in four-hour turns. Those that ain't on duty, sleep with one eye open. Be ready to move on at first light. We'll push on to Mountain Meadow and lay over there a day or three to recruit the horses. Should be plenty of graze there."

Boone drew the last watch before dawn. He had slept enough, and was nervous enough, to be alert. Nooch was on the same watch, along with another Ute and two Taos Mexicans. The riders, moving opposite directions around the herd, passed one another at intervals. They seldom spoke but whistled or sang out in passing. When a rider going by failed to acknowledge his whistle, Boone grew suspicious, turned, and heeled up his horse to catch up. The Mexican, whose name he did not recall, kept riding as he approached, despite Boone's calls to halt. Riding beside, Boone thought him asleep, slouched in the saddle as he was, and reached out to give him a shake.

Rather than awakening, the man fell out of the saddle, his foot hanging in the stirrup, to drag several steps until Boone could find a rein and stop the horse. Boone dismounted, tugged the wedged foot out of the stirrup, and it fell to ground without resistance. He knelt and in the dim light saw dark blood. Thinking the fall from the horse caused the injury, he rolled the Mexican onto his back and saw blood spilled down the chest, staining the poncho all the way to the hem. The head flopped sideways, and Boone saw the throat open where it was slit wide and deep.

He scrambled to his feet, backing away. Mind racing, he knew not how much time passed before he let out a whistle and a

157

shout, then hollered some more. Nooch reached him first. Boone fell silent with his arrival, his breath coming in gasps. The Ute knelt beside the body, then stood, looking into the dark in every direction, seeing nothing but irregular shapes and shadows of horses.

"Listen!" he said.

Boone held his breath. He heard the grinding teeth of grazing horses, their snuffles and snorts and nickers, a squeal as a horse somewhere in the herd bit or kicked another, and the shuffling movement of the hundreds of horses.

"Do you hear it?" Nooch whispered.

"No—what is it?"

"Listen. There."

Boone could just make out the direction Nooch pointed. He strained to hear and thought he detected distant hoofbeats, the occasional crackling of disturbed brush, the clack of displaced stones.

Then, other noise drowned out the faint noises he thought he heard.

"Halooo!" came a shout, accompanied by horses—two or three—forcing their way through the herd, shifting horses aside as they came.

"Over here!" Boone said.

The riders reined up and dismounted. Boone made out they were Wakara, Pegleg, and Beckwourth.

"What has happened?" Wakara said.

Nooch rattled off an explanation in Ute, leaving only Boone to wonder what was said.

"He right, boy?" Pegleg said.

Boone had no answer.

"Well?"

"How the hell should I know? I don't know what he said."

Pegleg snorted. "Tell us what happened."

Boone explained his suspicion when the dead rider passed by without signaling. And how he caught up the horse, and, thinking the man asleep, tried to wake him. "He fell off the horse, and then I seen his throat was cut."

Beckwourth said, "You didn't hear anything before that?"

"Nothin' out of the ordinary. Then Nooch came, and I might've heard somethin' goin' off up the hill yonder."

"Somethin'?"

"I don't know. Horses, maybe."

Nooch said it was horses for certain. A good-size bunch, he guessed. More than ten. Moving quickly.

As dawn approached, more of the party gathered round the dead man. Wakara attributed the death to Paiutes. "The killer leaped onto the horse's rump, grabbed this man, and slit his throat. He did not even know what happened to him. Then they drove away as many horses as they could gather in a hurry. It must be Paiutes. It can be no one else."

Pegleg looked off to the east. "It'll be light enough to read the sign soon enough. It don't sound like they got off with too many horses. But by damn, they ain't gettin' away with it. We'll be goin' after 'em."

CHAPTER TWENTY-ONE

Wakara and Pegleg rode a distance from the herd, out from where the dead Mexican fell. The sun was far from up, and they strained to see any tracks on the ground. Then Wakara raised a hand, and Pegleg stopped. Both men dismounted. Wakara squatted, pointing out faint tracks. Pegleg walked ahead, and the trail grew more distinct. They saw broken brush, displaced stones, and scuffs in the packed soil. The men remounted and followed the tracks a short distance to where they entered a shallow draw between two low ridges.

Pegleg turned in the saddle and waved the waiting riders back near the herd to join them. Nooch and another Ute, Patnish, Philip Thompson, and Jim Beckwourth would go with them after the Paiute thieves. The rest of the party would move the herd on to Mountain Meadows for a few days' rest and grazing.

The Paiutes drove the bunch of pilfered horses eastward away from the river, into broken country outcropped with red sandstone ledges and hoodoos, buttes, and cliffs. In places, Wakara dismounted to trace the faint trail over slick rock bereft of soil. At times the riders, in single file, squeezed through narrow passages between high sandstone walls. They broke out of the canyon and onto sand dunes hemmed in by black lava rock, the clear trail turning southward through the sand toward the valley of the Rio Virgin, far upstream from where it cut through the mountain wall to reach where they had camped along its banks days earlier.

Wakara, in the lead, reined up and signaled a halt as he rounded an outcrop. He backed his horse, slipped out of the saddle, and crept forward to watch the trail ahead from bended knee.

"They are not far ahead," Wakara said to the waiting riders. "They have crossed an open, brushy plain and have dropped into a ravine and are out of sight. They are seven, driving twelve of our horses. Only two are mounted, on Paiute horses. The others walk. If we hurry through the brush, we will be upon them."

The brush-covered bench land extended about a mile. At a fast trot, the riders covered the distance quickly. They slowed where the arroyo the Paiutes had followed connected the bench to the valley below. The thieves had just ridden up on a shaded campsite, greeted by women and children and old people of their band. The tired horses stood by, cropping mouthfuls of grass that grew along a small stream.

Pegleg studied the situation. "What do you think?"

Wakara did not answer.

"I say we attack," Beckwourth said. "We can be upon them before they know we are here."

But Beckwourth's suggested surprise was ruined when Thompson's horse whinnied. The eyes of every horse below, and those of every Paiute in the camp, turned toward the bench.

"Let's go!" Pegleg said, spurring his horse and pulling his rifle from its saddle scabbard as he dove into the ravine with the others hard on his horse's heels.

The Paiute men below strung their bows and scrambled into wickiups for additional arrows and other weapons as the women and children melted into the brush and cedar trees around the campsite. Pegleg did not see a firearm among them. Spreading as they poured out of the dry wash, Pegleg hollered out a command to stop and shoot. The men dismounted, some steadying rifles over saddles, others kneeling, Pegleg staying mounted and shouldering his rifle. Four Paiutes went down in the volley.

"Don't bother to reload, boys," Pegleg yelled. "Let's go get 'em!"

They charged the camp, dodging arrows. Only one found its mark, driving into Pegleg's wooden leg like a nail, striking just below the knee. Pegleg and Thompson used their pistols to advantage, each downing another Paiute fighter. Patnish chased down a runner and smashed his skull with a club; Nooch put an arrow into the shoulder of another who escaped into the brush. An arrow penetrated the cantle on Beckwourth's saddle enough to draw blood from his hip.

When the dust settled, there was not an ambulatory Paiute in sight. Those wounded and down and still drawing breath were soon dispatched with Patnish's club or Nooch's knife, which then went to work taking scalps.

The stolen horses had scattered during the attack, along with the two Paiute horses, but had not gone far. Thompson and Pegleg rode out to gather them. They came back to find Beckwourth and Patnish arguing.

"He wants to go out in the brush hunting women and children," Beckwourth said in response to Pegleg's question. "I say this is not the time to be taking slaves."

"Easy money," Patnish said.

Beckwourth countered. "We do not have food enough to feed ourselves. Besides, they will only slow us down."

"We will feed them only enough to keep them alive. If they cannot keep up . . ." Patnish shrugged.

Pegleg thought for a moment. "What do you think, Wakara?"

"I think Beckwourth is not concerned about food. Or about slowing our travel." Wakara smiled and looked at Beckwourth. "We all know the black white man does not hold with taking slaves at any time."

Beckwourth started to protest, but Wakara raised a hand to silence him. "But the complaints he makes are good ones. I see no purpose in taking slaves, only to let them die—which they may well do." He turned to Patnish and spoke in Ute. Patnish scowled but said nothing.

"These horses is near spent and could do with a rest," Pegleg said. "Howsomever, I ain't inclined to hang around here. What's left of them Paiutes could come back and do us a damage. Let's push on up the trail a ways, then stop and give the critters a blow."

With that, he started for the ravine. The others circled the horses and pushed them in Pegleg's direction, then followed them up the arroyo and onto the bench above. Pegleg set a course to avoid the sand dunes and red rock canyon, skirting the lava ridge and traveling northward along the foothills of the high mountains to the east. The rest stop they would soon make would be brief, as he intended to return the horses to the herd at Mountain Meadows by night.

Delegated to eat dust at the tail end of the herd, Boone and Juan followed the miles-long drove up the trail upstream along the Rio Santa Clara until leaving its course to shadow Magotsu Creek to Mountain Meadows. The work required only the occasional urging ahead of tired and lame horses, particularly the oldest and youngest of the survivors of the Mojave crossing.

Old Bill proclaimed a layover of four or five days in the lush grass of the Meadows. The somewhat sheltered valley atop the rim of the Great Basin offered a welcome, if temporary, respite from the barren desert highlands for both man and animal. Ute hunters were in the hills after camp meat, and, given the retaliation of the Paiute band for the plunder taken by the herders, guards were posted to detect the approach of any hostile Indians.

"What about Pegleg and them?" Boone asked Old Bill as they lazed in the long shadow of trees along the creek.

"What about them?"

"When do you reckon they'll catch us up?"

"Hard to say. Depends on how far they had to track them damn Paiutes. Could be back with the horses tonight. Tomorrow, I reckon. Next day, maybe, if they ran into trouble. Them Paiutes fight like badgers when they're cornered. But, for damn sure, our boys will be back. Ain't no Paiute alive a match for Beckwourth or Pegleg. Or Wakara, come to that."

Boone mulled that over for a bit. "I don't see why you-all care so much about losing ten or twenty or however many horses to those Indians. Hell, we left a thousand dead horses layin' in that desert—ever' one of 'em killed on account of bein' pushed too hard and dyin' of thirst."

Old Bill laughed a soft, mirthless laugh. "That's one way of looking at it, I reckon. Way I see it is, we got nigh on to two thousand of them through alive. And two thousand California horses and mules will turn a hell of profit in New Mexico—of which you'll get a share, boy."

After filling the clay bowl of his pipe and setting a flame to the tobacco, Bill went on. "But them Paiutes stealing from us is a whole 'nother thing altogether. Any Indians will steal from you if you give them a chance, but some of them—Paiutes, Mohaves, Navajos, Snakes—would as soon steal as breathe. You let them get away with it, they'll be back for more. Besides, there's honorable ways to steal, but sneak thieves like those Paiutes ain't no better than sniveling coyotes. They've got to be taught a lesson."

"Hell, we ain't nothin' but thieves our own selves."

Again, Williams laughed. "Like I said, son, there's stealing and then there's stealing. Once we get to Santa Fe and start selling off these horses, and some of that money ends up in your purse, you come talk to me about being a thief."

Boone stood and dusted himself off, then knelt beside the creek and slurped up a bellyful of the cool, clear water. "Reckon I'll turn in. I got the last shift on guard."

Old Bill only nodded and sucked on his pipe, blowing out a stream of smoke. Boone untied his bedroll from behind the cantle of his saddle, wandered away from the creek, ducked under the low-hanging limbs of a gnarly cedar tree, and rolled in his blanket.

Long before his turn to watch the herd, Boone—and the rest of the camp—awakened to the sound of drumming hoofbeats. He sat up and scoured his eyes and squinted into the moonlight to see a rider slide his horse to stop at the edge of camp.

"Someone comes!" the Mexican guard shouted.

Boone saw Old Bill Williams silhouetted in the glow of the low-burning fire, rifle slung in the crook of his elbow. "Is it our boys coming in?"

"*No lo sé. Maybe. Muchos caballos.*"

"Well, we had best be ready for them, whoever they be," Old Bill said. "Find yourselves a hole and prime your pieces. But—and I dearly mean this—don't nobody shoot unless I give the order."

By now, all could hear the rumble of many hooves. Boone swallowed hard and knelt behind a jumble of boulders. The hoofbeats drew nearer, the horses on the run. Then a shrill shriek cut the air.

"Hello the camp! Stoke up that fire, and get the coffee on!" came a holler out of the darkness.

The men in the camp breathed a sigh of relief, recognizing the voice as belonging to Pegleg.

Another shriek. "Make way for Pegleg Smith and his retinue of returning heroes! We have fought Indians, rescued fair maidens, wrestled bears, and killed ourselves a dragon!"

The driven horses, their breathing labored, streamed past the camp and slowed as the drovers reined up. Pegleg rode right up to the fire and loosed another whoop. "Well, hell, boys! Where's that coffee? Me and these other conquerors is thirsty—and hungry enough to eat the asshole out of an elephant!" He swung out of the saddle and dropped to the ground, staggering a bit until finding the proper balance on his pegleg.

Old Bill said, "For heaven's sake, Pegleg. You have awakened us out of a sound sleep with all this nonsense. You could have been shot. Besides, you know good and well we have not had coffee since abandoning it in our haste to escape the Californios at Resting Spring. There might be a bone from a mule deer in the trash heap you-all can take turns gnawing on. The rest of us, we are for going back to bed."

But no one went to bed.

Logs flared up in the fire, and everyone, save those on guard, gathered round. Pegleg and Beckwourth and Thompson took turns regaling the men with the story of the attack on the Paiutes, telling how they had caught the Indians napping and were upon them almost before they knew it. They told of the Paiutes gunned down in the initial volley, and of death meted out in close quarters. Wakara sat, silent but smiling, as Nooch and Patnish displayed the scalps taken, much to the pleasure of their Ute compatriots.

Boone's stomach turned at the sight of the bloody trophies. Without thinking, he lifted his hat and ran his fingers through his own overgrown and greasy hair.

"We got back every horse they stole," Pegleg said, "and two more besides. Thompson rescued a bag of last year's pine nuts and a parfleche of pemmican, which we would be pleased to share with you—howsomever, we ate it all—every bite—on the way here," he said with a chuckle.

By ones and twos, the yawning men drifted off to their

bedrolls, and the camp again grew quiet. With his turn on guard coming soon, Boone decided attempting to sleep would be futile. Other than the chirping and ticking of night insects and the occasional yap of a coyote, only the snap and crackle of the dying campfire kept company with his thoughts as he stared into glowing coals that flamed up from time to time as the fire clung to life.

Chapter Twenty-Two

The days at Mountain Meadows were long and lazy. Other than taking turns as lookouts, the men had nothing to do but repair saddles and bridles, mend clothing and footwear, rest and relax. On the second morning there, Boone watched Juan Medina ride among the grazing horses, studying a bunch, moving on to another, and, from time to time, dismounting to pat and rub a horse or mule or one of the big jacks scattered among the herd.

Juan had shown the same kind of interest in the horses before, but this time it piqued Boone's curiosity. He wanted to know what the young vaquero was up to. Boone found Nooch talking and laughing and playing some kind of game with whittled sticks with some of the other Utes and asked him to come along and translate to find out what the Mexican was doing. They rode out into the meadow and intercepted Juan.

Boone used up a good share of the Spanish words he had learned, asking Juan what he was doing. "*¿Qué estás haciendo?*"

Juan shrugged and said he was just riding among the horses. "*¿Por qué?*"

Another shrug. "I enjoy being with them. Sometimes I prefer the company of horses to that of people."

He told of growing up on the Rancho de Don Emiliano Peralta, and how his father had charge of the caballos there—breeding and training horses for ranch work, and breeding the *machos* and *yeguas* to produce mules, for which the rancho was known. He told of his years assisting his father; how he knew many horses and mules from their birth, and even before, as he took mares to be bred; how he helped with breaking and training for riding and driving and packing.

Then he said, "Some of these horses I know—and they know me. You have taken from Don Emiliano his best brood mares. And the *machos*—the big burros—taken from his rancho have fathered the finest mules in all California."

Boone stared at Juan and said to Nooch, "Y'know, I reckon this boy's told me all that before. But I didn't understand a word of it."

The boys rode among the horses, Juan pointing out some he knew. "Most of the horses and mules here are *ordinario,*" Juan said. "They are common, of no special quality." But the horses he pointed out as having come from his home ranch, particularly the mares, were of noticeably better size and conformation. "This is one I have trained," he said of a leggy sorrel gelding. "Or, I should say, I started the training, and my father—who is—was—without equal—put the finish on him. *Usted verá.* You will see."

Juan dismounted and walked toward the gelding. The horse, head high, ears pointed, and nostrils flaring, watched. Juan spoke, and the sorrel lowered his head, stretching his neck toward the approaching boy and his extended hand. Juan scratched the horse between the eyes, then patted his neck as the gelding pressed its forehead against the boy's chest and rubbed.

Grasping a fistful of the horse's mane, Juan clicked his tongue and led the horse to where he had left his mount and where Boone and Nooch waited. He pulled the bridle from the horse he had been riding and hung it on the sorrel and followed with the saddle. He talked with the horse the entire time and kept up the soft talk as he led the horse in a tight circle a round or two before stepping into the stirrup and swinging into the saddle.

The horse snorted and stiffened but relaxed when Juan leaned down and rubbed and patted its neck and shoulder. He touched the horse with his spurs, and it walked a ways. He urged it to trot, tracing a circle through the grass and clumps of brush. Soon, he pressed the gelding into an easy lope around the circle, then cut the circle in half, signaling the horse to change leads as he circled back forming a figure eight, all with such a light rein that Boone and Nooch could not see the cues.

With the horse warmed up, Juan increased the speed of the figures. Besides tracing the eight, he slid the horse to a stop, then walked it backward. He spun the horse in both directions, the circles so tight its hind legs could have been pinioned to the ground. Then, starting a spin, the gelding would stop and reverse direction, leaping back and forth like a fast pendulum.

Juan stopped and again rubbed and patted the horse's neck and shoulders, talking all the while.

"I don't reckon I could do any of that," Boone said. Then, with a smile, "For one thing, I can't talk Mex, and it appears that's the only lingo that horse understands."

Nooch only shook his head. He was both familiar and experienced with the training of horses, but on a more basic level, Ute horses needing no further refinement than the ability to respond to pressure from either rein or leg.

When Juan rejoined them, Boone asked, with help from Nooch, why the horse had been taught such fancy moves. The boy explained the responsiveness was necessary to the vaquero ways of working cattle. But, he admitted, much of it was machismo—a man's pride in his mount, and a desire to show off. He told of riding contests and games among the vaqueros, as well as the men of the upper classes. When roping grizzlies, Juan said with a laugh, an agile, fleet-footed horse was all that kept you from getting hugged by the bear.

"That why you wear them fancy spurs, too? Them rowels is

'bout as big around as a fryin' pan, but you don't hardly even touch the horse with them. Them just for showin' off, too?"

Nooch translated the question, but Juan's smile and shrug required no interpretation. The Ute checked the position of the sun. "We had better be getting back. It will be my turn to act as lookout soon. And I am feeling hunger."

"Me too," Boone said. "And I do believe Old Bill and them brought in a couple of fat does this morning."

The three horsemen started toward camp, the horses at a long trot. As they rode, Boone studied the way his companions sat in the saddle and moved with their horses—each a little bit different, and both a whole lot more comfortably than he did.

"What the hell you three young bucks doin' out there?" Pegleg said when Boone sat down in the shade near where the mountain man sat. His wooden leg lay on the ground beside him as he massaged his stump.

"Just lookin' at the horses."

"There somethin' special about 'em?"

Boone thought for a time. "Some of 'em. Some of them horses we stole at that one ranch—the one where we lost Ankatash—was broke by Juan."

"He say so?"

Boone nodded. "More'n that. He caught one of 'em up—big ol' sorrel gelding—and put us on a ridin' show. That boy made that horse do ever'thing but sprout wings and fly. I ain't never seen nothin' the like of it."

"Some of them vaqueros is mighty fine riders, all right. But you say this boy trained horses on that ranch?"

"So he says. Says his daddy was more or less in charge of the horses and mules, and he's been helpin' him longer'n he can remember—leastways that's what Nooch said he was sayin'. I can't make hide nor hair out of most of that Mex talk."

Pegleg strapped his appendage back on, stood, and worked it

back and forth until it seated properly, then sat back down on his rock. "He say much about mules?"

"Nah. Only that some of them big jacks is from that place, and some of the mares they bred 'em to. I don't give much of a shit 'bout mules, so I never asked."

"I know what you mean, boy. A horse does seem a more noble beast. Howsomever, a good mule ain't nothin' to take lightly out in this country. This trail we been on all this time has seen more mules than you or me know enough numbers to count. Long pack strings of 'em haul goods out from Santa Fe to where we was in California, and most of what they trade for is mules. Back in Santa Fe, they run 'em down into Old Mexico and sell 'em for a right smart profit. Even take some of 'em back East to the States."

Boone stood, dusted off the seat of his pants, and fetched a tin cup from his bed nest. "Well, just now I'm hungry and damn glad I don't have to eat one of them mules. Or a horse."

Pegleg laughed. "You don't know what you're missin', boy. A steak from a colt goes down mighty easy and sits right well on a man's stomach."

Boone shivered at the thought. But the hunters had been busy, so there was nothing equine on the menu this day. Two gutted deer carcasses, still in their hides, hung from the limbs of a cedar tree. Another, skinned and stripped nearly to the bone, hung next to them. A pile of bones under the tree attested to others already butchered. Manolo had strips of venison drying on willow racks over low fires. Slabs of meat hung on stakes over another fire, their juices flaming up as they dripped onto the coals. In one of the few pots the expedition still carried, a thick soup of venison chunks and some roots or bulbs dug from the meadow bubbled away, seasoned with bits of leaves Boone couldn't identify. The smell of the steam rising from the pot set his mouth to watering, so he dipped a cupful of the mixture from the kettle.

He ate slowly as the soup cooled, spearing out chunks with his knife blade and sipping at the broth. A way out from the camp, Juan Medina and some of the *mozos* from Taos and Abiquiu entertained themselves with their reatas. They spun loops large and small, flat and upright; loops that changed the direction of spin at the flick of a wrist. They made loops grow, or shrink, as they spun. They tossed loops into the air and seemed to direct them to land around a target by some magical means.

When he'd emptied his cup and then another filled with the soup, he fetched his rawhide reata from his saddle and joined the Mexicans, hoping to learn how to handle a rope the way they did. It did not take many twists and tangles to teach him there was more to it than he suspected. He coiled his rope and sat and only watched.

Juan tired of the play and coiled his reata. Boone stood, and they walked together back to the cook fires. Spearing sizzling slabs of venison with their knives, they sat on the ground under a cedar tree waiting for the meat to cool. Pegleg hobbled over carrying a leather bag and sat on a nearby rock. Setting the sack on the ground, he opened the throat and reached in as Juan and Boone looked on. Out came the pistol confiscated from Juan when he rode into the thieves' camp those many days ago.

"This is a mighty fancy shootin' iron for a workin' man."

He was right. The engraved metal, incised wooden grips, and finely tooled mechanism showed the pistol to be something more than simply a serviceable gun.

Juan nodded.

Pegleg went on, his questions a mixture of Spanish and English.

"The *pistola* was the property of Don Emiliano, owner of the Peralta rancho," Juan said. He told how it, along with an equally fine sword, were keepsakes from the Don's time as an officer in the Spanish army. The rancho the Don owned also resulted from his service; it was made up of the original properties granted to him by the government.

"How did you come to have it?"

"You will recall my telling you of killing one of the Californios before escaping from them to join you. He was Eduarado Peralta, son of the Don. He tried to kill me with that very pistol you hold in your hands but was unsuccessful. Instead, I took it from him and killed him." Juan hung his head. After a moment, he looked into Pegleg's eyes. "I am not sorry. I feel no shame. To be honest, I had wished him dead for some time and am content to have satisfied my desire." Again, his head sagged, and his shoulders slumped.

Pegleg reached into the bag and brought out the shot pouch and powder flask seized with the pistol. He handed them, and the gun, to Juan. "I reckon you might just as well take these. Truth is, I'm tired of packin' them around. It don't appear as you intend us any harm. Howsomever, if you take a notion to retaliate for what happened back there to your Pa, I will shoot you deader'n hell. *¿Lo entiendes?*"

"*Si.* I understand."

Pegleg stood and found his balance. "We'll be pullin' out come the morning. You boys best be ready, or you'll be left here sittin' in the shade."

Come the morning, the long shadows cast by the rising sun followed the strung-out herd of horses and drovers as they wound through cedar-stippled hills. As the day passed, the shadows overtook them and then led the way into a big valley, hemmed in to the east by a high plateau standing on broken cliffs of sandstone and volcanic rock. They made camp where a small creek out of the eastern mountains spread out in a shallow lake at the bottom of the valley. The herd, weary but in good shape from the respite at Mountain Meadows, scattered into smaller bands, content to tear at the grass and drink the water.

Boone recognized the valley from the outbound trip. He knew that tomorrow the trail would take them across the valley, climb a rise to the north, then drop into another valley much like this one. The trail would turn up a narrow canyon into the high plateau, along the course of a small stream coming down out of the mountains.

A few days from now would find the horses knee deep in the lush grasses of Bear Valley. But, for now, he once again straddled his tired and sore legs over his saddle and rode out to the perimeter of the herd. Old Bill had assigned him duty on the first watch, cautioning him and the others to keep a sharp eye out for Paiutes, as this valley was the sometime-home of the wandering bands.

Plodding along in a big circle around the horse herd, Boone fought to keep his eyes open, looking forward to the occasional passage of another guard and a brief exchange of words as they rode past one another in the night.

CHAPTER TWENTY-THREE

Pegleg Smith sat horseback on a ridge overlooking the Bear Valley, its elongated bowl hemmed in by high mountains all around. He found the place a more pleasant sight than it had been on the outbound trip weeks before. The two thousand and some sore-footed horses scattered across the grasslands, resting and fattening up for the trail ahead, made the difference. To his eyes, each of the grazing animals, wrapped in its colorful hide, looked for all the world like money. And a goodly portion of that money would, one day soon, fill his pockets. He reckoned this place, and the herd it fed for now, was just beyond halfway back to Santa Fe—and payday.

The horses, although stolen, had come at a heavy price. When next he saw his Ute wife, Song, he expected she would call him to account for the loss of two of her brothers, left dead in California. Other men—boys, some of them—had paid with blood as well. According to the ruled columns in the ledger in his mind, he had paid dearly for these horses and more than earned the profit the animals would bring, as had the other thieves, now lazing about in the valley below. Entered in the ledger columns were other assets as well. The youngsters—Nooch, Boone, and some of the *mozos* from Taos and Santa Fe—had acquired experiences that would have never accrued had they stayed in their towns and villages.

Despite the difficulties behind them and those perhaps to come, Pegleg calculated the California raid, on balance, amounted to what mountain men called Shining Times.

The one youngster who did not figure in Pegleg's equation was the vaquero who abandoned the California posse to throw in with the thieves. Juan Medina sat on a rock on a low rise watching, much as Pegleg did from above, the horses and mules scattered like summer raindrops across the valley. Nothing in the picture, save the four-legged animals, was familiar to the boy. The brush, the grass, even the mountains with their rugged peaks still draped with snow, were unlike the land he knew. Before setting out with the posse, he had never traveled farther from home than Los Angeles, and slightly beyond there to the beaches of the big ocean to deliver hides and tallow for the ships anchored offshore. The Utes, the white men, even the New Mexicans he had traveled with these weeks were as exotic to him as those sailors and ships and the goods from their holds.

Juan picked up a pebble and tossed it at Boone. It bounced off the back of the boy's neck, and he swatted at it as if it was one of the deer flies that had been pestering him as he lazed in the afternoon sun. Another pebble followed, this one thrown harder. Boone yelped and clapped a hand over the sore spot on the side of his head. He knew now it was no fly that tormented him and turned toward Juan with a curse.

The Californian only laughed. Nooch, who sat nearby, laughed with him. Juan's laugh settled into a smile as he watched Boone. After a moment, he said, "What will you do?"

Boone stood and brushed off the seat of his pants. "I'll kick your ass, that's what."

Again Juan laughed. "Not that," he said, then paused to find the right words. While he grew more conversant with the unfamiliar language by the day, this time his grasp of its nuances failed. He spoke in Spanish to Nooch, who told Boone what he meant to say.

Boone thought it over for a minute or two, dropping again to his seat on the ground, resting his back against an outcropping boulder. "Can't think of a thing." He plucked a stem of grass and chewed on it as he kept thinking. He shook his head. "Nope. Ain't nothin' comes to mind. How 'bout you-all?"

Juan understood the question but looked to Nooch to hear his answer.

"I will go back to my people," the Ute said. "Back to my band to the north."

He spoke in English, but Juan had understood. *"¿Qué harás ahí?"*

Boone understood only the *qué*, the what, in Juan's question, but assumed the rest.

Nooch smiled. "There is a girl. She is called Siah. When I return, I will take her for my wife. Her father demands many horses, but now I will have more than enough. She will be mine." He told Juan the same in Spanish.

Nooch's smile faded. Neither of his friends shared the prospect of his happiness. He did not understand why.

Boone pulled the grass stem from his mouth and tossed it aside. "Best of luck to you, Nooch. Me, I ain't had much luck with girls or *muchachas* or women or however the hell you want to call 'em. It's on account of a young lass that I find myself away out here so far from home."

The boys plied him with questions, and, bit by bit, Boone's story played out. He spoke of his attraction to Mary Elizabeth Thatcher, the prettiest girl in all of Clay County, Missouri, with boys and young men and even some older men in pursuit of her hand. But her father, a straitlaced preacher of the hellfire and brimstone variety, believed her too young to wed at age fourteen and sent every caller packing with a stern warning to stay away. Boone was persistent and sought the girl's company on the sly, and he claimed she encouraged their clandestine meetings.

It was during one such encounter that the Reverend Thatcher

caught them—and that, Boone said, ended in a fight with the preacher. "I busted his head with a singletree and left him for dead. And that's how I come to be clear the hell out here in the West stealin' horses." He shook his head and looked at Nooch with wet eyes. "I ain't had much to do with womenfolk, and what little I did brung me nothin' but trouble. So you'll have to forgive me if I ain't all too fired up about you hookin' up with that girl of yours."

The boys sat quiet for a time. Then Juan said, "It is much the same with me."

Nooch translated as Juan told of his infatuation with Magdalena Peralta and her love for him. He spoke of the futility of their love, as Magdalena, daughter of Don Emilano Peralta, owner of the rancho where Juan lived and worked, was of a social class far above and beyond the reach of a simple vaquero, a peasant, a peon.

Juan told of the intervention of Magdalena's oldest brother, Eduardo, and the beating he took from him. How Eduardo accused him of theft and had him jailed. And how his incarceration led to his being impressed into service on the posse pursuing the horse thieves, then the vengeful killing of Eduardo that led to his fleeing the Californios and joining the *ladrones de caballos* he now rode with.

"You must forgive my distrust of a fortunate future where women are concerned," Juan said. "As with *mi amigo* Boone, my limited experience tells only a sad story."

Nooch said nothing. The three boys sat, lost in thought, as the sun slid below the crest of the mountains to their back, and the mountain air cooled in the absence of the sun.

Nooch shivered, then stood. "Come, you two. Let us find something to eat. Your love stories are sad but do not dissuade me from finding happiness with Siah." He smiled. "And make her happy, I will. For while you are but boys, I, Nooch, am a man. And it is well known that only a man can make a woman happy!"

As Nooch walked away, Juan scooped up a handful of pebbles and tossed them at his back. He did not react as the stones plunked off his bare skin, nor when Boone joined the game and threw his own handful of rocks. The boys looked at one another and shrugged, then rose and followed Nooch toward camp.

From all the day's stories and conversation, four words clung to Boone like cockleburs to a horse's fetlocks—it was the question asked by Juan Media that had started it all: *What will you do?*

Through a fitful night and all the next day, Boone searched his mind for an answer but found none. He felt as untethered as the thousands of horses wandering the valley—no notion of where they were going, and fading memories of whence they came. Wanting to satisfy his curiosity about the fate of the horses, at least, he plopped down next to Pegleg's bedroll, where the mountain man sat airing his stump and sucking acrid smoke through a clay pipe borrowed from Old Bill.

"What's goin' to happen to all these horses and mules once we get back to Santa Fe?"

Pegleg laughed. "Hell, son—we sell 'em, every one. What do you think we'd do?"

"Well, I know that. What I mean is, how? Who's goin' to buy 'em? How do you go about it?"

The mountain man mouthed the pipe for a moment, drifting smoke rising to settle under the brim of his hat. He waved the cloud away with his hand. "It'll take some doin', I reckon. We ain't never ever brung back so many before. Wakara and his boys'll likely take some of their share with 'em when they go home . . . use 'em to build up their herds and for trade with other bands. Howsomever, they'll leave most of 'em with us to sell, and we'll settle up later."

He sucked on the pipe again, the tobacco in the bowl glowing red, and blew out a long stream of smoke. "We'll divide 'em into bunches and put 'em on grass here and there around Abiquiu and Santa Fe and Taos and thereabouts and put the word out we got animals to sell. Buyers'll come, and we'll dicker a fair price. Some'll go down into Old Mexico on the Camino Real—that's a road the Mexicans been usin' for trade since they was Spaniards. Some of 'em will go in bunches back to the States—'specially the mules. Them freighters that come out from Missouri trail 'em back there to sell. Make a right handsome profit, too, if things goes well."

"Mules? Why mostly mules?"

"You come from back there. You know there's always a market for good workin' stock. And them California mules is better'n anything they got in the States."

"How long 'fore you figure to get all this stuff sold?"

The bowl of the pipe rang as Pegleg tapped it against a rock to dislodge the dottle. "It'll take us some time, I reckon, to shift all these critters, but we'll get it done. Why you askin', boy? Worried about gettin' paid?"

"No. Not really. Just wonderin', is all. Been kind of at odds about what to do with m'self from here on."

"Well, hell—you'll have money enough to do whatsoever you want to—at least for a while—years and years, maybe."

"That's kind of the thing. I ain't got no notion as to what it is I want to do. Don't know that I'm cut out for this country out here."

"Can't help you there, only to say you've held up your end on this trip. Way I see it, a young feller like you could likely do well at whatever he set his hand to."

Boone shook his bowed head, eyes fixed on the earth between his crossed legs, and exhaled a long, slow, deep breath.

Pegleg strapped on his wooden leg and set about dealing with the fasteners. "One thing I can tell you—you had best do *somethin'*. It's for damn sure it won't do no good to sit around stewin' about it. Even if you do somethin' that turns out to be wrong, it's a hell of a lot better than doin' nothin'." He rolled over onto hands and knees and hoisted himself to his feet, then hitched up his britches. "Take me, for instance. I'm goin' to take a leak. Might not be the best thing I could do—but it'll sure beat the hell out of sittin' here doin' nothin'."

In one fluid motion, Boone stood up from his seat on the ground. He brushed off the seat of his pants. "I suppose you're right. My mood will improve once we get back on the trail. All this waitin' around wears on me, I guess."

"Well, you won't have long to wait. Unless I miss my guess, Old Bill will have us on the way come mornin'."

Pegleg clapped a big hand on Boone's shoulder and gave him a jostle, then hobbled off into the fading light.

CHAPTER TWENTY-FOUR

The day was already bright, but the sun had yet to clear the eastern peaks when Old Bill Williams, hunched over in the saddle and preaching a morning sermon to the mule beneath him, took to the trail. The riders scattered across the valley stirred the stolen horses and mules into motion bunch by bunch, the herd taking shape in a long line behind the mountain man's lead. Come afternoon, the leaders spilled out of the foothills into the long valley of the Rio Severo.

Upon reaching the slow-moving, meandering river, Old Bill followed it downstream a ways, then turned onto its banks and into the water. The point of the herd followed him to the water and stopped to drink. The animals behind slowed, and the riders pushed them to the riverbank, the maneuver putting each animal into clear water rather than the stirred-up, muddied flow below. It took the better part of an hour and more than a mile of river before all the horses got their fill.

Carpeted with grass in the bottom and brush-covered elsewhere, the valley here offered nothing in the way of shade. The men pulled the saddles from their mounts and staked out replacement horses, then sought comfort on the ground to rest and gnaw on slabs of cold, roasted venison and strips of jerky dried from the deer meat. Even as Boone chewed his ration into a pasty wad, he thought it fortunate the hunters were still bringing in plenty of meat so there was no need for the party to butcher horses. He wondered if such would be the case upon reaching the dry and barren red rock country yet to come. But that was a worry for another day, and he swallowed the meaty mass and chased it down with a slug of river water from his canteen.

Wakara took the lead as the caravan of rested horses ambled ahead. The valley soon narrowed, and the river flowed for two or three miles between the confines of steep hills, outcropped here and there with sheer rock cliffs. The stream soon broke out of the mountains into another broad valley. Boone recognized it as the home of the first band of Paiutes they encountered on the outbound trip. But well before they reached the site of the village across the valley, Wakara called a halt, and the herd slowly spread across the brushy plain, horses and mules snatching mouthfuls of grass. Riders unsaddled their mounts, and those horses sought room to lower themselves to the ground and roll the itch of sweat from their backs.

Boone saddled another horse, as he was among the first watch. He rode to the other side of the herd beside Jim Beckwourth, also assigned guard duty.

Beckwourth said, "Do you know where we are, boy?"

A twinge coursed through Boone at being called "boy" by a black man. Although somewhat accustomed to the lack of class distinctions among the mountain men by now, he still felt a mild shock at times because of it. "I do," he said and nodded toward the other end of the valley. "There's some Indians live up yonder. They hid from us when we come through here before."

"You are right. But I do not believe we will find them there now. Unless I miss my guess, they will be up in the mountains somewhere, where the weather is more pleasant."

"Then why we standin' guard?"

Beckwourth chuckled. "Because the Paiutes are a wily bunch. It could be they have seen us coming and will lie in wait and attempt to make off with some of these horses. Could be they will offer to trade for some."

This time, it was Boone's turn to chuckle. "From what I seen, most of these Indians out here ain't even got proper clothes to cover themselves with. What the hell they got to trade?"

"You will recall from our earlier conversation that the Utes and Mexicans and white men will sometimes take Paiute women and children to be sold as slaves."

Boone nodded. "I remember."

"Well, on occasion, in some circumstances, a Paiute will trade away a youngster for a horse."

Boone gasped. "They'll sell off a child for a horse?"

"Sometimes. Not always."

"But who'd do such a thing? Why?"

Beckwourth shrugged. "Horses are scarce among their people. Children are easier to come by—and they can always make more."

By now they were through the grazing animals, and the riders separated, skirting the edge of the herd in opposite directions, watching the valley beyond for any sign of danger as the shadow of night fell over it. If Indians were present, they lit no fires that night.

The herd lined out in the morning, on this day following Pegleg Smith down the valley. Boone wondered why when, rather than following the Rio Severo, Pegleg forded it and followed a fork that flowed out of the eastern mountains. With the herd strung out through the canyon, he had no opportunity to reach another rider and satisfy his curiosity.

Hours later, the canyon ended. The stream they were following split, the larger fork coming down the long narrow valley from the south, the smaller creek mirroring it from the north. The herd turned north, continuing on for a few more hours before settling in for the night.

Boone found Pegleg, sitting at a small fire, massaging his stump. "Where we goin'? This ain't the way we came."

"That's right observant of you, son," Pegleg said, still rubbing at his leg.

"Well?"

"Since your memory is so good, you'll also recollect all that desert country we come through since the Green River, and on both sides of the Grand River."

"I remember."

"Well, here's the thing. There wasn't a whole lot of feed nor water out there then, and there's a whole hell of a lot less of it now. And, now, we got all these critters to think of that we didn't have back then."

Boone nodded. "I see. So we'll be missin' all that desert by comin' this way?"

"No, son. We still got to go through it. Howsomever, up this here cutoff a ways we climb way up into the mountains—higher than we ever been before—to where there'll still be fresh feed a-growin'. We'll put some fat back on these horses, then push 'em on down off that mountain and back through the barrens. They'll come out in a lot better shape for it."

When the drive left the valley to climb to the heights, the ascent was long and steep, with frequent stops to let the horses catch their breath in the thinning air. The trail passed through scrub oak, aspen, maple, and pine forests, stretching the herd over long distances as they plodded along. The narrow road followed a side hill above a basin between steep slopes, the basin filled with a deep, clear, cold-water lake that spread more than five miles, playing hide and seek below through the narrow white trunks of thick growths of aspen. Patches of brittle snow still lay in places where the sun seldom reached.

Boone smelled wood smoke before seeing it through the trees.

He saw the source of the smoke later, when a cluster of a dozen or more cone-shaped brush huts appeared down on the lake shore. Near the center stood four posts, joined by a lattice of limbs and branches creating a shady roof over what he assumed must be a gathering place. Fires still burned but were mostly down to smoke and ashes. Baskets in the camp looked to be filled with seeds or nuts of some kind, and what must have been dried meat or fish. Save for one wrinkled old woman sitting in the entrance of one of the brush huts, watching the long procession of horses pass along the hillside, there was not an Indian in sight.

The lake fed a small stream at its north end, and Boone saw other evidence of Indians around the outlet in what looked to be drying racks, discarded tattered and torn baskets, tumbledown brush shelters, and smoke-blackened fire rings.

By the time he reached the meadow that continued down the valley, the herd was already spreading out to graze. Boone reined up when Philip Thompson and Jim Beckwourth rode toward him, accompanied by three of the Utes. Thompson peeled off and stopped to talk. Boone said, "Where you-all goin'?"

"Fishing."

Looking back at the lake, Boone wondered aloud if there were many fish there.

"Lots of 'em," Thompson said. "Leastways that what the Utes say. That's what them Paiutes is doin' here. A while back, when the fish was spawnin' in that there stream, they say there would've been a whole passel of Paiutes up here. They scoop fish up by the basketful. Regular slaughter, they say. They come back every year—the fish and the Indians."

"Well, good luck with your fishin'."

"I hope we catch us some. I've growed a mite weary of eatin' nothin' but deer meat."

"I know what you mean," Boone said. "Still, I'd lots rather

187

it's venison than horse meat."

Thompson nodded and spurred his horse into an easy lope to catch up with the other fishermen. Boone rode on to where the other men were setting up camp. He unsaddled his horse and turned it loose into the herd, wondering whether he would be called upon to catch another for a turn on guard duty. With Paiutes in the vicinity, he assumed that would be the case. In the meantime, he meant to rest up, feeling saddle weary, the fatigue heightened by the altitude.

He found Nooch and Juan talking at the edge of camp and dropped his saddle to the ground beside them, then plopped down and leaned against it for a backrest. Given the long days moving the herd, the trio had spent little time together since the layover in Bear Valley. Boone pulled off his boots and wiggled his toes, nearly every one of them poking through threadbare socks.

"*¡Huele como si algo hubiera muerto!*" Juan said.

"*¡Sí!*" Nooch said with a laugh.

Boone yawned, then said, "What'd he say?"

Nooch smiled. "He says it smells like something is dead."

Boone wiggled his toes again. "Well, you-all don't exactly smell like my Mama's roses." He squirmed his way into a more comfortable seat on the ground. "Say, Juan," he said around another yawn. "That what you asked me before, about what I was goin' to do—I'm askin' you the same question."

Juan understood much of what Boone said, his grasp of English growing at a much faster pace than the American's facility with the Spanish language. Still, Nooch passed along a translation. Juan said he did not know. He hoped that in New Mexico, as in California, there would be ranchos requiring the services of vaqueros, and that he could once again make his living horseback. Even more, he hoped to be able to train horses, as he had learned to do from his father, and to breed and raise fine mounts.

"What do you think about mules?" Boone said.

"*Las mulas son mulas. Nada más y nada menos,*" Juan said with a shrug.

"Hell, I know a mule ain't nothin' but a mule. What I want to know is, do you think a man like yourself, wearin' them fancy silver spurs, is too grand to take care of a bunch of them long-eared canaries?"

The blank look on the boy's face called for an interpretation from Nooch, who was likewise stymied.

Boone said, "Canaries. Them's these little birds we got back home that people keep for pets on account of they sing songs. Some folks call mules canaries on account of how they sing . . . Aw, hell, never mind." Boone said to Juan, "Do you think it's beneath a man to raise mules?"

Juan said, "No! The Rancho de Don Emiliano Peralta is known throughout California for the quality of the mules we raised. My father and I cared for the *machos,* the jackasses who sired the mules. And we selected the *yeguas,* the mares, for breeding. The Don insisted we use only the finest mares, and to keep only the biggest, strongest *machos.* Peralta mules were much in demand and highly prized."

Dropping his head, Juan said, "But now, I do not know. I cannot say what has become of Don Peralta's mules." He raised his head and waved his arm, sweeping across the herd grazing in the meadow. "Much of his breeding stock—the *machos* and the *yeguas*—is now here. I do not know what will be the future of the mules on his rancho." Juan sighed and turned to Boone. "*¿Por qué preguntas?*"

Boone studied his friend for a moment. "Oh, nothin'. Just somethin' I been thinkin' about. Somethin' Pegleg said."

Chapter Twenty-Five

If the climb to the lake meadow was long and tedious, the cutoff trail down off the plateau kept horses, mules, *machos*, and men alike alert and anxious. It was single file all the way, so the herd stretched for miles, and the riders and their mounts and the loose-herded horses found themselves in ever-changing terrain. They tippy-toed along the thin crests of ridges and clattered down the rocky bottoms of narrow canyons. Often, the trail took them in between, knifing across precipitous slopes too steep to go either up or down in a direct way, often reversing course in a series of switchbacks. The riders—scattered along the long line of the herd—sometimes had to dismount and scramble afoot, leading their mounts through rockfalls and washouts.

Never, in all his miles and months on horseback trails, had Boone encountered anything like this ride. At times, he leaned back until his back brushed the horse's rump as they slid and skidded down. Other times found him so busy ducking low-hanging limbs and sweeping branches aside he hadn't time to pay attention to the trail. At all times in the saddle, knees, thighs, and backside clung to the leather, and, on occasion, his hands gripped the horn before him or the cantle behind.

Boone rounded a switchback and heard a horse scream from somewhere up above. He looked up and saw, two switchbacks up the ridge, a horse down, its forelegs folded beneath it and struggling to find purchase with his hind legs, so his front hooves could claw their way out and he could pull himself up. A dust cloud, and dirt and rocks rolling down the hill, signified a stumble, or perhaps ground that gave way. As the horse whinnied and clawed, the horses above and behind on the trail kept coming, the one directly behind crashing into the downed horse just as it found its feet. Lashing out with its hind legs, the stumbling horse kicked the offending animal in the chest. That horse panicked and tried to turn around to go back up the trail. But the horse behind him knocked him down and off the trail, and he slid down the steep slope, with windmilling hooves and legs pointed uphill.

From the switchback above Boone, Juan Medina watched the wreck coming at him. He saw no way to avoid the falling horse, trapped in line as he was, with no escape front or rear. He could not go up the slope, as the horse was coming down it. On his downhill side he was atop a sheer rock face that descended several feet, then disappeared back into the steep slope. All he could do was brace himself for the impact. The sliding horse hit him about knee high before he had time to pull his foot from the stirrup. His horse tipped sideways and fell on his side, spilling Juan over the edge of the trail. Only the stirruped foot kept him from falling into the empty air, the leathers drawn tight across the seat of the saddle. But the interrupted fall was temporary, as the movement of his struggling horse and the force of gravity soon pulled his foot loose.

Boone watched his friend free fall several feet until he dropped into the top of a spruce tree. He could hear Juan crash down through the limbs, then strike ground. Rocks and pebbles rained down on him as the two fallen horses above scratched and clawed, then regained their feet on the trail. Then Juan came tumbling out onto the trail ahead, spooking the horses in line there. He scrambled out of the way, and the horses kept moving and soon calmed down, averting another wreck. As he rode past the quivering Californian, clinging to tree limbs to stay on the steep slope, off the trail and out of the way of the passing horses, Boone reached out a hand, grasped Juan by the forearm and lifted him over his horse's rump to a seat behind the saddle.

Meanwhile, the mad scramble on the switchbacks above had sorted itself out, and all the horses, including Juan's mount and the stumbling horse that caused the wreck, were upright and, though still skittish, making their way down the trail. Boone could feel Juan shaking and listened as his breathing slowed.

"You all right?"

"*Si. Bueno.*"

"That was quite a fall." He cocked a leg and turned to look at Juan.

"*No fue nada,*" he said with a shrug.

"Nothin'! What do you mean it was nothin'? Hell, you could've been killed!"

Another shrug. "*Estoy bien.* I am fine."

The switchback trail eventually made it to the bottom of the ridge to a place with room for Boone to turn out of line. Juan slid off from behind him and stood beside the passing horses, and, when his mount arrived, appearing no worse for wear, he reached out and grabbed a dangling rein. The saddle was tipped and hanging to the side but had not slipped under the horse's belly. Loosening the cinch, he shifted it upright. Outside of a few more scratches and scuffs to the already marred leather, it looked to be in good shape. He spent several minutes passing his hands over the horse, feeling for sore and tender spots, rubbing up and down the legs, and examining the hooves. A patch of hide scraped off one foreleg, and a long but shallow cut on the shoulder above, appeared to be the only damage.

One of the Abiquiu Mexicans, who had been next in line behind Juan, but with many horses between them, stopped. He and Juan talked in rapid-fire Spanish for a minute or two, and, other than a stray word here and there, Boone could not begin to keep up with the conversation. The Mexican smiled and clapped Juan on the shoulder, which caused him to wince and shy away.

"*¡Lo siento!*" the rider said.

Juan waved him off, saying it was nothing—he was fine—just a few aches and pains—no need to be sorry. The horseman rode back into the line. Boone waited while Juan tightened and tied off his latigo and swung into the saddle with a grimace. He followed Juan into the passing parade of horses, thinking it best to keep an eye on him in case his injuries were more severe than the boy let on.

After a time, the cutoff bottomed out in a canyon facing a high, steep wall. Here, they rejoined the main trail, and not far down the canyon reached a valley with a small mountain stream and enough grass to hold the horses overnight. Already, camp was organized, and fires were burning, with venison sizzling on willow skewers and boiling in a few pots.

"Smells mighty good, Manolo," Boone said. "Though I confess my taste for deer meat ain't what it used to be."

Manolo smiled. "Mine as well. But it is all we have. And soon, we may not have *el ciervo* to feed us."

Boone grabbed one of the willow sticks with a slab of meat dangling from it. It looked to be cooked enough to be edible. He pulled up another from over the fire for Juan and carried it to where he sat, back against a fallen tree. The boys were working the meat over, nibbling—gobbling—around the edges as it cooled, grease dripping from their chins.

Before the meat was in them, Nooch and one of his Ute friends came by and squatted before the eating boys. Not far behind, Pegleg hobbled his way over, in company with Thompson and Old Bill and Beckwourth with a few of the New

Mexicans. The rider above Juan who saw the wreck must have spread the word, so an audience was assembling to hear the story.

Juan had little to say, only that a horse had fallen off the trail and knocked his horse down, and he had lost the trail for a time.

But the audience demanded more, so Boone related the story in greater detail, starting at the top and following the calamity all the way down. "Truth is," he said in summary, "Juan here is damn lucky to be drawin' breath, takin' a tumble like he did. Could've been a whole hell of a lot worse."

Old Bill probed Juan with questions, assuring himself the boy was unhurt and fit to ride come the morning. Others asked questions of their own, most of which Juan shrugged off or answered with few words.

"I got to tell you-all," Boone said, "when I was a kid playin' around back in Missouri, I seen plenty of my friends fall *out of* trees. But till now, I ain't never seen nobody fall *into* a tree."

For the next few days, the horse thieves trailed their herd through familiar terrain, albeit they were seeing it in reverse order. The trade route skirted the high plateau they had crossed before setting off into the rugged, barren desert to flank even rougher country of sandstone spires and defiles, canyons and crevices, gorges and gulches. The small streams they had passed on the way out were now but trickles or had disappeared altogether into the sandy bottoms of arroyos wide enough to hold a raging river. The scant bunch grass on the plain was withered and brown, the leaves on the occasional bush dusty and curled.

But, much to Boone's pleasure, the trail did eventually bend toward the southeast and Santa Fe, its long course to the north complete. Although still far from the end of the road, at least they were headed that direction.

Boone, Nooch, and Juan stopped one afternoon at a seemingly nondescript place in a shallow canyon. Juan watched as the other two studied the terrain, pushed their mounts to the top of the low canyon rim, rode back and forth, then skated their horses back to the bottom.

"I believe this is where it happened, all right," Boone said.

Nooch nodded.

Juan said, "*¿Lo que pasó aquí?*"

"I'll tell you what happened—ol' Nooch here damn near drowned at this place."

"Drowned? What does it mean, 'drowned'?"

Nooch thought for a moment. "*Ahogarse, en el agua.*"

Juan looked around, the dust from the horse herd, long since passed, still hanging in the air. "But there is no water here. I do not understand."

Boone and Nooch described the flash flood that ripped down the arroyo following a far-distant rainstorm and told how the riders and the pack string barely got out of the canyon in time to avoid being swept away. And how Nooch's horse slipped and slid as it clambered up the canyon wall and was washed away, with the Ute surviving only because of Boone's intervention.

"I was fortunate," Nooch said.

"Damn right you was," Boone said. "Damn lucky I didn't turn loose the end of my reata. Which, had I any sense, I would've done. Then we'd be rid of you."

Nooch smiled. They rode along the bottom of the ravine until it took a sweeping bend. Jumbled against the wide side of the turn was a tangle of trash left behind by the water. Rocks and boulders, tree trunks, bare and broken limbs and branches, brush and heaps of sand. The boys reined up and examined the piles, then Nooch slid off his horse and pulled away a mess of raveled sagebrush and greasewood and kicked away a drift of sand to reveal the desiccated remains of the horse he had ridden that day.

The saddle—what was left of it—was still cinched around the dried hide and rib bones. The head and neck of the horse were somewhat in place, but most of the rest of the animal was gone, likely dragged away and scattered by scavengers. With his knife, Nooch cut through a brittle saddle string behind the seat and tugged loose the roll of leather it had secured. Sand leaked out from every fold as he prized the stiff leather open. Inside, a spare shirt was stained and falling to bits, but a beaded buckskin vest, while hardened, could be salvaged with care.

But what pleased Nooch the most from the buried treasure was a necklace, with silver beads and baubles—dulled and darkened with tarnish—strung along a now-fragile leather thong, interspersed with bright turquoise stones and what looked to be bear claws.

"That's right handsome, Nooch," Boone said. "How'd you come by it?"

"My first raid against the Navajo. I took a scalp from a man when we overran their village. This I found in his dwelling. Except the claws from the bears. Those, I added myself." With the ball of his thumb, he attempted to polish one of the beads. He sprayed spit on one of the claws and wiped away the clinging dust turned to mud. Shaking the string gently to loosen some of the dirt, he folded the necklace twice and rolled it and the beaded vest in the remains of the cloth shirt for what protection it might offer and stuffed them into his saddlebag. "I will give it to Siah when she becomes my wife."

The boys rode on and found the herd scattered and pawing and nosing the barren desert, searching for something edible among the scattered sagebrush and shadscale but having little luck. For another night, the camp would be a dry one.

Pegleg hobbled over as they unsaddled their horses and shooed them away to the herd. "You youngsters find what you was lookin' for?"

"Yessir," Boone said. "Found what was left of the horse Nooch lost in that flood. He even found a few things still useful in the stuff that was tied to the saddle."

Pegleg shook his head. "Hard to believe there could be that much water in this here country. Howsomever, I have seen such floods as that on bare rock before. Places you wouldn't think has ever been wet. Rainstorms out here in these deserts ain't like they is in other places."

"Wish to hell we had some of that floodwater now—only if it was better behaved," Boone said. "Them horses out there look mighty thirsty. I sure hope we don't end up killin' a bunch of 'em, like we done before."

Juan pulled off his hat and wiped the sweat from his forehead with a shirtsleeve. "I will never forget the stink of *caballos muertos*. Not even the *matanza*, where we slaughtered cattle, smelled so bad."

"They'll be all right," Pegleg said. "We might lose a few of the weaker ones, but the rest'll make it. We'll be to the Green River tomorrow, and there'll be plenty of water there. If there's enough grass there, which I suspect there will be, we'll lay over a day, maybe two, and let the critters rest up a bit." He paused and looked at the ground as he stirred around the dirt with his peg leg.

"But you boys got to understand that these horses and mules ain't pets. We may yet ag'in have to sacrifice some of 'em so as to get as many of the rest as we can to Santa Fe. If we have to push 'em hard and lose a few doin' it, that's a hell of a lot better than losin' 'em all because we dawdled, thinkin' it would be the kinder thing. I'm here to tell you, it ain't."

With a grunt, the mountain man turned and stomped away, his wooden leg leaving deep depressions in the desert soil as he muttered something under his breath about the stink of dead horses.

Chapter Twenty-Six

Juan stretched out, slid his hat down over his face, and crooked an arm behind his head for a pillow. The sun had slipped below the horizon, but the sky above the rough-hewn red rock desert south of the Grand River was far from dark.

Boone watched Juan at rest for several minutes, then kicked the sole of his friend's boot with the toe of his. The big rowel on the vaquero's spur jingled.

Juan tipped his hat back and glared at Boone. *"¡No me molestes!"*

"I ain't goin' to leave you alone. I want to talk. What you thinkin' about?"

Juan sat up and drew his legs up and wrapped his arms around them. He studied Boone's face for a moment, wondering at his friend's question and trying to discern his purpose. He shrugged. "I think of home—the rancho. My father." He watched for any reaction from Boone but saw nothing in his face. "And I think of Magdalena—*pienso mucho en* Magdalena."

Boone gathered a handful of pebbles and, one by one, tossed them away, watching them click and clack as they rolled and bounced down the rippled sandstone slope, the patterns on the rock looking like waves in water. "I know what you mean. Sometimes I still think about Mary Elizabeth." He tossed a few more pebbles. "Not so much anymore. But sometimes." He gathered and lobbed more stones. "What do you aim to do, Juan?"

"*¿Qué?*"

"What I mean is, after we get to Santa Fe and get done with these horses, what will you do? Where will you go?"

Boone watched Juan's furrowed brow and pursed lips, but, after a time, the face fell and he shrugged slowly and shook his head.

"You think you might go back to California? Maybe stay in New Mexico?"

Another shrug. "*No lo sé.* I cannot go to California, I think. I will be locked up. Or killed. *¿Nuevo Mexico?*" Another shrug.

Three more stones rattled away at long intervals. "I been thinkin', Juan."

His friend did not reply.

Boone launched two more pebbles. "You recollect when I asked you 'bout mules? What you thought of 'em?"

"*Si.*"

"Well, I maybe got an idea. Somethin' Pegleg said one time 'bout how valuable mules is." He tossed another stone. "Back where I come from, it's farmin' country. Near 'bout everybody that don't live in the towns and some that do is a farmer of one kind or another. And all them farmers need mules, or horses, to work the land. Mules bein' the best for that work."

Now that he was started, Boone's thoughts poured out of him. "There's lots of mules back in Missouri, but they ain't near the animals these ones we stole out of California is—like them mules you said come from the ranch you worked on. Them mules look to be bigger and stronger and just all-around better lookin' than what they got back home. I guess it's on account of them big jackasses."

"*Si.* The *machos.* And the *yeguas* we choose for mothers."

"I reckon so. Here's the thing. Supposin' I talk to Pegleg and Old Bill and them and see if I can take my pay in a pair or three of them jacks, and some mares. We trail 'em back to the States and set ourselves up in the business of sellin' workin' mules to all them farmers. Hell, we could maybe outfit some of them freighters on the Santa Fe Road, too, I'll bet. We could get more mares back there, pick good ones. But there ain't no jacks like these ones. We'd be puttin' out the best mules anywhere."

Juan watched his friend's face in the fading light but said nothing.

Boone stayed silent for as long as he could. Then, "C'mon, Juan—what do you think?"

"Did you not kill a man? Should not the same reason I cannot return to California keep you away from that place, from your Missouri?"

"Aw, hell, Juan. I ain't worried 'bout that. I reckon the excitement died down long ago. I sure won't go back to Clay County. But if things looks too hot around Independence with the law and all, we can go to Saint Jo, or down to Springfield. Hell, it don't even need to be Missouri. There's Illinois and there's Arkansas and there's Kentucky and Tennessee—we could go anywheres we took a notion to! Anyplace there's farms they need mules, and there's farms everywhere!"

Juan said nothing.

Again, Boone waited. Then, "You don't have to make up your mind now, Juan. Just think on it, that's all. You got any questions you can't put into words, well, we'll get Nooch to explain. Or we can ask Manolo. He knows English good. Maybe even Pegleg can help." Boone stretched out, using the seat of his saddle for a pillow, rolled on his side, and closed his eyes.

Juan set his hat aside and stretched back out on the ground as before, turning his attention to the stars appearing in the sky, a sky in which he saw no beginning or end.

Even in the quiet of night, a resting herd of more than two thousand horses and mules is noisy. Nickering and snuffling.

Coughing. Pawing. The grind of teeth on coarse desert grass. The clatter of dislodged stones and rustle of disturbed brush.

Pale light from the sky cast moon shadows on the desert, most slow and still, but some, at the edges of the herd, flitting and ephemeral. Those shadows followed the skulking forms of coyotes, stalking the edges of the herd and whining, sometimes yipping, in their fevered excitement. The horses paid little attention; a coyote presented essentially no risk to a healthy and mobile—if tired and hungry—horse. Still, the curs persisted, ever hopeful. An occasional yelp split the night air when a swift kick answered an impulsive snap at a tempting leg.

The coyotes slipped away with the dawn. Horses drifted aimlessly, stomping and stamping and tossing their heads about, pointed ears and flared nostrils searching the air for the scent of water.

The long, hot, dry days through the barrens leading to and beyond the Green River and Grand River crossings had cost the herd as many as a hundred head of the weaker horses, the carcasses left lying in the wilds, food for opportunistic coyotes and other scavengers.

The water sources that had quenched man and animal on the outbound trip—potholes, seeps, springs, and small streams—had either dried up with the season or were insufficient to water so many animals. Many of the horses showed hip bones and ribs that grew ever more prominent as they trudged and lumbered along. But, Pegleg and Old Bill promised, better conditions lay ahead. Once they reached the country around the Dolores River, there would be plenty of water in streams coming off the western slope of the Rocky Mountains, and enough grass to recruit the horses, even fatten them up some, for the last leg of the trip to Santa Fe.

The herd had further diminished by two hundred head following the crossing of the Green River when all the Indians, save Wakara and Nooch, drove those horses eastward to Ute villages and camps there. Wakara would collect the rest of his people's share of the take in New Mexico.

"You miss your friends?" Boone said as he rode beside Nooch at the tail end of the herd on the way up a low, wide ravine leading out of a dry valley.

Their mounts plodded along for a time before Nooch said, "Yes. Some. They will be almost home by this time—close to where my Siah is." He smiled. "It is Siah I miss."

"Reckon she's missin' you?"

Nooch's smile turned to a frown. "I hope so." Again, he smiled. "I have sent her a reminder! I chose from among the horses a fine mare. It is the color of gold, with a mane and tail like snow. The Mexicans call a horse of such colors a palomino."

"I know what you mean—I have seen some horses like that in them that we stole. They're right pretty, for sure."

Nooch smiled and nodded. "With such a beautiful mare, I do not think Siah will forget me."

"How come is it that Wakara never sent you back with the others?"

Nooch smiled bigger than before. "Wakara says he believes that one day I may become a leader of the People. He keeps me with him to teach me. I will learn how to bargain with the whites and the Mexicans." Leaning closer to Boone as they rode along, Nooch said in a whisper with a still bigger smile, "In trade, the People always take advantage of the whites."

Boone reached out with a fist and gave Nooch a soft poke on the arm. "Maybe so—but you-all ain't never bargained with me."

They rode on in silence for a time.

"Listen, Nooch. I got me a plan . . ." Boone explained the idea he had proposed to Juan of trailing mares and jacks to the States and going into business raising mules. "I don't suppose you'd want to come along . . . you're a good hand with horses, and you ain't afraid of work."

Nooch declined the offer, claiming Siah had too strong a hold on him.

"Hell, bring her along. You-all can be as much married in Missouri as out here."

"I think not. There are too many of you white people out here, and I do not think I would like to live among more of them back there. And I do not think the whites would like to have an Indian living among them. If Juan agrees to go with you, I do not know if he could live happily with your people. The whites seem to like only other whites."

"Ah, to hell with 'em. We'll do as we damn well please." Boone turned off to the side to chouse a skinny, sore-footed horse that was falling behind. He followed along, urging it ahead until they topped out of the long ravine in a low saddle between rocky hills. Ahead lay a big valley, stretching away far to the south and eastward until running up against a mountain range. Boone reined up for a look. While far from the well-watered land he knew in Missouri, there was more green in this view than he had seen since the forested high mountains on the cutoff trail around the big lake.

The herd pushed on into the big valley and by day's end reached a creek flowing strong enough to water the horses. As promised, the land proved much more accommodating, with sufficient grass for feed, and each day the trail crossed at least one creek, and sometimes more, to keep the herd watered. Moving at a slower pace, the horses were able to graze as they moved along, as well as overcome the fatigue of days past.

Upon reaching the Dolores River near the base of a high mountain mesa, Old Bill declared a rest, and for three days the horses cropped the grass in the meadows lining the stream. Wakara and Beckwourth led a hunting party into the mountains.

Other than the usual tasks of refurbishing worn tack, there was little for the rest of the men to do beyond taking their turn on guard.

Boone spent time with the vaqueros and *mozos*, improving his handling of a rawhide reata but also talking with Juan about his ambition to return to the States to raise mules. He intended to carry out the plan no matter Juan's decision but told the Californian his—their—prospects for success would be much greater should Juan come along and bring with him his knowledge and experience in breeding and training the long-eared animals.

For his part, Juan remained noncommittal, claiming uncertainty about life among the Americans.

"Aw, hell, Juan! You won't be the first Mexican folks back there has seen! Them freighters on the Santa Fe Road, least-ways all the ones I seen, has got as many Mexican bullwhackers and muleskinners as what they do white men. It ain't so much that way where I growed up in Clay County, but down around Independence they got every kind of people you ever thought of. There's always folks comin' and goin' through there—Mexicans, Indians, negroes, and what all. Hell, even the white folks come from all over—every part of America and some from places I don't even know where, talkin' lingo I don't get. I don't reckon anybody'd take much notice of you."

Juan chuckled. "*Sí*. I think you are right. But a man deserves to be noticed. Every man. Is it not so?"

"I don't know what you mean."

Juan searched his mind for a meaningful explanation. "In my home, in California, the people of common parentage, people like me, are not respected. We are peons, good for nothing but for work; our opinions or thoughts are of no consequence. The ranchos are owned by the *gente de razon*, the people of reason, who believe no one else worthy. They are of Spanish blood, and look down on those with *indio* or mixed blood. And so we are—how do you say it?—invisible, unseen. We are of no account. I think in your country, among the *hombres blancos*, the white men, it would be much the same, or perhaps worse. Even the low-born white men will look down on me. Is it not so?"

Now it was Boone's turn to ponder an explanation. He found none. "I don't know what to tell you, Juan. I ain't never thought about such things. I know that preacher daddy of Mary Elizabeth's never thought much of me. I don't know . . . Ain't nobody pays darkies no mind, but they mostly know their place, so it don't cause no troubles for no one. But, like I say, it ain't somethin' I've thought much about.

"Still, I reckon we could do as we please, and to hell with anyone what don't like it. That's what I told Nooch when he told me 'bout the same thing you did, and I'm tellin' you the same thing. You decide to come in with me, we'll figure it out. What d'you think?"

Juan smiled. "*¿Yo?* But I am not of the *gente de razon.* I have no thoughts."

"Oh, bullshit."

"I will think it over, my friend."

Boone clapped him on the shoulder. "You do that. But you been thinkin' a long time already. I think it's a damn fine idea, myself. We could make us a heap of money; then it won't matter one damn bit what anyone thinks. I'll talk to Pegleg . . . see if we can get us some of them jacks and mares when the time comes."

Chapter Twenty-Seven

Climbing into the mountains, the trail followed broad canyons and valleys upward. Storm clouds obscured the high peaks, but rain did not fall on the herd. Lightning bolts rained down all around as the horses poured over the summit, and the flashes both led and followed the drive downslope. Wall-eyed horses snorted and danced in the electrified air, agitated by the thunder that rolled off the ridges and through the canyon as they followed the creek running down its bottom.

Boone sawed on the reins, attempting to keep his mount from running and keep the horses around him, unsettled and skittering, headed downhill. Then the horses ahead bolted and ran, and there was nothing for it but to join the stampede.

Soon, he overtook Jim Beckwourth. A few rods up the slope of the canyon ridge, Beckwourth's horse pawed at the air as it leapt against the strength of the rider hauling back on the reins. "Run 'em boy!" the mountain man hollered over the cacophony of booming thunder, pounding hooves, and shrill whinnies of frightened horses. "Push 'em! Hard as you can!" Beckwourth's voice faded, but he continued his cries, encouraging the drovers farther back in the herd to do the same.

The smell of wood smoke in the air hinted at the cause of the panic, and, as they rounded a bend in the canyon, Boone could see the reason. Pine trees, underbrush, and grass were aflame on both sides of the canyon—higher up the ridge and further down the canyon on one side, but near the creek bottom and eating its way up the canyon toward him on the other. The flames burned bright orange in the dim overcast, shooting upward and casting blazing embers into the wind, the glare of the flames fading only when overwhelmed for an instant by the flash of lightning.

Boone let loose a trilling scream and hollered as much from fear as to keep the distressed horses on the run. The distraught horses shied away from the flames as they neared the blaze, pressing and jostling one another as they crowded toward the opposite ridge. For a moment, Boone feared his horse—or another—might go down, upsetting and spilling dozens more. But, once past the infringing inferno, the spooked animals separated as much as the confined canyon allowed. In the confusion, Boone had barely noticed the heat of the flames or the sear of airborne embers, but, once out of the worst of it, he slapped and rubbed at his shirtfront and sleeves, wiping away the smolder and smoke of a dozen small burn holes.

The canyon opened, and the thundering herd poured out into a wider valley where a river flowed. Ahead, the drovers ran the horses into and across the stream without slowing, raising a curtain of mist and splash. On the far side, the race continued. The riders made no attempt to slow, turn, or mill the herd until well beyond the river so as to avoid a jam at the crossing. But, once clear, the horses were easy to stop, heaving for breath and streaming sweat from the miles of hard running over rough terrain.

Riders, too, gasped to fill their lungs, hoping to cool the effects of hot smoke with clear air. There was no attempt to establish an orderly camp, each man seeking shelter from the still-threatening sky, stripping his saddle and shooing his horse back toward the herd, then collapsing to the hard earth, few even bothering to unfurl a blanket for warmth against the blustery mountain air.

Thunder and lightning made it difficult, if not impossible, to relax. There was no telling the time, beyond knowing the sun had yet to set. Dark clouds rolled overhead; fog and mist settled into the creases in the mountains. Lightning dissipated and moved on, but the clouds turned loose torrents of rain in thick curtains that swept through the river valley. The juniper tree Boone huddled under protected him from the worst of the rain until its scaly limbs and leaves overflowed, then water poured down in thin streams too numerous to dodge, though he did scoot back and forth in the attempt. Huddling under his blanket helped, but that, too, soon became saturated and offered little protection.

The intensity of the storm faded and turned to a drizzle, and, one by one, the drovers crawled out of their hidey-holes. Most of the horses stood with heads hung low, dripping water, steam rising from their backs. Clouds to the west parted, and sunbeams shot through, fanning light into the valley. To the east, a rainbow glowed. Spindly streams of thin smoke rose from hot spots on the canyon ridges, but the deluge had drowned the fires.

Scratching through the duff under pine trees, the men uncovered enough dry needles and twigs to serve as tinder and kindling, feeding the flames deadfall that sizzled and seethed and smoked until it was dry enough to burst into flame. Sodden drovers huddled around the fires, the warmth welcome in the crisp mountain air. Manolo boiled dried meat to make a broth of sorts, and the men gulped it down. Piece by piece, clothing came off, hung to dry on sticks rammed into the ground near the fires . . . blankets the same.

Juan Medina sat spraddle-legged on the ground, his booted feet extended toward the fire. His poncho hung behind him, reflecting heat from the blaze. Boone sat nearby, shirt in hand, holding it out to toast in the warmth.

"Looky there," Boone said, nodding toward the tiny burn holes in the fabric, orange firelight peeking through in the darkening evening. "I done caught fire. Hell, I could've been killed!"

"*Sí*. I thought *relámpago*—the lightning, you say?—would get me, then I believed I would die in *el fuego*, the fire," Juan said with a shake of his head. "And then, the rain. Tell me, *mi amigo*, is it like this in Missouri?"

"Not that I ever seen." Boone smiled. "But this ain't nothin'. Just wait till you see a twister."

"Twister? What is a twister?"

"Sometimes when you get a big storm—like this one we just had—out in that country, the clouds get to spinnin' 'round and 'round in the wind, and it spins up into a twister. Them spinnin' clouds and wind drop down out of the sky clear down to the ground and make all kinds of a mess. Busts things up and blows things away. It can knock a building plumb to pieces and blow the pieces away. Why, I heard tell one time that one of them twisters picked up a whole cabin in Jackson County and set it down pretty as you please over by Sedalia. Them folks moved, house and all, without ever meanin' to."

"Is this true?"

"Oh, hell yes. That twister carried their milk cow and all their chickens to the new place, too. Even pulled up and replanted their corn crop."

"*No te creo.*"

"Huh? What you babblin' about?"

"I am saying what you say is not true. I think it is—how do you say?—bullshit."

Boone laughed. "Well, some of it is. We do have twisters, and they do wreck things. Even kill folks, sometimes. But I ain't never been nearly struck by lightning, burned up in a fire, and damn near drowned in a rainstorm all in the same day. Missouri is right calm compared to this."

Boone felt the sleeves of his shirt and determined they were dry enough. He slipped it on, enjoying the warmth of the cloth against his skin as he fastened what buttons the shirt still held. "You plannin' on comin' to Missouri with me, Juan?"

With a shrug of his shoulders, Juan said, "I do not know. I am thinking about it. Have you talked with Pegleg about *los machos*? Without *los machos,* there is nothing to consider."

"Not yet, I ain't. But I will . . . I will."

Come the dawn, with silver light washing away the stars as it filled a clear sky, Old Bill, Pegleg, Wakara, and Beckwourth palavered for a time and determined to stay put for the day, allowing the horses—and the men—to recover from yesterday's ordeal.

"I don't recall the name of this here river," Boone said, sitting himself on a rock next to Pegleg.

The mountain man did not answer right away, chewing and swallowing a mouthful of dried deer meat as he watched the boy. "They say some old Spaniard named it Rio de las Ánimas Perdidas. Means, River of Lost Souls. Mexicans just call it Las Ánimas these days. To trappers, it's just plain Animas." Pegleg squirmed his backside into a more comfortable position on his boulder and gnawed off another bite of jerky. He tucked it into his cheek with his tongue and said, "I got a feelin' that ain't what you want to ask me."

"That's so." Boone ducked his head and cleared his throat. "What I'm a-wonderin' is how we get paid for this trip."

Pegleg studied the boy's face for a minute. "You ain't gettin' greedy on us, are you, boy?"

"No. Just wonderin', is all."

The trapper's stare continued.

"There's somethin' more I want to ask you about, but after."

Pegleg said the payout was simple, but it did not seem so

simple to Boone. Each member of the party was entitled to one share of the take, with the leaders—Old Bill, Beckwourth, Wakara, and Pegleg—each claiming three shares. Thompson would get two. Once the average value of the animals was established, the division would be based on that price. It was unlikely, impossible, really, that all two thousand, give or take, of the animals could be shifted in a short time, so the money from the initial sales would go to those wanting to be on their way, while the mountain men would see to the pasturing and eventual sale of the remaining horses.

"What about the people that got killed back there?"

"If we know of any kin—like Song's brothers—their share gets paid out just the same."

"How 'bout them horses the Utes took?"

"That'll come off their share. Where the Utes is concerned, we give all their money to Wakara, and he spreads it around as he sees fit."

Boone thought it over for a few minutes, asking other questions as they came to him. Then he got to the point. "Suppose I wanted to take some of them jacks and some mares instead of money?"

"What you got in mind, boy?"

The boy shook his head. "Save that for later. If I can't do what I said, it won't matter none."

Pegleg scratched deep into his beard, then pulled off his hat and raked his fingers through tangled hair. He put his hat back on and said, "I don't see why not."

Boone sat up straight, smiled, and slapped his thigh.

"Howsomever, by hand-pickin' the animals you want, you'll be gettin' better critters than the run of the herd, so we'll have to figure how to balance that out." Pegleg watched the boy some more. "Just to keep it fair, you know."

Boone nodded. "Sounds fine to me. If I get what I want, then it don't matter to me 'bout gettin' any more. There ain't no way what I want would amount to anything like a share of two thousand horses. You-all are welcome to the rest."

"What you figurin' to do with jackasses and California mares?"

Boone told Pegleg that if Juan agreed to come along, he would trail the jacks and mares back to Missouri and go into business breeding mules.

"What the hell you want to do somethin' like that for?"

"Well, Pegleg, I sort of got the notion from you. One time you was a-carryin' on 'bout what fine animals mules was," Boone said with a smile. "Guess I kind of took it to heart. I figure there's always folks wantin' mules, and, with these California jacks, seems to me we'll have the best mules there is."

"That ain't what I mean, boy. I mean, what the hell you want to go back down there for? You come all the way out here thinkin' to be a mountain man; now you're a-wantin' to go back where you come from."

Boone shrugged and screwed up his face as he searched for words to answer. "I guess when it comes down to it, I just ain't cut out for this country."

Pegleg snorted. "Hell, kid, you done just fine. You've more than held up your end."

"It ain't that. It's just that it's too . . . too . . . *different* out here, I guess."

"Different?"

Boone nodded.

"You mean the country—the deserts and mountains and such?"

Boone shook his head. "No. It ain't that. I like the country fine. It's the people, I guess. It's stupid of me, I know, but I never knowed there'd be so many Mexicans and such. I guess maybe I knowed there would be, but I thought there'd be more white folks."

Pegleg laughed. "Hell, kid, you're in Mexico. Hell of a place to be if you don't like Mexicans." He laughed again. "And here you are fixin' to take Juan Medina to Missouri as a business partner."

Boone reddened. "It ain't that I don't like Mexicans—well, at least not one at a time. But when there's bunches of them, like in Santa Fe, it just don't set right, somehow. Supposin' I was wantin' to get married? I don't know as I could find me a white woman, and I don't know as I could marry up with a Mexican woman."

"You could always marry an Indian gal," Pegleg said with a smile. "Hell, once you blow out the candle, all womenfolk look alike."

Boone shook his head. "Can't see doin' that, neither."

"You know I've got me a Mexican woman and a Ute woman, too. I could have more if I wanted 'em. There sure ain't no shortage of women out here."

"That's another thing. It don't seem right for a man to be hitched to more'n one woman. Seems like all you men do it, but, like I said, it don't seem right."

"It's a big country, Boone my boy. Havin' a woman to keep you warm at night no matter where you find yourself is right handy. Ain't nobody out here thinks any worse of you for it."

Boone had no answer.

" 'Course womenfolk can be a trial, as well. They can run a man ragged with all their notions. And they can sure flay you with their tongue. Tell you the truth, I ain't lookin' forward to what Song's likely to do to me next time I see her. She sure as hell won't take too kindly to two of her brothers gettin' killed out in California. That'll be my fault in her mind, for damn sure."

"That's another thing. Folks out here don't seem to think twice about dyin'—or killin'. All them horses we lost, and all those boys what got killed, and them Paiutes . . . I don't know, Pegleg. That don't seem the way it ought to be."

It took the mountain man a few minutes to answer. "Everything, and everybody, dies, kid. Ain't no gettin' away from it. When it comes to dyin', why, one day ought to be 'bout as good as any other. Indians got a sayin'—nothin' lives forever but the rocks and the mountains. As for killin'—well, sometimes it's you or them. And sometimes it's just them. If you don't kill 'em now, you might have to kill 'em next time—or they could kill you. Out here, dyin' and killin' is all part of livin'."

Pegleg stood and adjusted his leg harness and hitched up his pants. "I'll talk to Old Bill—see what he thinks of what you're wantin' to do with them jacks and brood mares. Beckwourth and Wakara'll go along with whatever we decide."

CHAPTER TWENTY-EIGHT

None of the men talked, their mouths and jaws working furiously on the food before them. Boone only picked at the roast *cabrito* and mutton stew, his appetite for meat sated by all the flesh—and little else—he had consumed for all the weeks since the party lost most of their supplies and camp equipment to the Californio posse on the Mojave Desert.

He folded and stuffed tortillas into his mouth whole. Spooned up squash and corn and tomatoes and beans and roasted chilis and cheese as fast as he could work his elbow. And coffee. The way his belly sloshed, he thought he must have swallowed at least a barrel of the steaming stuff.

The women of Abiquiu kept busy at cooking and serving the hungry men, and it took the better part of two days until the last of them laid down his spoon and pushed back from the table. Drink was as alluring for some of the men as food, but Old Bill and the other leaders allowed limited access to aguardiente—pulque, mezcal, tizwin, and the more potent Taos whiskey—while discouraging over-indulgence until the work was done.

Since the fire, the trip to Abiquiu had gone without incident. The horses forded the Florida, Los Pinos, and San Juan Rivers in turn, as well as many creeks and arroyos and ravines, before cutting through the Carracas rim and passing through the long canyon of the same name. Later, La Puerta Grande passed between Apache Mesa and Tierra Amarilla and poured them into the valley of the Rio Chama. Abiquiu, other than a few impoverished and usually vacated Indian villages, was the first settlement the men had seen since racing through the ranchos of California.

Besides food and drink, Abiquiu offered the opportunity to sleep under a roof for the first time in months. But the row of small rooms in the long adobe building Boone remembered from his first visit provided few comforts. Packed dirt floors, fetid air, no ventilation save the low doorway, dim illumination during the day and candlelight at night, and vermin that represented the only permanent residents of the hovels kept many of the men, including Juan, Nooch, and Boone, under the stars.

Nooch sighed following a slow, rolling belch. Juan and Boone laughed at the emission, wishing the same satisfaction for their own overstuffed selves.

"Nooch, *mi amigo*," Juan said, "I fear that soon we shall part company, perhaps never to meet again."

"It is so," the Ute said. "Wakara says we will go on to Santa Fe to see to the selling of some of the horses. Then we will take some money and supplies to our people."

"Say, boys—you-all sure you don't want to come on back to Missouri with me?" Boone said.

Nooch snorted. "Not I. My Siah awaits, and she is much better company than the two of you."

"What about you, Juan? You made up your mind yet?"

Juan shrugged, unseen in the dark of the night.

Boone waited for an answer. "Well, what about it?"

Juan said nothing for a time, then, "I do not know. It is a decision I cannot make until the idea you have becomes real."

"I done told you what Pegleg said."

"*Si*. But he said he must talk to Old Bill. I think the decision must come from *el viejo*, not the one-legged one."

Boone wrapped his blanket tighter around his shoulders and lay down, shifting his saddle to a more comfortable position as a pillow. After so many nights, it almost felt like the saddle had molded itself to the shape of his head—or, perhaps, the opposite had occurred.

The answer to the lingering question Juan voiced came with the rising sun. Pegleg's shadow fell across the still-sleeping Boone. He hauled back his wooden appendage and swung it into the boy's ribs. Boone shot up with a grunt, squinting through the glare of morning for the source of the thump to his midsection.

"What the hell, Pegleg?"

"Get up, boy. You other lazy bastards best roll out as well. You got work to do."

Juan and Nooch stirred themselves awake, and the three youngsters struggled to rearrange their minds to cope with the confusing transition between the real world and that of interrupted dreams.

Pegleg waited a bit for them to get their wits about them. "We'll be gettin' to the business of cuttin' the herd tomorrow morning. We'll leave a couple of bunches here along the Chama and send another bunch up to Taos to pasture. The rest we'll push on south to Santa Fe. We'll sell what we can right away and split the rest into bunches to graze in that country."

He tossed a ball of wool yarn, dyed yellow from the flowers of *chamisa,* into Boone's lap. "What I want you to do is pick out what critters you think you want. Take this here twine and tie a hunk of it in their manes. We'll keep 'em with us till we get to Santa Fe, then take a look down there and come to an understanding."

"You're sayin' I can do it, then? I can take my share in mares and jacks?"

Pegleg nodded. "Most likely. Howsomever, if Old Bill thinks

you're tryin' to take advantage, he'll cut you off like a rattlesnake's head."

"Oh, I wouldn't do that. No such thing."

Pegleg nodded, then turned and walked away.

The boys saddled horses and rode out into the herd, slowly working their way through the scattered horses. Boone left it to Juan to identify the mares likely to throw good foals and choose the best of the jacks. The three of them would look over each selection, and, if in agreement, Nooch would ride around and to the other side to cut off any escape. The horses were not wild, and all, save a few of the youngest, had been handled by humans; most were broke to ride. But their manners had dimmed some over the time on the trail, so they were wary and sometimes skittish, heads up with ears pointed and nostrils flared as the riders came near.

Juan would dismount and approach the chosen horse and, most times, with a slow advance, could make contact, talking softly and rubbing and scratching the horse's neck. Then he would tie a hank of the yellow yarn into the mane and, with a few more gentle words and pats, walk away. Should a mare prove too nervous to stand, Juan would remount, shake out his reata, and ride up close enough to drop or toss a loop over its head. Then Boone or Nooch would knot the yarn into the mane hair as he held the horse fast.

By day's end, the trio had marked thirty-four mares, ranging in age by Juan's estimate from two to ten years old; several were horses he had helped raise, train, and breed at the Rancho de Don Peralta. Many of the *yeguas*, he said, were already with foal by one of the *sementals* or *machos* on the trail, or from earlier breeding. Whether the issue turned out to be horse or mule, the offspring would be an added bonus.

Also sporting yellow yarn were three jacks—a proven five-year-old from the Peralta ranch and another a yearling of good breeding from the Peralta stock; the third was a *macho* unknown to Juan but of superior size and conformation. Juan guessed it to be seven or eight years old. They had also chosen three young mules to use on the trail as pack animals. With so many four-legged animals at hand, saddle stock would be a matter of deciding which of the dozens of horses to wrap a cinch around each day, so riding horses were not much of a consideration.

Every man of the raiding party was horseback the next morning. Old Bill sat facing a crescent of mounted men, spelling out orders for the day. First, the men were to cut out some five hundred head and move them up the Chama. Beckwourth would stay behind with the Abiquiu New Mexicans to keep them on good grass. Another three hundred head were to be trailed by Philip Thompson and the Taos *mozos* up to pastures near that mountain village. Old Bill, Pegleg, and Wakara—with Nooch, Juan, Boone, and Manolo—would push the remaining thousand or so head down to Santa Fe and find pasture and put the horses and mules on the market.

"Don't worry about whether you get horses or mules, mares or studs, geldings or jackasses in the cut. Just take them as they come, with only this one difference—if you see a critter with a yellow ribbon in its mane, turn that animal back into the main bunch."

Old Bill stopped to fill and light his clay pipe. Once lit, he tipped his head back and blew a thick stream of smoke into the air. "Gentlemen, we've done well with this trip, and you shall all reap the rewards. I daresay each of you will have a poke full of gold and silver coin for your work once we shift these animals." He sucked another mouthful of pungent smoke from the pipe and let it drift slowly out of his mouth, curling and clouding under his hat brim. "Well," he hollered, "what the hell are you waiting for? Get to work!" With a smile, he held the pipe aloft like a standard, then turned and rode away, knees cocked and back hunched, his mule's ears turning and twisting to hear the rider's mumbling monologue.

The horsemen followed, riding alongside the herd. Jim Beckwourth hurried past, taking up a position beyond the herd. He and Old Bill separated and created a gap through which the horses would be driven as they counted them. The riders pushed them through until the counters reached five hundred. Beckwourth and several riders herded the cut on up the river valley, then let them scatter to graze.

The next cut, destined for Taos, took place at the opposite end of the herd. Again, Old Bill took the count, along with Philip Thompson. When the three hundred head were through the gap, Thompson and his drovers continued down the river valley, where, upon reaching the San Juan Pueblo, they would turn to the northeast and parallel the Rio Grande up to Taos.

Pegleg, Old Bill, Wakara, and the remaining men and animals, destined for Santa Fe, would wait for the morning to depart. Boone eyed the herd as they rode back to town. The thousand or so head remaining seemed a small bunch compared to what had left California. Those here, he realized, were about the same in number as those left dead on the dry playas of the desert. Boone's eyes were not the only ones studying the grazing horses. Old Bill and Wakara, in particular, paid close attention to the animals with yellow yarn in their manes.

Back in Abiquiu, the remnants of the raiding party sat down to a meal.

"This grub goes down a whole lot easier than horse meat," Pegleg said with a smile as he licked a dribble of chili stew off his finger. "I do confess to missin' it some, howsomever."

Wakara grunted. He waved his heavy knife in the direction from which they had come, where the herd grazed. "The caballos are there. I will slit a throat and bring you a haunch if that will satisfy your craving."

Laughter rose around the table, but, even as he smiled, Boone could not stifle a shudder.

The laughter subsided, and Old Bill said, "Not now, Wakara. Them horses is too valuable now to be eating them." He pushed his bowl and plate aside and filled his pipe, tamping the coarse tobacco into the bowl. "Speaking of such," he said with a nod toward Boone, "from what I've seen of them California caballos sportin' ribbons in their hair, you boys have a fine eye for horseflesh."

Boone shook his head as he swallowed a mouthful of a meat and egg dish spiced with onions and chilis the women called *machaca*. "Not me. I ain't got nothin' to do with it. That's Juan's doin'."

Old Bill looked at Juan Medina, who only shrugged. Old Bill looked back to Boone. "How many horses and whatnot did you hang that yarn on?"

Boone cleared his throat. "Countin' mares and jacks and three head of mules, we marked about forty, I reckon."

"That how many you think you got comin' as your share?"

"I believe that's for you-all to say."

Old Bill nodded and puffed on his pipe as he thought. Then, "The way I figure, dealing in rough numbers, every man that took that trip had coming the proceeds from maybe sixty or seventy head or so. That's rough figures, as I say. 'Course them mares you boys have marked are as good as any horses we got and better than most—so they'd bring a better price. Then again, you ain't wanting but a few mules, and a mule is worth a whole lot more than any horse."

He again paused and mouthed his pipe, the smoke drifting from his lips and the bowl in faint wisps. "What's hard to figure is the jacks. Those animals are worth a heap of money to the right buyer. If you were to sell them in Missouri, you'd be a rich man."

Boone nodded. "Likely as that may be, I don't aim to sell 'em. I aim to get rich sellin' the mules I can get out of 'em. Me and Juan, that is."

Nooch had listened to the conversation. Now he spoke. "What about Juan Medina?"

All eyes turned to the Ute boy.

"What about him?" Pegleg said.

"Does he not deserve something for his work? He rode with us for most of the way back. And he has worked as hard as any man among us."

Nooch's thought had not occurred to anyone else, including Juan. The men exchanged glances, eyebrows cocked, foreheads furrowed, and lips pursed.

"I reckon that's an idea worth chewin' over," Pegleg said. "Me and Wakara and Old Bill will palaver on it—Beckwourth, too, when he comes in from his herd. But me, I've heard enough of these business dealin's for now, and I intend to rest my weary leg and have me a drink of this fine Taos whiskey." He held a bottle aloft, swishing its contents.

Old Bill snorted. "That stuff will peel the hide off your insides like the skin from a beaver."

"The hell you say! This is tonsil varnish of the finest kind! I ought to know, as I have a hand in its makin'."

"That's just the thing," Old Bill said with a laugh. "You know what goes into it, so you ought to have better sense than to drink it. It will likely kill you."

"Just never you mind, Bill Williams. You will be dead and buried long before this child, and when you are gone I'll dance on your grave, wooden leg and all!"

CHAPTER TWENTY-NINE

Dust hung heavy in the air above the pens. More than two hundred head of horses milled in the big corral. Boone dismounted and closed and latched the gate after the last of the bunch passed through. Among the animals were the mares and jacks with their yellow-yarn markings, as well as the three mules likewise marked.

Boone had spent the morning—along with Juan, Nooch, Wakara, Manolo, and Pegleg—separating the horses he had chosen from the larger herd out on the plain. Then the men had cut out another two hundred head or so and driven them to the *corrales* on the outskirts of Santa Fe, the first of the herd on offer to livestock buyers. Old Bill was in the city, spreading the word that caballos and *mulas* were available for sale to any buyer with ready cash.

The riders next eased through the herd with coiled reatas, dropping loops over the heads of the yarned horses and jacks and mules, leading them through a gate to a smaller holding pen. When the job was done, Boone and Juan rode out of the corral, dismounted, tied their horses, and squatted in the scant shade of the fence. The other riders, meanwhile, cut out another ten head of horses and mules at random and pushed them into the pen with Boone's herd. Boone and Juan watched, not knowing the reason for the labor.

"Well, boys, I don't know about you, but I'm hungry enough to go back to eatin' these horses. What say we ride on into town and find Old Bill and get some grub into us."

Pegleg reined his horse around and lit off at a trot in the direction of the plaza, with Nooch and Wakara and Manolo close behind. Boone and Juan snugged up their saddle cinches, mounted, and followed the now-distant riders. Pegleg knew right where to find Old Bill. By the time Boone and Juan tied their horses to a hitch rail in front of a small cantina near the plaza, Pegleg and Manolo and the two Utes were already seated with Old Bill at an outdoor table on a flagstone patio in the golden light of the late-afternoon sun.

The boys pulled up chairs to join them just as *la camarera* came out the door bearing a tray filled with clay mugs and a jug of vino. The litter of identical, but used, mugs on the table and a nearly empty wine jug told of Old Bill's long day entertaining potential buyers. The waitress gathered the empties as Pegleg reeled off a list of foodstuffs to feed the group from the bill of fare on a slate board on the wall. Diners and drinkers at other tables watched the roughhewn assemblage with curiosity.

Pegleg filled himself a mug of wine, swallowed off a long draught, then said, "How's it goin', Bill?"

"Right fine, gentlemen. There be plenty of interest in livestock. I have commitments to move a goodly number of horses come the morning. We can shift all the mules we want to near as quick as we can get them to town."

Boone watched and listened as talk of prices and terms occupied the time until the food arrived, then conversation came to a halt as the hungry men ate. When the plates were cleared away and another round of wine poured, he cleared his throat and spoke. "Say, Pegleg, I been wantin' to ask you. What's with them extra horses you put in my pen 'fore we come here?"

Pegleg smiled and took a sip of wine. "You got Nooch to thank for those. We talked about it and decided ol' Juan here did deserve some pay for helpin' us on the trail. Not that he was one of us, and worthy of a full share, but he ought to get somethin'."

Juan bowed his head, took a deep swallow, then looked in turn at Pegleg, Old Bill, Wakara, and, finally, Nooch. *"Muchos gracias. No esperaba nada. Eres muy amable."*

"No need to thank us, son," Old Bill said. "You maybe expected nothing, but you earned those horses—more, even."

They sat through the long evening twilight, sipping wine and talking. From time to time, visitors stopped by to inquire about buying horses and mules, and Old Bill answered questions and handled the negotiations, with Wakara and Pegleg chiming in on occasion. Boone studied with interest their deft handling of objections and amiable bargaining. He also absorbed the counter offers and haggling on the part of prospective buyers. If he were to become a dealer in horseflesh—muleflesh—bargaining skill would become a necessary tool.

When buyers were not present, the conversation followed a winding trail, veering from one subject to another, with the men telling story after story, some of questionable veracity. Old Bill and Pegleg outbid one another in turn, with one outlandish adventure, then another. Wakara chimed in from time to time, most often to report his people's saving of the ignorant white men, pulling their fat from the fire after their misadventures in the mountains—including Ute women nursing Pegleg back to health, even life, after losing his leg to an Arapaho arrow.

After yet another potential buyer asked about the horses, Old Bill claimed the expedition to California would prove more profitable than expected. He picked up his rucksack, reached in, and took out a long-barreled pistol unlike any the others had seen.

Pegleg said, "What the hell is that, Bill?"

"Man who came from the States with a freight outfit gave it to me to hold as security for a bunch of mules he wants. This here gun is made back East by a man name of Colt. Calls it a Paterson revolver."

Old Bill handed the gun to Pegleg, who looked it over and passed it along to Wakara and the others in turn. Its basic function was easily discerned by the examination, but the finer points of its operation were not apparent.

"Never seen it fired, but he showed me how it works," Old Bill said. "It holds five shots before you have to recharge it. Seems like it would come in handy in a shooting scrape." He explained what he knew of its works. With a tool, the shooter would remove a pin wedge from the frame, pull off the long barrel, then the cylinder, load powder and ball in each chamber, seal it in with tallow, seat a cap on each nipple, then put it back together. When the hammer was pulled to full cock, the trigger would reach down out of the frame for firing.

"Hell of a thing," Pegleg said. "Howsomever, I wonder if all them rounds would fire off at once, like some of them pepperbox pistols will do."

"Don't know. Can't say," Old Bill said. "I only just seen this thing this morning. Never saw it fired."

"It ain't much to look at," Boone said. "That pistol of Juan's is a whole lot prettier. Show 'em, Juan."

Juan handed his pistol to Old Bill, and each of them in turn admired—not for the first time—the elegant engraving and carving in the metal and wood, the silver embellishments polished to a high gloss—albeit a bit tarnished from the trail—and the rich finish of the wood. Boone admired the weapon, as he had on many occasions, then set it carefully on the table.

"She's a beauty, all right," Pegleg said. "But if I had a passel of Indians comin' at me with evil intentions, I believe I might prefer the firepower in that plain black piece of iron."

"But could you fire it while running away on one leg screaming like a woman?" Wakara said with a laugh.

Pegleg laughed in return, then said, "If them Indians was as handy with a bow or a gun as you be, Wakara, I could run a hell of a long way 'fore bein' in danger of bein' hit."

The banter went on until, just before full dark, three visitors approached. One, a giant of a man, looked even taller under his high-crowned sombrero. Beside him was a man in a fur hat, with a long fringe of greasy, light-colored hair dangling around his face. The two walked a step or two behind their smaller companion. As they drew closer, Boone thought the smaller man looked familiar. Then he realized it was the French-speaking trapper he had seen Pegleg fight all those months ago back in Taos.

"You had best be aware, my friend," Old Bill said to Pegleg in a low voice. "Trouble coming."

With his back toward them, Pegleg did not see the approaching men. He did not turn and look, instead reaching under the table as if for a weapon.

His two followers separated and stepped to the sides as the Frenchman walked into the dim glow of candlelight from the tables and sconces along the outer wall of the cantina. "We have business to discuss, Pegleg Smith," he said through his thick accent.

Pegleg turned, sliding his chair around as he did. "Go away."

"I will not. When last we met, you offended my honor."

"What I did was beat the hell out of you."

"It would have been preferable had you killed me, monsieur. To be beaten by a one-legged man, *l'impotent*, has tainted my repute."

Pegleg stood, scooting his chair to the side, and grasping the back with his hand for balance. In his other hand dangled his wooden leg. "Aw, hell, Frenchie. That weren't the first time you've had your ass kicked."

"No, monsieur. But it will be the last, so far as you are

concerned."

"You goin' to fight, or stand there workin' your jaws?"

Frenchie grinned without mirth. He slid a Green River knife from its sheath at his belt and raised it to the level of his squinted eyes as if taking aim at Pegleg. He stepped closer, lowered the blade, and waved it slowly from side to side like the weaving head of a snake. His grin hardened, and his eyes squinched tighter. Pegleg stood still as stone, and, if he moved so much as to draw breath, it was not evident to those watching. With a yell, Frenchie crouched and leaped forward, thrusting the blade at Pegleg's midsection.

It never reached its mark. The whoosh of Pegleg's wooden leg slicing the air ended with the crack of bone as the appendage-turned-bludgeon shattered Frenchie's forearm. His scream changed its sound and meaning as the knife fell from his grasp and clattered to the flagstones.

Eyes wide, Frenchie stood and stared at his right arm, the hand and wrist hanging useless at an odd angle, bent where there had been no joint an instant before. With a growl, he squatted and picked up the knife in his left hand. He lunged forward as he rose, again taking aim at Pegleg's belly. This time the wooden leg landed with a wet crunch on the top of his head, again widening his eyes and halting his motion. He dropped to his knees, and as they hit the ground the leg struck again, a sideways blow that smashed the side of Frenchie's head. He tipped to the side and was dead before reaching the stone floor of the patio.

Other than the arm holding the wooden leg, Pegleg had not moved. He still stood balanced on his one leg, braced against the back of the chair with his other hand. He did not see the big man in the sombrero behind him withdraw a knife even bigger than Frenchie's from its belted scabbard and start toward him.

Wakara, however, did see the move and in a trice was out of

his chair, his blade flashing like lightning, slicing through the air and barely slowing as it cleaved the Mexican's throat. Blood erupted from the cut, fountaining through the air and pouring through greasy whiskers and down the front of the giant's protruding gut. The look of surprise in the man's eyes said he did not yet know he was dead as he collapsed to the ground.

The greasy blond watched it all in horror from the edge of the light. Hesitant, he did not know whether to join the fight as he had been paid to do, or run away. Boone watched the man from his seat at the table and saw the man grasp the butt of a pistol tucked into a sash at his waist. Without thinking, Boone picked up Juan's pistol where it sat on the table before him and shot the man. The bullet smashed through his ribcage and tore through the bottom of his heart. He covered the wound with both hands, blood gushing through his fingers. He dropped to his knees and fell face-down, a red puddle staining the flagstones from beneath his buckskin-clad body.

Nobody moved. Powder smoke drifted through the still air. The *tabernero* rushed out the door, wiping his hands on a dirty apron tied around his waist. He looked at the bloody bodies littering his patio. He looked to Old Bill for explanation, but the mountain man only shrugged. Patrons at two other tables found their voices and told the tavern keeper how the fight unfolded, assuring him that Old Bill and his friends were innocent, and that the dead men had been killed in self-defense.

Pegleg scooted his chair and hopped a step or two to where he could sit down. He fitted his prosthesis to his stump and fastened the bindings. Wakara picked up a stained cloth napkin from the table and wiped the blood from the blade of his knife. Boone stared at the gun in his hand, wondering how it came to be there, tossed it into the air with a half spin and caught it by the barrel and handed it butt-first to Juan.

Old Bill stood. "Boys, I believe we had best be on our way."

He dropped a handful of coins on the table. "That ought to take care of what we owe," he told the *tabernero*, "along with some extra to clean up the mess. We're sorry for what happened here, but as these folks have said, it wasn't of our making."

The men walked out the opening in the low wall surrounding the patio, untied their horses from the rail, and mounted.

"If the *federales* want to see us, they'll find us camped out by the cow pens," he said to the innkeeper from horseback. "You know the place."

Chapter Thirty

Pegleg tightened the diamond hitch on one of the pack mules. "You sure you want to do this, Boone?"

"I reckon so. I got to go somewheres. If I don't get out of town, like them *federales* said, I'll likely get locked up. I left Clay County to stay out of jail, so I reckon I might just as well leave here for the same reason."

"Don't you worry none about them tin-pot lawmen. Even if that feller you shot's gun was still in his belly sash 'stead of in his hand, there's witnesses that'll say he was goin' for it."

"Well, even so, they can make it right uncomfortable for me."

"To hell with 'em. You can always come up to Taos. They don't bother us much up there."

Boone slid the latigo through the loop of the cinch knot and pulled it snug, then grabbed the saddle by the horn and rocked it back and forth to assure it was well-seated on the horse's back.

Since the visit from the Mexican authorities yesterday morning, he and Juan had spent their time preparing to leave Santa Fe. They sold three geldings from the horses given to Juan as pay and used some of the money to purchase pack outfits and supplies for the road.

It seemed such a long time ago since Boone had come out with the freighters on the Santa Fe Road. He had not paid a lot of attention along the way, as he did not intend to travel that way again, at least not anytime soon.

But, unlike the trail they had followed out to California and back, the trail to Missouri was well-traveled and accommodated wagons as opposed to only mule trains. He was confident he and Juan could make the trip without incident, finding their way to Missouri and into the business of raising mules. His only concern was traffic on the trail, which could cause difficulties keeping their stock from mixing with the herds of loose stock— mules, oxen, and horses—accompanying the freight trains. The possibility of outlaws rustling the animals also lurked in the back of his mind. Still, confident in the experience gained since leaving Liberty all those months ago, he considered himself man enough to respond to any circumstance that might arise.

That confidence waned some when he stepped into the stirrup and swung into the saddle. He gave Nooch a slight wave, and the Ute friend he would likely never see again nodded in reply from his station by the gate.

Wakara, whose quiet demeanor had kept Boone from knowing him well, only watched through eyes as sharp as flint. Manolo, leaning against the corral fence with elbows hooked over the top rail, tipped his sombrero. Old Bill Williams, sitting by the fire sucking on his pipe, raised it in salute.

Pegleg Smith clapped a hand to Boone's thigh and gave it a squeeze. "You ever come back this way, son, you come find me. You're welcome at my fire anytime." He handed Boone the lead rope tied to the mules.

Boone nodded. He looked back to where Juan sat horseback in the pen with the *yeguas* and *machos* that would make a living for the boys when they reached the States. "You ready, *mi amigo?*" he hollered.

"*¡Sí!*"

Boone touched spurs to his horse's belly and tugged the lead rope to set the three mules, tied head to tail, into motion. Nooch swung the gate wide, and Juan pushed the horses through.

Pegleg watched as Boone towed the mules along, with the horses and jacks strung out behind and Juan bringing up the rear.

By the time the dust settled, they were out of sight.

AUTHOR'S NOTE

Back in 1840, mountain men Pegleg Smith and Old Bill Williams, and perhaps Jim Beckwourth, with Ute leader Wakara, led a horse-stealing expedition, following the Old Spanish Trail to California. In widespread, coordinated raids, the thieves plundered ranchos and missions of some three thousand horses and mules. While being chased across the Mojave Desert by Californio pursuers led by Ygnacio Palomares and José Antonio Carrillo, as many as half the stolen animals died from thirst, hunger, heat, and overexertion.

That historical incident provided the inspiration for *A Thousand Dead Horses,* but the book is a work of fiction. While much of the story is drawn from history, including many of its people and places, they are used fictitiously, interwoven with characters, locations, and events that exist only in the author's— and the reader's—imagination.

ABOUT THE AUTHOR

Winner of four Western Writers of America Spur Awards and a Spur Award finalist on six other occasions, **Rod Miller** writes fiction, poetry, and history about the American West. A lifelong Westerner raised in a cowboy family, Miller is a former rodeo contestant, worked in radio and television production, and is a retired advertising agency copywriter and creative director. *A Thousand Dead Horses* is his eighth novel and sixteenth book. Miller's award-winning poetry and short stories have appeared in numerous anthologies, and several magazines have carried his byline.

The employees of Five Star Publishing hope you have enjoyed this book.

Our Five Star novels explore little-known chapters from America's history, stories told from unique perspectives that will entertain a broad range of readers.

Other Five Star books are available at your local library, bookstore, all major book distributors, and directly from Five Star/Gale.

Connect with Five Star Publishing

Visit us on Facebook:
https://www.facebook.com/FiveStarCengage

Email:
FiveStar@cengage.com

For information about titles and placing orders:
(800) 223-1244
gale.orders@cengage.com

To share your comments, write to us:
Five Star Publishing
Attn: Publisher
10 Water St., Suite 310
Waterville, ME 04901